Published by: Cinnabar Moth Publishing LLC
Santa Fe, New Mexico

Cover Design by: Ira Geneve

ISBN-13: 978-1-962308-30-4

Library of Congress Control Number: 2025934624

Shadowslayers

COLIN SEPHTON

For Raffy and Ally.
This whole cosmos is yours!

Acknowledgement goes to Stan Lee,
Jack Kirby and Roy Thomas, who presented
life to a younger me as a cosmic Marvel!

Prologue

As the cosmos rippled to the sound of the Cosmic Sitar and wave after wave of harmonic vibration traversed the great expanse of time and space, the Book of Consciousness rose up and down on each sound wave. It had been safely retrieved by the Omnisoul and the cosmos was calm once more.

On Earth, dawn paled the eastern sky and wispy tendrils curled up to meet the delicate clouds high above Park Town, Oxford. Ignatius and Indigo, both dirty and tired, reached the large but unassuming door to Ignatius's house in Summertown. He reached into his engineers' waistcoat for the key. The pocket was slightly torn, and the tweed fabric splattered in places with blood. Behind him, Indigo was trying to remain invisible, her undergarments ripped and slashed with cuts, her pale skin bruised and blooded beneath.

Before Ignatius could find his key, the door opened and the two Union Jacks were greeted with a frown from a white wizened old man with a shock of white hair.

"Ah! Lambeth, thank you."

Lambeth's eyes widened. "Welcome home, sir." He seemed unaffected by the state of Indigo's clothing. "I'll run you a bath, my dear," he said being careful not to look at her in any obvious manner, to protect her modesty. Lambeth closed the door behind them. The pale sky above looked like cracked glass as the streets began to fill, the people of Oxford all staring upwards at the curious sky. Nobody knew what it meant; this strange phenomenon that had never been seen before. In each shard of the splintered sky appeared the faint image of the sun. The average Oxonian thought, perhaps, that this was some kind of atmospheric aberration.

Upstairs, Indigo loosened her corset, removing her concealed short sword. It clattered to the floor. She reached into her breeches and removed a steam cannon and placed it next to the sword with a heavy thud. She reached in again and unclipped two small derringers and put them down. Her long slender fingers reached into the top of her boot and removed the dagger. She was a walking arsenal. Removing her boots, breeches and corset, her pale slender figure was cut and grazed in several places. Testimony to her adventures.

She sat in the bath staring at her bruised knees. *We have fought with gods*, she thought. Nobody would believe them. Staring intently, she began to ponder the nature of the cosmos, the split holographic Megasphere that could be seen in the sky, parts of which had drifted off, washed away on the cosmic ocean, every being in every shard become sailors on the seas of fate.

The events of the previous day ran through her head, although the time seemed much longer. Clearly their experience through the cosmos bore no resemblance in time to that on the earth. Ignatius and Indigo had been snatched away by seven terrible beings, the Charon, and taken to the Well at the Centre of Time to access the Book of Consciousness, written by the Creator of the cosmos, The Omnisoul, in an effort by the Charon to try and destroy time itself. *This will get us both put into an asylum!* was the alarm running through her head, a silent scream that made her begin to question her own sanity.

Meanwhile, Ignatius posted his report on their previous mission. He tried to keep it scientific. If he mentioned the two of them had travelled the cosmos, fought gods, and found a magical book, then helped to split time and space into an infinite number of identical fragments, then the Grand Commander, the First Lord of the Union Jacks, might think he was crazy.

A gentle tap at the bathroom door startled Indigo.

"Indigo, I've left you some clothing outside the door. It's the best I can do, I'm afraid," said Ignatius softly.

A little later, Indigo slipped the lock on the bathroom door and without seeing, tentatively felt around on the floor for the clothing. A few minutes later she appeared, her wet hair tussled around her shoulders, which were adorned with a slightly over-large white shirt. She had rolled the sleeves up and pulled it in at the waist with a large thick leather belt. Over this she wore a tweed waistcoat with one of her twin derringers protruding from each pocket. She wore tan-coloured trousers, and her boots, which no doubt concealed her dagger and steam cannon.

She joined Ignatius in his study. He too had somehow freshened up and was sitting behind a large partners desk. "Well, you do look dashing!" he laughed. "I wonder what you are wearing on all the other cosmic shards that floated away from us? Or are we having the same conversation elsewhere in the cosmos?"

"Who knows? It's all a bit much to comprehend. They were gods, Ignatius! Gods! Our world will never be the same again. Anyway, we will have to record all of this for the Union Jacks archives. Do you think our founder, Brutus of Troy, knew there were gods out there? Is this what our secret organisation was set up to do? Fight gods? Did the Trojans and Greeks fight gods? They have a rich mythology. This is all very surreal. We should dig through the archives."

Still exhausted, the two agents of the Empire talked well into the night until the dawn came.

"I think I should take my leave," she said. "We both need some rest before we get together again and discuss what we do next." With that, Indigo stood up and took her leave.

Chapter 1: Assaulted

Indigo made her way through the streets of Oxford, alert as always to her surroundings, always observing, always light of foot. It was often thought that this worldly adventurer, or now this other-worldly adventurer, was of high-born descent. But nothing could be further from the truth. Indigo carried with her many secrets. Her entire existence had been built on secrets. Her name, for starters; not even Ignatius truly believed her name was Indigo Gemstone. Her profession revolved around secrets for the Empire, and now she held one of the greatest secrets of all. That of the existence of other beings, gods, demons, the Charon. From here on, what would become of the Union Jacks? What would become of her and Ignatius? What would become of the world, indeed, the Universe as they knew it?

As she continued, a drone from the Administorium came zipping by, whirring its gears as it let out little puffs of steam every now and then.

Indigo crossed the road, avoiding the steam gurneys that trundled past on a regular basis, their wheels clattering on the cobbles. The sun reflected in the honey-coloured glow of Oxford stone lit her face from time to time, making her look somewhat angelic. At other times, shadows covered her face, giving reflections of some truths that Indigo would rather forget. Truths about her past, her role as a Union Jack and about her latest adventure.

She quickened her pace, crossing the road again and turning right. After some time, she turned right again and then again, diving into the nearest inky blackness of an alleyway, pressing her back hard up against the cold Oxford stone.

A short figure came past, moving like quicksilver. Without hesitation, Indigo grabbed the figure by the scruff of the neck, hurtling them to the ground. She landed on top, holding a long pointy dagger at her stalkers throat.

"Why are you following me?" There was no reply. "Who are you?"

She pulled the figure up off the floor just enough for their shoulders and head to be out of the shadows.

She was greeted by a small young face in a flat cap. *A boy?* No, she pushed back the cap and removed it. Long red unruly curls came falling about the pale face. It was a girl. At that moment, Indigo thought she saw a momentary glimpse of a red light flash across the girl's dilated pupils. But then it was gone.

"Who are you?"

The girl looked frightened, but Indigo thought that this was probably an act. The girl was far too adept, cunning, and stealthy to be some chancer or pickpocket. Eventually she stammered, "I am Skoto and I live in the darkness."

Without warning, Indigo felt a blinding pain in the back of her head, and the world became hazy and her vision swirled. Her consciousness swirled with it, and she collapsed into a heap in the dark alleyway, a crumpled body of tweed with a long pointed dagger lying beside her.

Two girls stared at the body before them with intense black eyes, their skin pale like alabaster. About their torsos, they each wore a belt of odd, sharpened, jagged knives, some of which looked like they were made from obsidian. Others looked like they were made from hellfire, and they illuminated the girls' pallid skin beneath their chins so that they glowed the same colour as their hair.

"Look what you've done!" said the girl on the right, opening her eyes wider.

"She'll be ok," came the reply from the girl on the left.

Realising that Indigo was now fully conscious again, the attacker on the left said, "We know what you've done! You are in great danger."

"Really? And what do you think I have done?"

"You've had a hand in killing Solomon." A sinister grin grew across the girl's face and the two of them chortled, almost hissing.

Indigo's blood ran cold, and the hairs stood up on the nape of her neck and she broke out into a cold sweat. Perhaps they worked for the Administorium and were spies. Perhaps they were clever automata or some kind of new drone. Who knew?

Then, without warning, a second blow rendered her unconscious once more.

Chapter 2: The Librarian

The large bulky figure moved in the darkness towards an ancient bookcase, the contents of which were great tomes of such antiquity that they made all the books in the Bodleian seem as if they were written only yesterday. The existence of this labyrinthine library had remained secret for centuries. The library formed part of the hidden tunnels that spread beneath the city of Oxford and, more importantly, beneath the Administorium.

The figure remained in the shadows and had not been on the surface or seen daylight for as long as his memory served. But this was just a moment in history. He was several thousand years old and had been confined to this subterranean world to carry out the quest he had been set.

As the shadowy figure moved from shelf to shelf, ornate gilt decoration caught what dim light there was on his grey-turquoise armour. Carvings of ancient scribes and tomes written to record the passing of aeons on many worlds across many planes. The books he tended were part of the vast repository of information that he had collected through his long lifetime. Books here took the form of sacred texts carved in clay, or written on scrolls of vellum, or even human skin. Enormous tooled leather-bound volumes with gilt pages or with golden clasps, some were chained and bound, their knowledge too dangerous to be shared or accessed by mere mortals. The shelves had been arranged by subject and ordered in a timeline for each category. There wasn't any index system. The Librarian worked using only his memory, knowing each and every volume, regardless of when it was written or when it was obtained. Nothing was forgotten, his memory was a storehouse of wisdom and knowledge from across the cosmos.

With his brother and sister, they had probably gathered the entire history of the cosmos. From time to time, they would travel the astral planes in search of new knowledge and rendezvous every millennium to discuss and compare notes to set quests for each of them to fulfil in the search of even more ancient texts. Legend had it the three siblings were born of the Goddess of Wisdom and their father was a High Priest of the Ti-Botta.

At the centre of the library was a great layout table made of crystal, which stood on four giant golden carved birds. Two were owls, two were eagles, their outstretched wings supporting the great slab of crystal that seemed to illuminate the space it occupied. On its surface was a map of some part of the cosmos, like a hologram, moving and flashing colours as nebulae and galaxies moved and evolved. Individual stars twinkled and rogue planets that had broken free of their solar systems drifted by. At one end, the tabletop had books piled high, the latest reading material used by the Librarian.

High above, a large eagle soared, this was the Librarian's eyes and ears in the infinite space that was his library.

The structure had seen several changes, each with their own architectural forms and style. The changes had been about relieving the boredom as much as anything else and not just the whimsy of their architect.

The figure moved to the table, his armour creaking with age and scraping over the crystal top as he moved his hands across the surface. The map changed, and different areas of the cosmos came into view. Galaxies were formed and moved on. The figure mumbled something incomprehensible and continued moving both hands across the surface. New areas appeared, new planes, new cosmic bodies, some obeying different laws than those that had been seen on earth.

Despite his size, he jumped a little as a figure appeared behind him from out of the gloom. "Well? Have you located it yet?" Her voice was sharp, as were her fine features. She wore a crown of flowers with horns, and apart from a black gold-lined cloak and some gold chains, she wore little else.

"It's here!"

"Yes, you've said before."

"No, I mean here! In this building. I don't just mean on this plane. It's been on this plane for millennia. But somehow it has migrated to here. Somewhere before us!"

"Since when?" She asked somewhat sceptical.

"From what I can ascertain, only recently. A century or two."

She looked at him in disbelief. "Then how did you not know this?" She bellowed. "How?"

He looked at her. "It is enchanted. It's not going to announce its arrival. Its enchantment is more skilful, more cunning than that!"

"Find it! Or I'll have your head placed on top of this building and your siblings can come and retrieve your carcass." She turned and with a dramatic swish of her cloak, she purposefully strode away.

The great armoured figure returned to his crystal map and began to zoom in until he could see a layout of the library in which he stood. He knew full well that the book would not reveal itself. For that, he would need the key.

High above him his eagle circled as if looking for its prey in a field. Over and over, it circled without ever moving its outstretched wings. An armoured arm was thrust out and the bird dived, pulling up and hurtling towards it with talons firmly pushed out in front, landing with some force on his arm.

"I know, Manjushri, we will soon have it and then be able to get out of here. We have spent too long with these lower-class beings and need to rebuild the library somewhere more suitable."

The bird replied with a squawk and stretched its wings.

"My siblings will be envious when I have triumphed and found the most elusive book in the cosmos. Then our library shall be the most complete in the thirty-one planes." The bird moved its head to the side as if agreeing with him.

"Now we have located it, we will need to work out the what the key is for actually finding it."

Chapter 3: A Glitch in Time

Ignatius was finding it hard to relax in his study and was now getting a little restless. *There can be no invention about this tale*, he thought. But no one would believe him, his peers would think him quite mad, and he would do well to try and avoid the asylum. Although he had no doubt that some swamis, gurus and mystics in the Far East of the Empire might have done so, presumably he was the first English man to have ventured forth to other worlds, conversed with gods and demons alike and, seen the Universe for what it really is. What's more, he lived to tell the tale, and returned in time for breakfast. His companion, too, had been the first English woman to engage in battle with these same gods and demons. This adventure would have sent others of lesser mind and stamina insane. The two adventurers were from an elite and secret organisation called the Union Jacks.

The task of the present-day Union was to defend the Empire and pioneer its technological advancement so the Empress could retain order across the globe.

As Ignatius paced about his study, Lambeth appeared with a silver pot of tea and a fine bone China cup and saucer on a gleaming silver tray.

"Some refreshments, Sir?"

"Thank you, Lambeth," replied Ignatius somewhat absently, glancing at the clock on the fireplace which indicated it was 11 o'clock.

"May I enquire if there is anything more I can assist with? Whatever adventure you and Miss Gemstone have been on, if I may, Sir, it's left you somewhat distant and you still seem tired." Lambeth's brow wrinkled into a concerned look.

Hesitating for a short moment, Ignatius said, "Well, Lambeth, as a veteran of the Union, I know you have been on many adventures of your own for the Empire."

"Indeed, Sir, as you know I've seen action in the Anglo-Afghan war, The Crimea and worked for the East India Company. I'm sure there isn't anything I haven't seen that you could shock me with."

"Then you'd best join me for a cup of tea and take a seat. I need to ask you, have you ever left this world Lambeth? Departed planet Earth and headed for the stars?"

Lambeth let out a small gasp and his brow wrinkled again, "Oh, no, Sir! What do you mean?"

Ignatius was beginning to regret starting this conversation, afraid a stay at the asylum might be on its way. He leaned in and lowered his voice, recounting his adventure of how he and Indigo had been transported by seven deadly and ruthless gods, the Charon, to the very centre of the cosmos aboard a ship that flew through space, powered by the souls of the departed. Along the way they obtained a magical book, the Book of Consciousness, fought and expelled the Elder God, Calabi-Ya who attacked them in the form of a dragon, and fought a band of naked tattooed warrior priestesses to eventually try and destroy the cosmos, to destroy time.

Lambeth's face had turned as pale as his shock of white hair, "I now remember why I'm too old for this game," he laughed nervously. "I think I'll get back to my chores, sir."

As Lambeth turned to leave, the room shook and both men became unsteady on their feet. There was a flash like lightning and the room rocked again as if there had been an earthquake. Ignatius thought he saw other people, other beings, walk through his study. Then all was calm once more.

As Ignatius paced his study, Lambeth appeared with a silver pot of tea and a fine bone China cup and saucer on a gleaming silver tray.

"Some refreshments, Sir?"

The whole scene played out once more. Ignatius glanced at the clock on the fireplace, 11 o'clock! "That's impossible!" he murmured. Since trying to destroy the Well at the Centre of Time, the Charon had created glitches in time and space. Lambeth said nothing. He was blissfully unaware of the event; he had simply carried out his duty, unaware of anything extraordinary. Ignatius rubbed his chin, unsure of how he had witnessed the repeat event. Was life destined to be like this from here on?

Ignatius needed some time to think. He needed to process what was going on. Clearly, the damage that had occurred to the cosmos was the causation of the strange events taking place.

Ignoring the tea and waiting for Lambeth to leave, he lay down and closed his eyes. His breathing was deep and regular. He felt his rib cage rise and fall, his diaphragm rising, and could hear his breath as it both entered and left his body, his lungs collapsing once more. He felt his limbs grow heavy and his whole body began to feel like it was being pushed into the couch. He could feel the room begin to spin. He focused his mind and no longer paid any attention to his breathing or his heavy limbs. He could feel the vibration of the earth, his body resonating at the same frequency. He could feel it spinning on its axis at a thousand miles per hour. He could feel it spinning through the void of space at sixty-seven thousand miles per hour. At this point, he was paralysed. He was moving at a colossal four hundred and forty miles per hour as the entire solar system traversed the galaxy. It was as if he could feel the ebb and flow of the cosmos, feel it breathing, feel its heartbeat.

Weightlessness took over his whole being, and he now felt like he inhabited only his mind, the mind of a an incredibly gifted being. All was quiet, nothing stirred in the blackness. Eventually the monotonous infinite void changed and was suffocating. Ignatius could feel the pressure squeezing his chest, his lungs. His ears felt they were about to burst. As his mind wandered, he began to grow anxious, to panic. But this great panic that was about to engulf him was all in his head. His body lay paralysed with the crushing endless nothingness that sat upon his chest.

His panic increased. His eyes opened, desperately trying to focus on anything in this inky world that was drowning him. His body felt clammy. Salty beads of sweat stung his wild-looking eyes, and he felt his chest expand, his arms felt like they had just burst, and muscles and sinew strained all over his body. The blackness was replaced with blood red and the world, alien and unfamiliar, was a sea of crimson. The scarlet haze flooded his every fibre and swallowed him. He could smell sulphur and brimstone. As he looked around this scarlet world, every surface began to seethe and explode with what looked like precious jewels shining with such preternatural brilliance it hurt his eyes.

He didn't notice at first, but his hands were starting to feel the weightiness of some object they held, perfectly balanced. Suddenly in one lightning quick, panther-like move Ignatius lunged forward and, bringing his arms up over his head, a great broad-bladed sword arced overhead and sliced through flesh and bone. A fountain erupted, spraying a warm, red metallic taste over his face. He was now Adonai, Lord of the Beautiful and the Damned, Lord of the Charon.

In his mind's eye, a mystic haze began to form. Swirling black clouds began to grow bigger before him and eventually envelop him. What looked like lightning illuminated parts of the dark clouds with flashes of orange and scarlet. Out of the cloud formation, Ignatius could see seven terrible beings, growing larger until they stood before him, each carrying a scythe encrusted with dried blood.

A scream ripped through the redness, and Ignatius awoke to the inky blackness of his study once more. His chest was wet with sweat, his brow wrinkled with fear and curiosity. He couldn't live like this. He had to find answers to these strange events. Born of Adonai, it was too much to bear. He had to get out of his present surroundings, his study, his current life for a while. Much like the Charon, he wanted freedom.

Putting on his great coat, he headed out and made his way along the Banbury Road to St Giles', where he was soon able to lose himself in the not-so-salubrious coffee houses and smoking dens. Tonight, Ignatius just wanted to be isolated, without any responsibilities to himself, to the Union Jacks or to the Empire. It wasn't long before he had an ale in one hand and a pipe in the other, and although he didn't quite know what he was smoking, he knew it would relax him and bring about the pleasure and comfort he currently needed.

After several hours, Ignatius opened his eyes and although his vision was blurry, he could just see the warm roaring fire, the smoky atmosphere of an unfamiliar room and could feel against his side the warmth of a new lady friend he had obviously acquired earlier. Who she was he had no idea, but without hesitating he put his arm around her and went back to sleep.

No matter how much he slept, Ignatius was unable to get his adventure with the Book of Consciousness out of his thoughts. Every time he closed his eyes, he could see it, sitting there, a huge green glowing tome of unbelievable age. He could still feel its vibrations and hear it murmuring with sentience at his touch. He felt his body move up and down as if on an ocean as the cosmos rippled to the sound of the Cosmic Sitar and wave after wave of harmonic vibration traversed the great expanse of time and space. He could see the Book of Consciousness rising and lowering on the crest of each sound wave. The great glowing emerald slab murmured in response to these ripples in time. Its green glowing bulk rising off the floor and lowering again, and again, and again. As it did so, its brightness began to dim and it began to fade in and out of its present position, its present plane, and its present place in time. As the book came back into view once more, it split in two and duplicated itself. There were now two books fading in and out. Then one was gone. It faded and did not return, whilst its duplicate began to grow dark, the emerald green turning an infinite blackness that seemed to absorb any light around it, and then was gone.

In the infinite lightless void, his head began to whirl and he felt like he was unable to move his limbs. Out of the darkness, wispy tendrils of blackness began to circulate overhead, gaining speed until faces began to emerge from the shadows. Terrifying female faces with sharp teeth and wide eyes. Eventually, a single face formed before him. It was beautiful and looked to be wearing some kind of tiara or crown. Smiling sweetly, the face moved closer until their noses touched. He felt the weight of a body climb on top of him, then, pinned down the nightmares began. The beautiful, sweet face wasn't so beautiful anymore, and as she opened her mouth her teeth appeared to be growing longer into full gangs. She locked her lips onto his and began to suck his lifeforce, draining him of all power. Ignatius could feel his body growing weaker and weaker and his temperature plummeting until all blackness enveloped and suffocated him until he could feel nothing more.

Opening his eyes, Ignatius could feel his head throbbing. His vision was still blurry, and as he looked about, he saw the fire had gone out in the night, the unkind temperature causing his breath to cloud before him. He raised himself off the bed and, looking back saw the body of his companion, whoever she was, her flame-coloured hair covering her pillow, and without saying a word, much to his own shame, he left, creeping along the passageway to the cold morning. It was dawn and as he made his way back home, he began to feel regretful and had a sense of foreboding about his dreams that night. They seemed very real, as if they were some kind of premonition.

Chapter 4: Kidnapped

When Indigo regained consciousness, she saw double. Her bleary eyes struggled in the gloom, but she could just make out two identical young faces staring at her with wide, unblinking eyes. She attempted to move, but her hands were bound and the pain in her head was excruciating. She swayed a little. As her vision returned some more, Indigo became aware that the rest of her view was in single vision. Just the girl was seen in duplicate. *Twins*, she thought.

She had been bound to a chair, her wrists feeling slightly grazed as she struggled with her bonds behind her back.

"Exactly what do you want with me?" she enquired, her eyes throbbing, her head splitting with pain.

She looked around her. She was in a dingy room, probably somewhere in the tenements of Cowley. The walls were bare except for patches of mould, and most of the plaster had crumbled away a long time ago, leaving damp exposed brickwork. The only light came from a single gas lamp suspended from the ceiling. Indigo thought she could make out mystical symbols or runes painted on the damp walls and floor. Despite her hazy vision, she could tell they had been painted in blood.

Her captors did not work for the Administorium, that much was clear. Her two assailants were in the far corner, whispering to each other in the gloom. A rat quickly ran past, following the line of the wall. Neither of them flinched, it was just another daily occurrence.

Indigo moved her two bound arms as best she could, trying to reach far enough to obtain one of the derringers in her pockets. She jumped as a bullet exploded in the wall just behind her ear.

"Looking for these?" said one of her captors, as she waved the two pistols about.

"So, what do you want with me?" snarled Indigo.

One of the girls leaned forward into the faint glow of the gas lamp, her dark eyes glittering. A sinister smile touched her full lips. "We know you have recently been in possession of a very valuable book. And whilst this book may not be available anymore, there are other treasures to be had, and we think you hold the key!"

"I have no idea what you are talking about."

"Really? Well I, and my other self, Skoto, think differently."

"Other self?"

"Yes. Surely you must know. You were there. I am she and she is me. We are Skoto. We live in the darkness and now live on a myriad of universes. We inhabit the Megasphere that you helped create with your meddling, with your allegiance with the Charon. The Skoto are now many thanks to the split cosmos" The two girls giggled and embraced each other, their evil giggling turning almost to the purring of a sinister cat about to rip its prey apart with its sharp claws. Indigo shifted uneasily in her seat.

"Are you doppelgangers?"

Again, the girls giggled insanely. As she looked on, trying to fathom what was going on, she thought she could see beneath the disguises the girls wore. Although dressed as boys, they appeared to be wearing a harlequin outfit.

"But so are you. You must know that. There is an Indigo on every shard, in every universe. If needed we will kill you all, only time eternal may prevent us from that. But you will suffer! Many times over, unless we get what we want."

"And what do you want?"

"Rahu."

"What is Rahu?"

"The Book of Shadows."

Indigo repeated it, "The Book of Shado…." But she was cut short by one of the girls. "Yes. Our master demands it. You will get his book for him. The great author demands it!"

"I have no idea what the Book of Shadows is. Plus, I don't see your master. So, you are just minions, a nobody. It doesn't matter how you think you will hurt me; you will never be more than the lowest there is, destined for nothing, on any world, in any part of the cosmos. You just blindly carry out orders." Indigo laughed. She was hoping the two assailants would not see through her bravado, see her real fear.

With lightning speed, one of the girls was beside her. She grabbed Indigo's hair and yanked her head back, holding an obsidian knife to her throat. Indigo could feel the cold glass-like stone pressing hard against her skin. A trickle of blood ran down her neck and onto her chest, staining the brilliant white shirt. Skoto's eyes were burning red and wild looking. The other Skoto called out, "No, we need her. Or you can explain to the master how we have destroyed any chance of obtaining the book on this plane. I have not travelled here from my own world to help you if you are just going to screw this up!"

The Skoto holding the knife snarled at her doppelganger. Indigo knew she would have to seize her moment just right. Whilst the two of them were distracted by each other, Indigo pulled her head back away from the knife, then, risking all, brought her head crashing down on Skoto's nose. She felt bone crunch and felt the knife bite into her throat a little. The girl gave a yelp and staggered backwards, her nose pouring with blood. "Bitch!"

Indigo didn't delay, she stood up as best she could and swung around, using the chair to which she was tied as a weapon, taking Skoto completely by surprise. The wooden legs came spinning into her, knocking her off balance. As she staggered and fell backwards, Indigo slammed all four legs onto the floor either side of her torso. The legs splintered with a cracking sound and the seat came slamming down onto Skoto's head and chest, Indigo's full weight crashing down on her. Her legs twitched in front of Indigo; then she was still. With no time to lose, Indigo was up. The other Skoto had pulled her knives. An obsidian point came whistling past Indigo's eye. She couldn't risk that again, so with full force she charged so she was in close quarters and Skoto couldn't throw any more knives. She swiped her leg and the girl's body crumpled to the floor. A blade lashed out and sliced through Indigo's shirt. Fortunately, the oversize shirt Ignatius had given her was enough to help cushion the blow and the blade became buried in cotton. Keeping her advance, Indigo kicked out again. She felt Skoto's ribs crack. And again. She knew if she was to survive, she had to get released from the remnants of the chair. Somewhat sluggishly and in pain, Skoto punched Indigo in the ribs, then again in the abdomen. Taking a primitive carved blade, she swiped past Indigo's belly. But she was too slow. Indigo pushed her buttocks out to avoid the knife and, losing balance, collapsed head first onto her assailant. Both of them groaned and rolled onto their backs, winded. Indigo felt around on the ground beneath her and discovered a knife. She quickly grasped it somewhat awkwardly and as she cut into her bonds, she felt blood wet her hands. But it didn't matter, she was free. Like quicksilver, she rolled over and straddled Skoto, pinning her to the floor, pinning her arms. The girl had underestimated Indigo's power. Holding her arms with a hand and a knee, Indigo held the blade to her throat.

"Who is your master? What is this Book of Shadows?"

The girl giggled. She looked like a ghoul, her face pale, her eyes burning. She raised her head as much as she could and her voice changed. It was a mere rasp, but an evil rasp, as if she was possessed.

"Ha! The Great One will destroy you. He will wreak vengeance upon you and this world will burn. Fire and brimstone will engulf this planet and his scales will crush all who think they can stand in his way. His wings will engulf this plane and destroy it once and for all."

Then, without warning the girl thrust her head forward, the knife piercing her throat.

"No!" screamed Indigo.

Skoto let out a desperate gurgle and blood spurted over Indigo's face as the girl's body fell limp, her head thudding to the stone floor.

Indigo recoiled. She was still no wiser as to why she had been kidnapped. No wiser about why she had encountered the girls or who had sent them. What's more, what was the Book of Shadows, where was it and why did they think she would know? Who was their master?

Gathering her thoughts, she stood up a bit shakily. It looked like she was in a basement, a cellar. There was a distinct damp smell about the place, but more than that there was a smell of death, of an evil darkness. At the far end of the chamber was a stone anvil, covered in dried blood and decay. Then she saw the end wall. Painted in blood was a pictogram of a winged beast with horns and scales and great wings. Her blood ran cold. She knew who the great beast was, she knew their master and had fought him before. Without wasting any more time, she did a quick search for her weapons and upon finding them concealed them upon her person, then headed for the door. She knew she had to get out of there and find Ignatius.

Chapter 5: Escape

As Indigo unlocked the door, she had no way of knowing what time of day it was. Her whole body ached; and her wrists were sore due to her bindings. The heavy latch creaked as she opened the door just a crack to peer outward. It looked like it was dusk. She slipped out quietly, keeping close to the wall, looking around constantly as she tried to gauge which part of the city she was in, looking for landmarks to get her orientation. In the distance, she could see the great black monolith of the Administorium looming over the city. She headed in that direction, nervously looking over her shoulder and avoiding others. The street bustled with steam gurneys and overhead she could hear the whirl of a propeller thrusting a dirigible forward.

By now her body was feeling its pain. She was bruised and cut from her encounter with the Skoto twins, and although she had stopped bleeding, she dragged her sore body across the city anxiously, still looking over her shoulder. She had to get some rest before heading back out to find Ignatius. She was too tired and in too much pain to continue. She needed time to figure out what was going on. When she got to her door, it had been forced, the doorframe splintered and the latch lying in pieces on the floor. Indigo carefully pushed the door open, pulling a derringer out and pushing it into the dark to lead the way should the villain still be here, although likelihood was that Skoto and her double were responsible. Looking around, she could see that her belongings had been ransacked and she was definitely alone. Closing the door and wedging a chair against it, she lit the room, and the full horror of the scene confronted her. Every drawer, every box, every tin had all been emptied. Her clothes had been swept aside and her wardrobe searched, her French linen bedding discarded on the floor and her writing desk prised open, letters, reports and sentimental items strewn everywhere.

"Well, I don't know what you were looking for, but I'm sure you haven't found it," she mumbled to herself, cursing the would-be thieves.

Indigo set about tidying up a little and tending to her cuts and bruises. She was tired and needed to rest before trying to find out what was going on. She lay down on her bed and although restless, it wasn't long before she was fast asleep. Night set in and she lay there in the darkness, the void, the emptiness of her own room.

Somewhere between wake and sleep, she began to have visions. Was she dreaming? Was it real? Although it was dark, she knew he was there. She couldn't see him, but she could feel the hotness of his breath on her neck. A foul acrid smell filled the air. Out of the darkness appeared a hawk-headed man, looming over her. Indigo screamed and woke suddenly. Her chest glistened with sweat, her hair sticking to her face with cold wet fear. The evil bird of prey, half bird, half human, but actually some kind of god-like being, morphed into a man dressed in combat leathers, his powder blue eyes matching his breeches, staring at her. At this sight of her father, Atman of the Charon, she was wide awake and resentful.

She sat up in her bed, and she peered out into the dimly lit room. A single shaft of brilliant light shone through a split in the curtains, which she hadn't opened for days. Her head felt fuzzy. Since her adventure through the cosmos, Indigo had struggled to come to terms with all that she and Ignatius had experienced. She felt empty. What was it all for? She was a mere speck of dust on an insignificant ball of rock hurtling through space, unimportant, unnoticed and of little consequence to the gods that played out events that shaped the human universe, the cosmos and beyond.

She was not herself and didn't want Ignatius to see her like this, vulnerable. She was struggling, fighting the demons in her mind, struggling with the horrific death of Skye at the hands of the Charon. She was a wreck. She wanted to neglect her duties and her allegiance to the Union Jacks and the Empire. She could not get past the empty feeling that all life on earth was fruitless, just a pointless existence. Life in its many varied forms, not just life on earth, was far more complex than any scientist, philosopher or astronomer on this tiny blue planet could possibly comprehend. What was it all about? What is the purpose of any religion or belief? Or were they valid? Did each and every god, supernatural being, monster or demon from all the legends on earth actually exist somewhere on some plane? Did all folklore and mythology really originate with an actual being or event somewhere in the cosmos? How could she ever return to a normal life as an agent for the Union Jacks with the knowledge she now had?

She decided not to go and see Ignatius, not yet. As she whiled away the time, her appearance denied any hint of her usual strength and clarity of mind and action. She no longer washed or dressed correctly. She took to drinking gin. Lots of gin. Usually straight from the bottle. A bottle that usually found its way onto the floor surrounding her bed. She was a shell of herself. She avoided leaving the house unless absolutely necessary, just for provisions usually, or more gin. Even then, only at dusk, quickly returning before the velvet blackness of night set in.

That night, Indigo climbed into bed, wearing just a loose nightshirt, and as she slumped back onto her linen-covered mattress, the room began to spin. Her head swirled as the effects of too much alcohol took hold. She felt nauseated, but she shut her eyes tight and felt the darkness of night envelop her.

The night passed quickly and as dawn pierced the room through a crack in the drapes, Indigo slid out of her bed and sat cross-legged on the floor. She closed her eyes and for some reason unknown to her, began to chant, a low-pitched incoherent set of syllables given to her by Tara of the Charon. She could hear the world around her, hear Ignatius pacing the room impatiently, even though he wasn't there. Too many worldly distractions. She continued undeterred, her words merging into one long musical tone. She became aware of nothing around her except the beating sound of her own heart and the rush of blood through her head. Her mind's eye saw nothing but inky blackness until in the distance a single faint and tiny point of light appeared. It grew in intensity and appeared larger and larger until it floated before her. She felt like she could feel every atom, every sound, every ripple in the chaotic cosmos. She felt like she had left her bedroom and was walking in the bright sunshine, waist deep in golden flowers and still in her nightshirt. She could feel the heat of the sun beating down on her back. A moment of escapism. As she ceased her contemplation and became aware of her surroundings once more, she felt invigorated, her aching body had renewed itself. She still had her cuts and bruises but felt decidedly energetic and stronger.

She washed and changed into a ruffle skirt and bodice. Looking at the lock on the door, there was no way she could repair it quickly, so she would have to hope for the best. She suitably armed herself as always, recharging her steam cannon and headed out to look for Ignatius, pulling the door carefully behind her to make it look like it was locked.

Chapter 6: Revelations

A few days had passed, and Ignatius was still thinking about the glitch he had experienced and how time had repeated itself, even though it had been for just a few moments. Pacing his study, he began trying to analyse the vision he had experienced immediately afterwards. He wondered if this was likely to be a common feature of the new Megasphere and if his visions would become debilitating. He had formed the opinion that it was best to say nothing to High Command of the Union Jacks organisation, for fear they would think him afflicted with some kind of madness, but wondered if any other agent had experienced anything like the event themselves. He hadn't seen Indigo for a few days and so hadn't even been able to ask her.

Since his last mission, Ignatius had been struggling with his nature, the fact he was descended from a god, a demonic, merciless god. As part of his own mental wellbeing, he had decided to take up meditation. The reasons were two-fold, firstly to stay calm, at peace with the world, with his circumstances, at peace with his status in the Union Jacks, and secondly to try and stay connected to the cosmos now that he knew it was far more complicated than he'd imagined, and that every living being was connected to it with their consciousness, a result of the Book of Consciousness written by the creator, the Omnisoul. During his meditation sessions, he wondered if he would ever come face to face with the Charon again, other than in dreams. Perhaps their imprisonment in Limbo was so restricted it no longer allowed for the wanderings of their consciousness. He knew on occasions, Adonai was able to escape and had been terrorising Britons disguised as the character the penny dreadfuls called Spring-Heeled Jack.

Ignatius needed to relax, but as usual he was combining his meditation with the occult knowledge he had acquired by studying the magicians of Persia and Nubia and the shamans of Kashmir, so had chalked a pentagram and strange symbols on the floor of his study. He checked the door to his study was locked then threw back a large Kilim rug to reveal his handiwork and, placing the rug aside, sat in the middle of the pentagram. Crossing his legs, he sat and placed his hands upon his knees. Closing his eyes, he began to breathe slowly and deeply, feeling every part of his body becoming invigorated with the oxygen travelling through his body, until he felt completely at ease and his mind was empty save for the sound of his soft, deep breath.

The world seemed to jolt, much like the time glitch before, and he felt unsteady, as if he was about to fall over, despite still sitting on the floor. Then he saw himself, as if in an out-of-body experience. He saw Indigo in the distance. He could hear faint music that seemed to envelop him, but he could not tell where it was coming from. It was mesmerising and it seemed to be calling him. As he looked on in a daze, he could now see several Indigos going through several doorways. He followed in his uncertainty, but which Indigo was the one to pursue? Which doorway was the correct one to enter? He placed his right hand, his eye-shaped birthmark, over his eye to try and gain insight. But to no avail. The view was confusing; he could see across too many planes. Too many demons and ghouls, too many copies of doorways and people he knew. He looked on as he saw himself walk over to a door, possibly to his study and lock it, he threw back a rug on the floor to sit on the pentagram exactly where he was now, and it felt like his spirit was re-joining his body so the two were one again. Another glitch in the cosmos? Or a mirror soul?

He returned to the here and now, to his empty mind, and sat motionless. His mind was a black empty void. After some time that blackness was interrupted by a single white point of light no bigger than the head of a pin. It grew larger and larger as if he was moving towards it, but no matter how much he moved forward, it didn't fill the entire void. The whiteness became blinding before starting to fade and Ignatius could feel a warm acrid breeze on his face. The fading light began to morph and take the shape of two enormous iridescent blue lips, which changed to create a sinister grin with blackened crooked teeth. Ignatius had seen this image before, this was the Voice, one of the Celestials, seven powerful sorcerer lords who had obtained god-like status from an otherwise extinct civilisation in the Netherworlds. The Voice was the Celestial who usually communicated with the Charon to convey the will of The Omnisoul.

The bodyless Voice spoke, "Know this, Ignatius, reluctant human, you have a quest to fulfil which only you and Indigo can achieve. It will repair the cosmos and secure the fabric of space and time once more. However, an ancient relic is at risk. If captured by the wrong people, it will lead to complete entropy. Through you is the way into the depths of knowledge. Through you is the way to the mystical city. Through you is the way to the lost people who hold the key. However, through you is also the way to unlocking this terrible relic and unleashing death upon all eternity."

Ignatius was confused. Was this a dream? Had he connected to the cosmos in some way, guessing this to be the goal for all who meditate or seek enlightenment? Could he respond? His body seemed restrained in some way, he couldn't move, but concentrating all his effort, he at last managed some words, although he didn't know if these were real, spoken from his mouth or just his mind's inner voice.

"What do you mean?" he seemed to croak, although he didn't believe a single word actually left his lips. "What kind of quest? And why are you telling me? I thought your role was to inform the Charon of their quests. This does not concern me."

"Oh, it very much concerns you. Heed my words, there is much you do not know, but you and your counterpart, Indigo, have much to offer the cosmos. You are now messengers of divine will. You must fulfil a prophecy. However, be cautious, a life may be forfeit but it will save many."

"What do you mean?"

"I cannot remain any longer, for I have risked much to come here, keeping my presence a secret from the Omnisoul has exhausted great energy from the other Celestials."

"And the Charon? What of they? Have you told the…" He didn't get a chance to finish.

"You must not involve the Charon!"

Then as quickly as the Voice had appeared, he disappeared again, leaving Ignatius alone once more in his study but feeling somewhat breathless and fatigued from the incident. He opened his eyes. He was still sat on the chalked pentagram, his study exactly as he had last seen it, except it was now nightfall. He had been meditating for a considerable amount of time, yet if felt like moments. Checking his pocket watch, he realised it had stopped. That was unusual. It was a precision piece from Switzerland and seldom needed correcting. As he got up off the floor, he noticed two neatly folded newspapers on his desk. Unusual! Had Lambeth started ordering other newspapers? As he picked them up, he realised they both displayed the same header logo, that of the Times, but they were different editions. He looked more closely at the dates, they were different. On his side table was the Times he had been reading. Ignatius staggered backwards; how could this be? He had been meditating for three days without any break. He headed for the door, but it was locked. Turning the key, he opened it and headed for the drawing room. "Lambeth! Lambeth! Where are you, man?"

The grey-haired gent appeared in the doorway, "Yes sir. How may I assist?"

"How have I been out of it for so long? Why didn't you tell me?"

"Well, sir. I didn't wish to disturb you, you looked so peaceful and I thought you needed the rest. You did have me worried the first day when I couldn't get a reply, so I took the liberty of using the spare key to enter and check you were ok. A bit difficult as your key was still in the lock, but with a bit of wiggling and some persuasion I gained access. But since your last adventure, I thought you needed the rest, sir. Sorry if that was a mistake."

"No, not at all. Thank you, Lambeth, you have been most helpful."

"Tea, sir?"

"Good idea Lambeth, yes. Make it Lapsang Souchong will you, I need something a little more invigorating."

"Very well sir," and Lambeth headed for the kitchen.

Ignatius returned to his study, replacing the rug back to conceal the chalked symbols on the floor. He paced up and down for a while, rubbing his chin whilst thinking. Duly, Lambeth arrived with his tea. He placed the tray down and left. As Lambeth walked back into the hallway, he heard the key turn once more as Ignatius locked his study again, saying, somewhat muffled from behind the door, "I do not wish to be disturbed."

Chapter 7: A Sound Invention

Lambeth was increasingly more concerned. He hadn't seen Ignatius for two more days. He had locked himself away in his study again but this time with strict instructions he was not to be disturbed, no matter what. The last Lambeth had seen of him was when he came rushing out like a man possessed. Wild-eyed, his hair unruly, his shirt sleeves rolled up and without his necktie. He'd gone clattering around the house grabbing musical instruments. An Indian flute or two, piano tuning forks, singing bowls from Tibet, a small drum from Africa and the metronome off the piano. Then returning to his study, he locked the door again.

Lambeth didn't like to skulk and spy, but he pressed his ear against the study door, a frown upon his brow and concerned eyes that could just about see in the gloomy corridors. Where there had been noise at first and faint music, flat notes, and the odd curse or two, he could now hear nothing. Silence filled the house.

The following day, Ignatius waited until he heard Lambeth leave the house on errands. He cautiously peeked out of the window of his study and watched Lambeth head off down the street, his white hair blowing in the breeze.

He turned back to his desk and, opening an ornately carved wooden box, took the miniature qanun out. This was the instrument he had acquired in the mystical city of Sagharta on his cosmic adventure with the Charon. He placed it carefully on the leather inlay of his desk next to a device that was covered with a piece of linen. On the other side of the study, he lifted a large heavy tome and placed it on top of a stone plinth. Returning to the instrument, he removed the linen, revealing a curious steam instrument shaped a little like a steam cannon. It let out a hiss and a plume of steam rose into the air.

Ignatius braced himself and very lightly ran his fingers delicately across the strings of the qanun. An empty sherry glass on his desk shattered and books in the bookcase opposite began to tremble and vibrate to the edge of the shelf and suddenly burst, scattering pages all over the study.

"Too hard!" he cursed.

After all the pages had floated back down to the floor and the air was clear once more, he tried again. He rubbed his fingers together and flexed them. He gently ran his fingers over the strings once more, as lightly as if he were caressing an injured bird. A faint melodic sound could just be heard over the silence of the study. On top of the stone plinth, the heavy tome began to vibrate rhythmically. It oscillated with each corner of the book lifting in turn until the rhythm settled down and matched the natural resonance of the music Ignatius was playing. He then lifted the weapon and, turning several dials, was able to mimic the sound coming from the qanun. As the sound of the mystical musical instrument began to die down, the steam device continued. Turning the volume down, Ignatius was able to gently lower the book back down onto the plinth.

"Excellent! Success at last." Ignatius could feel his pulse quicken and hear his heart pounding in his ears with excitement,

He turned the volume on again and the book levitated again, He had complete control over it and could raise and lower it at will. His weapon was far more predictable than the qanun.

Moving confidently across the study, Ignatius removed the book and replaced it with an ancient stone tablet carved in some forgotten language, although it was most likely a fake. Then, returning to the qanun, he ran his fingers once more across some of the strings. The sound that emanated travelled across the study and focused on the stone artifact, which resonated briefly before shattering into thousands of pieces and falling to the floor, mainly as powder.

Sweeping his hand across the top of the plinth and removing the remaining debris, Ignatius placed a similar tablet on top of the plinth. Once again, he took to the dials of the steam contraption and eventually replicated the instrument's sound and the second stone tablet shattered with a large cracking sound that split the tense air of the study.

A large grin appeared across Ignatius's face; he had achieved his goal. He now had a steam cannon that could move and destroy objects by the power of sound alone. He now had the Union's first sonic blaster.

He straightened his tie and put on his great coat, tucking his new weapon into the poacher's pocket inside. He unlocked the study door and headed towards the front door. As he turned the handle, Lambeth appeared behind him.

"Oh, sir. I am pleased you are well, I was beginning to worry."

"Fear not, Lambeth. Fear not! I must dash, I need to do some research."

Then he turned quickly disappeared into the street, blending in

with the bustle of the horse and carriages and the steam gurneys
as they raced by scaring the horses.

Chapter 8: Ransacked

Indigo appeared at the wide door to Ignatius's house. Knocking, the old figure of Lambeth appeared, opening the door guardedly, just enough for one wizened eye to look out cautiously to see who it was.

He mumbled "He's still not here. You're not coming in again," and pushed the door to. But Indigo was too quick for him and wedged her foot in the door.

"Ouch! Lambeth, whatever's wrong? Why can't I come in?"

"I'm still recovering from your last visit," he shouted as he swung the door open and thrust a steam cannon towards her, his bleeding skull following. "This time, I'm prepared!"

"Lambeth, I have no idea what you're talking about. Why do you think I'm responsible for hurting you?"

"Don't act all innocent, you were here about an hour ago, making all sorts of demands regarding Ignatius's artefacts. But I'm not… why have you changed your clothes? When you came here last, you were dressed differently. It's only been an hour or so…"

Indigo looked on, rather confused, "I can assure you this is my first visit today, Lambeth. Please let me come in so we can work out what's going on."

Lambeth conceded, "very well, madam," and lowered his weapon.

As Indigo entered it was clear that Lambeth was very shaken "Where's Ignatius?"

"I'm not sure, miss. I briefly saw him this morning. I think he said something about research. But you were here earlier and have left his study in a real mess. What's going on, miss? Why did you turn everything over? What were you looking for?"

"I haven't been here, Lambeth!" Indigo protested. "Let me see his study."

Before he could answer, Indigo walked past him and headed to the study. She stood in the corridor and listened intently at the door. Nothing. Placing her hand on the doorknob she turned it slowly and without a sound. Entering cautiously into the gloom, she let out a slight gasp at the sight before her.

The room looked like it had been ransacked. Books had been indiscriminately pulled from bookshelves. Arcane tomes, so very ancient they had started to fall apart, odd sheets in fragments on the Persian rug. Individual pages were scattered about the room, on the desk, the floor, the chairs, some were in small piles, others lay cast aside still open. Some looked ancient with yellowing pages coming loose from their bindings. Her eyes drifted towards the partners desk; an empty bottle of whiskey lay on its side. Another was open and only half full. Two empty bottles of absinthe had been cast aside, a milky louche still in its glass on the edge of the desk. Several empty bottles of red wine lay staining the leather inlay of the desk. Hand saws, drills and chisels lay amongst them, the resultant saw dust and wood shavings littering the floor. Elsewhere, the floor was littered with small rocks and rock dusk.

Technical instruments, broken glass and brass components were scattered around. The lock on the desk had been forced open and the drawers pulled out and emptied. Musical instruments littered the floor, some had been partially dismantled, a violin with strings missing, various flutes, some with keys missing, exotic drums and singing bowls, some filled with water. The scene was obviously not the usual behaviour for Ignatius.

"Do you know if anything was taken?" asked Indigo.

"I have no idea, my dear. But I'm confused. The culprit looked like you!"

With concern on her face, Indigo said, "Clearly something is not right. Let me help you clear this up."

After the study began to look at least something like its usual organisation, Indigo asked Lambeth, "Do you know where Ignatius was going when he left?"

"He said he was off to do some research, so he'll probably be in the Bodleian or one of those penny universities in the coffee houses in High Street."

"Thank you, Lambeth. I'll go and look for him, but please be assured, it was not me who plundered his study. Something very strange is going on."

Indigo left and began walking to the city centre, quite certain she would find Ignatius at the library, his favourite place in the whole city. As she looked skyward, she saw an airship gliding silently overhead, heading for the south-eastern part of the city. The streets of Summertown were quiet, with fewer steam gurneys and horses even. The long silent walk allowed her to ponder the events that had played out recently, but she couldn't make out what was going on. She felt the hairs on the back of her neck bristle, her usual sign that she was heading for some excitement and danger, the usual experience for an agent of the Union Jacks.

She tucked her head down and increased her pace, walking briskly in anticipation.

Reaching the city centre, dominated by the university, with its honey-coloured glow of Cotswold stone, gradually darkening as the steam-powered pollution from the surrounding areas crept in, an ever-tightening blanket of smog. On the horizon to the south-east of the city, Indigo could see the buildings were darker and altogether more imposing, angry and brooding. Watt's monstrous engines dominated the skyline, as the steam cylinders forged steel, spitting out sulphur and coal. The squalid houses and tenement blocks of the poor were dwarfed by the money-making machines that towered above, polluting the skies. To the north-west, hangars housing the great leviathans of the air disturbed the peace and tranquillity of the Oxfordshire countryside. Yet despite the industrial revolution choking and polluting the skies above the city, the gears of the universities, both official and backwater, continued to grind on, feeding the insatiability of her associate, Ignatius.

Chapter 9: A Peculiar Occurrence

Ignatius sat in the furthest corner of the Bodleian, the darkest corner where he could see the rest of the library. He had waited for some time for the book he was interested in to be fetched from the stacks in the labyrinth of tunnels beneath the library. He was beginning to think this was a deliberate act, delaying tactics whilst the Administorium were called. Eventually his request was fulfilled, and the librarian handed over the book.

Still seated, he turned on a desk light to see by and opened the ancient tome he had so often consulted recently. The author, Enoch Slipnot, seemed knowledgeable about recent events related to the Charon, which was impossible. This was an ancient book, so Enoch must have lived thousands of years in the past. He couldn't possibly know of recent events. Ignatius began to think that maybe he was a prophet or a seer, or maybe could travel through time. He scanned the pages in search of anything related to the creation of multiple universes, about the infinity shards that the Charon had inadvertently created when they tried to destroy the Well at the Centre of Time. It was becoming obvious that time was not linear, it somehow flowed in parallel and could be different on each plane, or perhaps it could flow back and forth. He looked for information regarding fractures in time, reading the faded ink once more.

After time stood still and the stars were split, the world did falter in its rotation, and it came to pass brothers would see apparitions of themselves like twin brothers, and confusion reigned with tribes not knowing themselves and upon visiting themselves took up arms once more and brother killed brother.

And the chaos heralded the great Unholy One setting foot upon this plane once more with even more power and destruction, acrid sulphuric death poured forth and the land was laid barren as he read from the indestructible dark book. That which is the dark twin to rival cosmic consciousness, and which wrought chaos and shadows bringing unknown darkness to the land and upon all who observed its pages. These two are the germ, and the germ is one concealed in the Divine thought of the First Cause. From the first born the thread between the all-seeing and the shadow grows ever stronger.

Yet behold the two righteous ones who are to fulfil the prophecy that shall banish the primordial root cause and restore order to the cosmos, when the heavens are splintered and the basilisk falls from the heavens like a flaming star.

Know this for once more, I am unswerving in my task as the last remaining warrior-priest of the Charon – the Dragon-slayers of the ecclesiarchy…

Suddenly, Ignatius was distracted. The door to the Bodleian swung open, causing the desk clerk to look up. She frowned at the abruptness. Indigo strode confidently into the library, letting the door close behind her with a clatter. Some of the readers looked up, their faces displaying annoyance and displeasure. The clerk let out a loud tut and sighed disapprovingly. Indigo didn't look as if she cared. She looked and acted differently to usual. *Maybe it's the result of the recent adventure,* thought Ignatius.

She was dressed in a large white blouson, a tight black leather corset that finished beneath her breasts, a crimson skirt and black thigh-high leather boots. She made no secret that she was armed with a small derringer tucked into her belt, and a large steam cannon hanging from her right thigh. Her hair fell about her shoulders and on her head she wore a pair of brass goggles with emerald-green lenses. She looked like a woman on a mission. To Ignatius, she looked decidedly odd somehow, but he couldn't quite put his finger on how. With her plunging neckline, her very demeanour and swagger made her look indelicate. Ignatius didn't feel comfortable. She skirted the edge of the library and soon located him in the shadows. She was looking for him. As she approached, a soft breeze brought her scent to his attention. Ignatius was alarmed internally at how he kept getting distracted. He fidgeted, unusually so.

Talking in hushed tones he greeted her, "Indigo, how lovely to see you. I was beginning to worry. Where have you been?"

"I've been lying low," she said. "It's all been a lot to take in. I've been exhausted." Her voice seemed to tremble a little.

"Well, quite, my dear. But I fear there is still more to do."

"What do you mean?"

"Well, I believe there is another book.

"This place is full of them!" she said sarcastically.

He didn't rise to it but showed her the familiar small ancient tome he had been studying, "You've heard me mention Enoch Slipnot before. Some kind of archivist or historian who seemed to know of the Charon. Well, here he alludes to another book. Maybe a twin to the Book of Consciousness. See here?" As he pointed out the relevant passages, Indigo was quick to pick up the book and read. Her face seemed to light up involuntarily until she realised and reverted back to her previous composure.

"Oh! I see. And where do you think this book is kept?"

"Well, your guess is as good as mine. Although I am sure there are more clues in this ancient tome."

Indigo looked irritated with that answer. "Well, you must have some idea!"

Ignatius thought he detected some irritation or desperation in her voice. Unusual for her. She was usually calm and collected, somewhat of an enigma, like her name. That's why he liked her and together they got on so well when they were out in the field on missions for the Union Jacks. No one else seemed to quite figure her out, and they definitely didn't mention her name with any inquisition. Even Ignatius knew not to question Indigo Gemstone. But today, she seemed different. Had recent events really affected her that much?

Indigo could see in his face the curiosity of her behaviour. She softened a little. Smiling, she moved closer to him, more into the shadows. Her lips were slightly parted, and she seemed to let her blouson open a little more so Ignatius could see the full swell of her breasts as she inhaled deeply. She put her arm around him and could feel his muscular frame hot against her body as she looked into his eyes. Ignatius was very fond of Indigo, but they had to work together, he didn't want to complicate their relationship. He began to feel uncomfortable and blushed. He could feel her hot breath on his neck.

"We need to keep this professional," he said, a slight tremble in his voice. She had never behaved like this before. His mind began to race, wondering if there had ever been any signs previously that their relationship was anything other than professional, with common goals to serve the Empire.

She moved her head directly in front of his and looked him squarely in the face. "But we can all benefit from the situation we find ourselves in, can't we?"

At which point she took his cheeks and, with her full red lips, planted a kiss on his. Ignatius pulled his head away and to one side. "I say!", he exclaimed, at which point the librarian gave out another loud tut. Then, beyond the reading desks, he thought he saw Indigo enter the library, dressed in her usual attire with a ruffle skirt and bodice. But that was impossible. He didn't want to upset her or embarrass her, and wasn't quite sure how to react. Besides, this was a public place! He stood up and gently grabbed Indigo by her waist and pushed her away, noticing her face change into a scowl. Realising she had dropped her façade, she smiled again.

"But Ignatius, together we can solve this, I'm sure."

Ignatius assumed she meant the riddle of the other book, and not the relationship, but he was too busy scanning the rest of the library looking for the other Indigo he thought he'd seen.

"There you are," exclaimed Indigo. "I assumed you would be in here as usual, oh! I'm sorry, you have company," Indigo said, seeing another woman standing in a white blouson and thigh high boots with her back to her. "I'll wait. No rush, Ignatius."

At this point, the woman turned around and Indigo saw herself staring back at her. Her other self took advantage of the confusion and grabbed the book Ignatius had been reading, rushing towards another reading table and sliding along it to the other end, books and lamps being swept aside as she went, much to the disgust of other readers who grumbled and tutted, albeit quietly. They turned to Ignatius with angry disapproval painted on their faces. Ignatius shrugged.

Without sparing any more time, he was up and gave chase, grabbing the Indigo he knew by the arm pulling her with him. "You have a doppelganger, my dear!"

The two gave chase, much to the dismay of everybody else in the library.

A stern-looking man with a balding head and very large moustache dressed in a black suit bellowed, "Mr Ignatius! Really! And you haven't returned your book!"

Ignatius shot him a quick apologetic glance and continued out the door, hot on the heels of the two Indigos, failing to see another man who, dressed like he was, must have been a cleric from the Administorium.

"I'm not exactly sure what I do when I catch her, Ignatius." Indigo could feel her heart pounding in her chest, mainly at the realisation that she was chasing herself. She gave chase down Broad Street, dodging in and out of steam gurneys and the crowds.

As they turned left into Cornmarket Street Indigo dived at her other self and tackled her to the ground. As they fought, Indigo lashed out and cut her doppelganger's right cheek. With her momentarily stunned, Indigo was able to grab the book and throw it out of reach, where Ignatius picked it up. Indigo and Ignatius took a few moments to catch their breath. Whilst she had the advantage, Indigo held her doppelganger to the ground, pinning her shoulders back and kneeling on her arms. It felt really strange to be face to face with herself, and she had to think twice, not really wanting to hurt her.

"Who are you?" demanded Indigo.

Her identical twin just laughed. "I'm you of course. A bad omen, come to find what should be mine. But I have to say, I didn't expect to meet myself, my twin soul.

"Then where do you come from?"

She laughed again, this time heartily. "Oxford, of course. I told you, I'm you!"

She could see the total look of confusion on Indigo's face. Ignatius, on the other hand thought he was beginning to understand.

"I'm from a parallel world, another universe, identical to yours. It exists on another plane running parallel to yours. We both occupy the same space. The planes are entangled and co-exist. But on my world, we have learned to travel across the planes, to search out hidden worlds, made easier since the Charon fractured the cosmos and inadvertently created the Infinity Shards. Now there are even more versions of ourselves. You can't blame me for trying to obtain Enoch Slipnot's book, for trying to obtain what you both seek. It's my adventure too!"

Indigo thought for a time, "but surely that same book exists on your world, does it not?"

"Not anymore. The Administorium destroyed it!

"Destroyed!" Indigo couldn't believe what she was hearing.

"Although we exist in parallel worlds, events do not happen the same. The Bodleian no longer exists on my world. The Administorium deemed it too dangerous and capable of perverting the Empire. So I have been sent here to obtain another copy. I was visited by Calabi-Ya's minions, who called themselves Skoto."

Indigo gave a knowing look and before she could speak, her other self said it, "They've been here too, haven't they?"

"Yes, they kidnapped me, but I had no idea what they wanted. They spoke of the Book of Shadows."

Her other self looked horrified. "We are all seeking the Book of Shadows, written by Calabi-Ya, but nobody knows where it is. Or on which plane it lies. But whatever you do, if you find it, tell me you won't open it! Do not open that book! My aim is to destroy all clues on all planes that may lead to the Book of Shadows."

"But why...." Indigo never got to finish her words.

"I have to go. Please get off me. I have to go! I do not want to be here if that book is ever opened! I beg you to keep Enoch's book safe, do not let anybody else read it, or destroy those pages that allude to the Book of Shadows, so there are no more clues to it. I need to cross to other planes to seek and destroy all copies of Enoch's book.

Indigo looked at Ignatius. He gestured slightly to indicate his thoughts. Indigo climbed off her other self and helped her up.

Brushing her clothing down and straightening her crimson skirt, she said, "Indigo, Ignatius, I wish you all the luck. You will need it if you find the Book of Shadows. But luck will not save you or any of us for opening that book will destroy us all!"

She turned and walked a little further up Cornmarket Street and casually threw a brass grenade of some kind that exploded before her, resulting in a flash of brilliant blue light and a shrill symphony of notes that pierced the ears of those nearby. Then she charged into the light and was gone, the portal she had created snapping shut immediately behind her.

"I am intrigued why you have a doppelganger and how she could open a portal, presumably back to her own world. I don't think we appreciated the significance fully when the Charon fractured the cosmos."

"Somewhere else in the cosmos our other selves have figured out a way to create or use these portals." Indigo raised her eyebrow, before continuing, "Makes us look a bit lame if there are Union Jacks with that kind of technology."

"My guess is when the Charon tried to destroy time, they unwittingly created a more complex cosmos. They have caused weaknesses in space and time, causing portals to other planes, other worlds, and the *other* Union Jacks have found a way to take advantage of this and utilise these weaknesses."

Indigo wasn't really listening. "It's really strange, chasing yourself. It's made me somewhat apprehensive."

"We need to try and figure this out. But we can't talk here." A few people had already stopped to see what the commotion was all about. Ignatius gave a cautious glance around.

"No, I know."

"We'd better return to my house where we can discuss what little knowledge I have gleaned and what our next move is."

"Your study has been ransacked. I called round earlier, and Lambeth was somewhat shaken. He thought I'd searched your study, but I guess that must have been the doppelganger. My rooms have been searched, too. I need to make them secure again."

"When we get back, I'll send Lambeth round. He can get the Union Jacks technician to take a look and see about making your rooms more secure from here on."

Indigo held her chin thoughtfully. "She must have been looking for clues for the Book of Shadows in Enoch Slipnot's book. But what does it contain that we have missed?"

"I had already discovered there is another book. I was reading about it only this morning. I think it's some kind of twin to the Book of Consciousness."

As they turned around to make their way through St. Giles to head for Summertown, where Ignatius lived, a dark shadowy hooded figure followed and then hid behind a large fig tree in the graveyard of St. Giles' church.

Chapter 10: Summoned

In Ignatius's study, the two Union Jacks sat hunched over the great desk that lay at one end of the study. They were both concentrating on Enoch Slipnot's book.

"Does this tome have a name?" asked Indigo.

"Yes, it's known as the Tamas Codex. It has something to do with darkness, shadows, perhaps and is an apocryphal work. Most believe it to be a hoax, but I have never been sure. I have always thought it to have some thread of truth or historical accuracy. Believe it or not, most myths and legends do. These stories are passed down orally from generation to generation and have to start somewhere, some significant event or person. But for the most part the book is about the cyclic nature of the world, destruction and rebirth after a great cataclysm or a deluge. It's my belief that the world has been populated by humans several time over, with advanced technology, before being wiped out only to start again."

"Each epoch different to the last?"

"Precisely! The last time I used this book was to learn of the Charon and of Turiya, The Book of Consciousness. So that's proof the text does contain some amount of truth, we need to look at what happens next. But it also begs the question, how did it get here, what are its origins? It is written like a historical record, so how are events only just happening? Unless of course history does repeat itself."

"Well, we know there are several planes in the cosmos, running parallel, and that travel across them is possible. Maybe, the book has traversed planes, changed its position in time? Who knows?"

"Well, now I have it, I'm not returning it to the Bodleian, at least not until we have some more answers and know what is going on. I think it will be safer here with me."

Turning the ancient, yellowed pages carefully, Ignatius scanned the text for anything of use, any scrap of information that might help them.

"Can you see anything related to doppelgangers?" asked Ignatius.

Indigo squinted her eyes and searched, focusing wholly on that word.

"What if Enoch used another term? Twin, evil twin, copy, double, even Didymus, it could be anything!" She continued to follow the text carefully. Page after page, event after event, none of it good.

"There's more death and destruction in here than the rest of the library put together!" she said.

"Here!" exclaimed Indigo. "I've found it!" Pointing with her finger so Ignatius could follow.

When the evil twins shall come out of the shadows in great numbers to walk the earth and great confusion shall reign as duplicates shall be seen in the streets and it shall be like watching through a looking glass as citizens shall see themselves. They shall look upon their darkest selves and recoil in horror as true malevolence shall manifest upon the planet and lead to its destruction.

Beware the signs, the bad omens that shall signify the start of the end of times and the great washing away shall begin, to begin once more with the seven strong fiery whirlwind and bright space shall cease to be and only dark space shall remain.

"So, your doppelganger really is a bad omen," said Ignatius giving a slightly nervous laugh. "Do we believe the end times are here?" he said, questioning Indigo.

"Who knows? But after our latest revelation, that the cosmos holds other life, other intelligence, and horrors and above all else gods, I wouldn't rule anything out!"

"I know that Enoch lived in a time when a group of people called the Duranki walked the earth. Do you remember it was through their land that Calabi-Ya came. Ragnar of Roc had opened a portal. But look here…"

Ignatius pointed at another page of the codex.

"I'm not sure these pages are even in order, you know. Whoever bound them may have got it wrong. It looks like each page was a separate sheet of parchment. Look at this part of the book, it is written in the present tense. This is a record of what took place, whereas so far, we have only read what will happen. Enoch Slipnot must have been some kind of prophet."

Looking on, Indigo read aloud.

When the gods of the earth had not yet appeared, the Duranki descended from the heavens in their fiery chariots and populated the land. They fulfilled the prophecy that had been written by those practiced in the art of Al Kimiya.

To document their great deeds, they brought with them scribes. The brothers two and their sister, possessors of great wisdom built three magical repositories that drifted across the planes of heaven and earth. And these near immortals recorded all that is, all that was and all that shall be.

It was the magic of the Duranki that set the repositories in motion and the siblings were sacrificed by being forever linked to the structures they built. Thus,

Indigo lifted her eyes from the manuscript, and looking at Ignatius spoke, "So what do you think? Is the Book of Shadows in one of these repositories?"

"I'm not sure!" said Ignatius, "But even if it was, we don't know anything about the book or where these repositories could be. I'm inclined to forget all about it. I mean, what does it mean to the Empire? At least we knew something about the Book of Consciousness. However, this business with the doppelgangers is bothering me. I'm convinced there is more to them. It's not all about the weaknesses brought about by the Charon splitting the cosmos."

The college bells rang out across Oxford to announce evensong as the sun began to set. Outside, the light was beginning to fade. The golden hour forced its light through the windows of the study. The noise of the steam gurneys diminished with the light, allowing the more traditional hansom cabs to dominate the evening streets.

"I think we should call it a day," said Ignatius, closing the codex and placing the ancient and delicate tome into one of the drawers in his desk.

A loud knock came at the front door, bringing Lambeth scurrying to open it. A tall slender man stood wearing a black hooded cloak. What part of his face was on display looked youthful, but gaunt and pallid. His eyes were in shadow cast by his hood. He said nothing, then thrust a small white card into Lambeth's elderly hand, swiftly turned and walked away. Lambeth stepped out and peered after him, but he was quickly out of sight.

Looking down, Lambeth read the card. It was addressed to Ignatius and was written in a fine copperplate script. Turning it over, Lambeth's blood ran cold. Ignatius had been summoned to the Administorium.

Turning, he headed back in, securing the door and making his way to Ignatius's study. Knocking he entered.

"Sorry to disturb, sir. But you've had an invite. Well, been summoned…"

Handing the card over, he watched Ignatius's face carefully for his reaction. Undaunted, Ignatius answered, "Very well, Lambeth. That's ok."

Chapter 11: The Administorium

Ignatius crossed the city and headed for the black monolith that was the Administorium. Turning his face to the spires above him, he looked beyond them, beyond this world, his mind wandering as if drifting through other dimensions, searching for answers. As he approached his destination, its long shadow cast a foreboding blackness across the honey-coloured stone buildings around it. A few more steps and Ignatius was enveloped by that blackness. He looked up to observe the patination on the building's surface. It had been constructed out of a single huge meteorite and highly polished to reveal the Widmanstätten pattern. As he approached the monolith, there wasn't any obvious sign of any doorway. As he got nearer, he had to slow his step for fear of walking into its stony iron wall.

Just then, a small spherical drone appeared from nowhere. It had a large mechanical eye at its front and its brass casing gleamed. Ignatius saw his own reflection looking back at him on the golden-coloured surface. A small hiss of steam emanated from the device and its large mechanical eye blinked. Then as quickly as it had appeared, it vanished again and an invisible doorway opened on the smooth surface of the monolith.

Cautiously, Ignatius entered and the doorway shut tight behind him, leaving no trace of its presence and blocking any external light, leaving Ignatius standing uncertain in the low light of the interior.

He stood in a large entrance hall where two enormous and intimidating statues stood either side carved from beautifully orange-veined and black-coloured marble. They depicted ecclesiastical knights in full armour with their arms stretched out and leaning on broad-bladed swords. Their faces were covered by sinister and grim-looking helmets. To either side of them hung long narrow banners attached somewhere in the vaulted ceiling and descending to the floor. They were richly coloured silk, embroidered with intricate imperial emblems that Ignatius didn't recognise. The rest of the hall was empty and stark except for its striking black-and-white checked floor.

The silence was broken momentarily by another spherical brass drone hissing by before it disappeared again. After a few moments, a robed figure appeared, an ecclesiastical-looking man dressed in black with a white collar and stockings to the knee, with buckled black shoes.

"Greetings, Mr Ignatius. Thank you for gracing us with your presence. An unusual request, I know. I am Brother Aelfric, the Grand Wizard of the Administorium."

Ignoring the pleasantries, and the pretentious title, Ignatius got straight down to business. "So tell me, why am I here? What possible reason could you have to speak to me?"

"I see you are impatient, Mr Ignatius. Patience is, of course, a virtue." He gave a faint thin-lipped smile, if indeed it was possible for a minister of the Administorium to smile.

"I know a brother of mine has observed you more than once in the Bodleian. You have a liking for strange reading materials."

"Well, the last time I checked, the Empire didn't have any laws regarding reading, or the type of material I choose to educate myself with. Perhaps the Administorium should try it. You may learn something."

A brief moment of anger flashed across Aelfric's face, but as usual he was soon restored to the same stony-faced composure typical of all those that worked for the Administorium.

"We are not exactly sure what you and your kind do, Mr Ignatius, but the higher echelons of the Empire, including the Queen, seem to hold you in high regard."

Ignatius could see that Aelfric was longing to ask what it was he did, but refused to, believing that, in his mind, it would be beneath him and so he was seeking ways to find out with more obscure questioning. Amused, Ignatius remained silent, only speaking when spoken to. Ignatius knew that well-placed silence was always a good tool to use.

"I'm sure your contribution to the Empire is invalid," he said mockingly. "Tell me, the events at the Professor's house recently, Solomon, you were there, were you not?

"What makes you think that?" Ignatius was determined to continually answer a question with a question.

"I have my sources. But on the night in question, I believe a book was obtained. Do you know the nature of this book?"

"You really have a great suspicion of books. Do you not read?" He could see Aelfric was getting irritated. "Why would you think I was there and have knowledge of any book you refer to?"

"Please! Drop the pretence, Mr Ignatius. The book has great significance apparently regarding the fate of not just the Empire but the universe."

"Has it? If you know the contents of such a book, then why not just say so. Have you a title? It may speed up your enquiries. In fact, if you give the title to the librarian at the Bodleian, I'm sure he'll send someone below to the underground stacks to fetch it for you."

Ignatius gave a wry smile.

"Although what if it falls into the wrong hands? Will the Administorium be taking responsibility for that?"

At this point, Ignatius thought Aelfric was going to explode. He could see the whites of the man's knuckles on his clenched fists, but he remained rigid and straight-backed, refusing get drawn into an argument or loss of temper.

"You have no evidence, Brother Aelfric, that there is a book or that I was indeed, as you say, there, wherever there is. Have you asked this Solomon about the book?"

Aelfric spluttered the smallest of ironic laughs. "That will not be possible. He is dead. A young girl was found with him. Disembowelled."

"Hey, what professors get up to in their spare time is nothing to do with me! Perhaps he didn't want to pay her!"

Aelfric was now fidgeting. Ignatius thought he was about to let rip, or that steam would blow from his ears. Ignatius thought this was a good point to probe further and find out what else the Administorium knew. "And this book, is it the only one, or are there more? Do you have a publisher's name?" He waited for an answer but received none. Aelfric just stood firm, staring blankly at him. "Or you could try old Ben Blackwell in Broad Street, he may be of some assistance."

Ignatius continued, "I don't believe you will ever find the book you mention, it's as if it didn't exist." He knew full well it had long gone, back to its author the Omnisoul. "But is that what the Administorium do, collect books? I often wondered."

Aelfric gave the resemblance of a smile but was clearly irritated by Ignatius's insolence.

"So, tell me, is this place a library? It does rival the grandeur of the Bodleian. Is that what the Administorium is for? You read a lot in the comfort of this grandeur, whilst others support or defend the Empire? I've often wondered, as have most other citizens."

By now, Aelfric's body was taut with rage, his eyes burned with scorn. Ignatius had irritated him enough for his cool to break slightly.

"The Administorium is, as you well know, there to advise the Queen, and to keep the lower classes of society from harming themselves with poor technological advancements, the like of which should not be tainting this great Empire. To do this, we gather knowledge, and that knowledge tells us that you need to curtail whatever it is you do. Your reading material is dangerous and yes, we do have a library, more magnificent than that of the Bodleian and it contains the rarest, finest manuscripts in the world, kept safe for your security, Mr Ignatius. The people out there," he gestured slightly with his hand towards the walls of the building "do not understand that they can live their lives safely due to us, our governance over certain aspects of the Empire that they are oblivious to, but only because of the Administorium."

"Well thank you for that information, now at least I know what you do. My visit here has been most enlightening. So, tell me does your interference," Ignatius stopped and corrected himself, knowing full well he was making Aelfric angrier by the second, "sorry, I mean governance, help those at war in India, or the continent of Africa? Those suffering from malaria, cholera and smallpox, those that risk their lives so the people can be provided with provisions, goods to trade, wealth and commodities that even the Administorium could not live without? Does your governance extend that far, Brother Aelfric? Do you think those in the outposts of the Empire give you thanks for your existence because you make such a difference?"

"I think it is time for you to take your leave, Mr Ignatius."

"Really? Oh! well I'm still not sure why you summoned me here." Ignatius knew he was outstaying his welcome, and it would be better to leave, but he wanted more information. He had flustered Aelfric enough to start getting information regarding the raison d'être for the mysterious Administorium.

"Will you not be showing me your library?"

"Not today, Mr Ignatius, but it is worthy of a visit. When the Empire crumbles, as inevitably it will, and when indeed this world does too, our repository will be invaluable. It rivals that of the Library at Alexandria, and will be the source on which the world and a new empire shall rise. Now, if you don't mind, Mr Ignatius, I must ask you to leave, I have other matters to attend to. I bid you a good day."

He led Ignatius towards the wall upon which the invisible door opened. As he left, a figure behind him peered out of the shadows, the light from the door just catching enough to highlight her fine cheekbones and dark hair. Ignatius squinted to readjust his eyes to the daylight, oblivious to the woman who stole back into the shadows as he turned to see the door shut tight once more, leaving the familiar black building looking impenetrable as usual. Ignatius grinned to himself, knowing that he had successfully annoyed the Grand Wizard himself and pleased in the knowledge that at some point, he didn't know how, he would be visiting their library, even if it was by stealth.

Aelfric turned and seemed slightly surprised by seeing the woman, he gave a slight nod of his head in way of a bow, "High Priestess, I didn't see you there. Forgive me."

"You are less than competent, Aelfric. You let Ignatius get the better of you. If he has any knowledge of any books, he now has reason to want to visit the Administorium's library now you have explained to him its vastness and importance. We are trying to ascertain what he knows and why he owns reading material consisting of the ancient grimoires he reads so voraciously! Get out of my sight."

Aelfric bowed again, this time more elaborately and backed away, never once daring to turn his back on the High Priestess, who was still keeping to the shadows.

Chapter 12: The Celestial

Ignatius sat cross-legged on the floor. He really wanted to rest, to sleep, but knew he couldn't, not until he knew what the Administorium were up to. As the patriarch over all the Chapters in the Union Jacks and the Master of his own Chapter, he had a responsibility to keep going. But this was fast becoming a burden he didn't want to carry. With Indigo, he had been dragged into a cosmic war and had not fully explained this to the First Lord or to other Union Jacks for fear of being declared insane. This sat uncomfortably with him.

He sat still and closed his eyes. This would have to serve to recharge his energy. Time was likely to be short after being interrogated by the Administorium. He slowed his breathing and concentrated on his vitals. His breath, his limbs, the sound of his heart as it pumped blood around his body. At first, his mind wouldn't settle. He was trying to remember when he first started to meditate but couldn't. He was sure this was a result of his recent adventures and discovering he was descended from one of the Charon, although this still didn't sit easy with him. He could feel his slow, regular breathing. He could feel his lungs expanding against his ribcage. His breathing slowed further and all he could hear was the pounding of his own heart. Eventually, his mind emptied until there was nothing. He saw nothing, he felt nothing, he heard nothing. He was totally oblivious to everything around him. In his mind's eye, he stood in total blackness. The world was empty. He was weightless. That was, until a small spark appeared before him in the duskiness of his consciousness. It grew until his whole subconscious view was a rich pink in colour. There was an amorphous shape. It moved. It had a form like a human. It was another being. A visitation. He could feel his body growing warm, and the pink grew a slightly darker shade and began to swirl and undulate, surrounding him like the walls of a well. Then, one by one, thousands of eyes opened in the pink fleshy surface of his mind, forming a vortex as they surrounded him. Occasionally a single eye would grow larger as it moved towards him to inspect him more closely before retreating and another taking its place. As much as he tried, Ignatius was unable to open his own eyes, so felt captive in this cyclone of surveillance.

Without warning, the eyes began to move further away and an indistinct figure began to emerge from the fleshiness. He was dressed in a purple cloak and a purple harness across his chest with a huge blinking eye at the centre. His alien face had sunken empty sockets where a human would be expected to have eyes, and his forehead was elongated upwards to form a fan shape, at the centre of which was another huge eye, identical to the one on his chest. From his neck, another fan grew upwards to surround his forehead, and this contained another four eyes, two per side. His mouth was a vertical slit, and Ignatius couldn't tell if he was capable of speech. On his back he carried a large, curved telescope. Ignatius knew only one being who could have six eyes. This was the Watcher, one of the Celestials.

Ignatius thought this was a dream, a vision. He realised he could move again and so, just to check, he reached out and touched the Watcher. Pulling back quickly, he realised this visitation was real. He opened his eyes and was back in his study. So was the Watcher. Whilst meditating, he had somehow managed to connect with him. Or the Watcher had sought him out across the planes to make an astral connection. Either way, Ignatius was confused and concerned. He scrambled to his feet and reached for a weapon. The Watcher raised an arm and, using some kind of magic, removed the steam cannon from Ignatius's grasp and casually placed it aside.

"Greetings, Ignatius," spoke the Watcher, who was hovering a few inches off the ground, his cloak gently swaying behind him.

"I know this is unorthodox, and usually I would not get involved with the affairs of humans, but this is of grave importance. My eyes are enchanted, my telescope an extension of my own powerful sight, and I have looked at the cosmos and travelled in time to see the outcome. I have looked out across all thirty-one planes and must inform you your behaviour is about to endanger the whole cosmos. You are already on another adventure, whether you know it or not, and depending on the outcome, the whole cosmos shall be destroyed. But unlike your failed adventure with the Charon, where they tried to destroy time, this danger will create all kinds of evil, all kinds of suffering for every living being across the heavens. Once started, it is unlikely these events will be able to be stopped. As fear and anger and thoughts of reprisals grow, so too will the power of the darkest of these evils. Your nightmares and dreams shall accumulate and add to the black legion of shadows, they shall feed on your darkest thoughts, your darkest vibrations, and your inability to grasp the consequences you have unleashed, creating incalculable might!"

Ignatius tried to move but found he was once more unable. He tried to speak, but found it difficult to find the words.

"My role as a Celestial is merely to watch. To watch the Charon for all eternity and to report to the Stalker to fetch them back to Limbo for the Keeper to incarcerate once more when necessary. I am the eyes of the Omnisoul. I inform the Omnisoul of the Charon's actions. The Omnisoul would not take kindly knowing I have visited you. I have used great magic to keep this visit a secret. It is the Omnisoul that lets us all exist, and you have no right to interfere with the great eternal creation.

The Celestials have a complex history, and our role is to wait for the end the cosmos. To await our final task, whatever that may be. What we do know is we have been tasked with bearing witness to the collapse and destruction of all things, all matter, to record the evidence for the next cycle. Humans are of small consequence in the great architect's design, but I fear I must intervene where you and Indigo are concerned."

Then it was as if the Watcher released his grip, and Ignatius found his voice. "So why are you here?" he said.

"Because circumstances dictate it. It's possible that time is against us. It's possible you and Indigo have unwittingly started the end of times. Your assistance given to the Charon to try and destroy time itself has caused such a fragmenting of the cosmos that even the Omnisoul is finding it difficult to align the collective consciousness in the splintered Megasphere that now exists. This is such a fundamental change to creation that it has not been received well. You are a disturbance. But I fear there is more here on earth that I do not yet know. Your Administorium have a greater significance, but I am yet to discover what. But I will."

Ignatius laughed, nervously. "The Administorium are a nuisance.

They meddle in affairs they do not understand. In affairs of state and the Empire. They hamper change and the advancement of technology that could make the Empire even more powerful on this earth, and maybe beyond. But they are blind fools."

"You underestimate them severely. They have a great secret, and you need to find out what it is. They will destroy this planet if you let them. They will destroy much more. Much is at stake here."

The Watcher placed his peculiarly curved telescope to the large eye in the centre of his fanned forehead and peered out into the cosmos.

"Place your birthmarked hand over your eye," he instructed Ignatius. Ignatius lifted his right hand and placed the eye-shaped birthmark over his right eye and gasped. He could see what the Watcher could see through his telescope.

Far off, beyond the solar system, beyond the galaxy and beyond the gaseous nebulae and black dust that filled the void between earth and interstellar space, he could make out large structures that linked great swathes of the cosmos together like a road network. These were like the neurons in a human brain. Perhaps these were the neurons that formed the consciousness of the Omnisoul. They formed a helical structure like that found in DNA. Then, deep within the structure he saw an eye staring back at him. A large bright yellow eye with an iris like a vertical slit. It momentarily disappeared, then reappeared. A serpentine membrane had moved across it and now the glowing eyeball was visible once more.

"Calabi-Ya?" he enquired.

"Yes," said the Watcher. "He is no longer in exile and is concealed by the shadows. The fragmented cosmos has given him means to enter once more. It's possible he is awaiting the Administorium fulfilling their part of these events… whatever that is. If I am unable to determine this, then you must find out."

"What do you mean, he is concealed by the shadows?"

"When you dream, you are producing brain waves. You are producing energy at a certain frequency. Your nightmares are the most powerful of all. This energy travels out across the planes and into the cosmos where it gathers and forms dark energy, shadows in the cosmos. These dark thoughts help to feed the demons, monsters of your nightmares, and beings like Calabi-Ya. In turn, these beings inhabit new nightmares, the brain waves of which produce even more energy, and so it is a self-perpetuating system.

But now, I must go. You must tread carefully, Ignatius, or the cosmos will be destroyed."

The Watcher placed his telescope back on his back, then with the merest wave of his hand he became transparent, then solid again. He continued to fade in and out for a few seconds. Then, as quickly as the Watcher had appeared, he vanished, leaving no trace of his visit.

Ignatius let out a large gasp, as if he had stopped breathing some time ago. Fighting for air, he became aware his eyes were still shut. He opened them to find he was back in the room, his chest wet with sweat, his heart beating faster now. He tried to move, to get up, but his legs were weak. He slumped back down onto the floor and tried to process what he had been told. From what he recalled, his thoughts were going to be his greatest enemy. They were going to feed a legion.

After some time thinking about this, he had regained enough strength to stand upright and, moving to his desk, sat to ponder what he had been told, not really understanding what he and Indigo had supposedly started.

Chapter 13: The Mortuary

Ingatius rested that night, rose early, and sent word for Indigo to join him. He knew that whatever events were building, they would need assistance. If this latest magical book was anything like the Book of Consciousness, this mission would be too big for them to handle, or maybe comprehend.

"I don't know what the Book of Shadows is about, but we're going to need help. I think we should call the Charon!" he told Indigo.

She let out a gasp of surprise. "Really? I'm not happy with that idea. I don't want to be associated with them. Learning our heritage was too painful. I'm not comfortable in their presence!"

Ignatius wanted to agree with her but chose to ignore the comment.

"We need to find a corpse," declared Ignatius, "so we can call them. But I'm no cold-blooded killer,"

"So what do you suggest?" said Indigo. "And I must protest!"

"We go to the mortuary." Indigo looked at him with surprise, but she realised his thinking made sense, although she wasn't comfortable with the plan. After about an hour of conversation, Indigo found herself reluctantly carrying out orders from her Chapter's Master.

The Radcliffe Infirmary, Oxford's first hospital, stood along the Woodstock Road. A large fountain with a statue of the Greek god Triton sat out front. Ignatius and Indigo had decided the best approach was probably just to boldly enter the front door of the imposing grey walls and then refine their rough plan as they went on. They had chosen a time when visitors were likely to be in the building so they wouldn't attract any attention. As they passed the fountain, Indigo said, "I wonder if we will ever meet Triton? I mean, now we know gods are real." She grinned, but it was more of a scowl, and Ignatius raised an eyebrow.

Once inside, they followed the corridor, looking for a staircase. "I'm sure this is where they would have brought her," said Ignatius. Deeper into the hospital they found a plain-looking staircase leading down into the darker basement. Silently and unchallenged, they scurried into the depths. A strong smell of carbolic and chemicals hit their senses, and then the smell of rot and decay cloyed the air.

"Are you sure this is a good idea?" asked Indigo.

"Not at all, but at the moment, it's our only hope to discover what is going on. We are obviously involved in something much bigger and more complex than just our last adventure."

As they rounded the next corner, an old man stepped out of the shadows. They both froze. It was just a patient. "Good day," bluffed Ignatius. They received no reply, just wide eyes staring through them. At the bottom of the stairs, they could see a sign ahead: Mortuary.

"I'm not sure about this, Ignatius."

"Neither am I, my dear, neither am I," he replied, but he continued headlong into the mortuary. The smell hit them first. It brought bile into Indigo's mouth. They both covered their noses as best they could and Ignatius began scanning the slabs, lifting labels attached to the big toe of each dead body.

"Just be quick," said Indigo. "Any corpse will do, won't it?"

"Well, yes. But I don't wish to be disrespectful." But before he could continue, Indigo interjected.

"It's a bit late for that!"

"I think we should use one of our own, albeit a hired hand. See if you can find her."

After a little more searching, Ignatius announced, "Here we are. I've found her." He peeled back the sheet just enough to reveal her still horror-stricken and contorted beautiful face, the heart-shaped tattoo on her left cheek confirming it was Skye.

A blue light suddenly came to life in the dark recess of the mortuary. Swiftly, a small brass ball came hissing over, gears clanking and cables sweeping behind its gleaming body.

"Drone!" rasped Ignatius in a low voice, trying not to attract any further attention. The mechanical spy beeped and hissed louder, its bright-green glass eye memorising the intruders, imprinting them onto the collodion glass plate buried deep within its heart. Without delay, Ignatius pulled the sheet from Skye's corpse, throwing it over the drone and pulling it to the floor, preventing it from flying off to raise the alarm. The drone fought back, trying to raise itself back into the air, beeping louder, the green light of its eye glowing through the sheet and steam hissing. Ignatius took a steam cannon from his coat and clubbed the drone repeatedly with the butt, dent after dent appearing in its perfect sphere until its movement stopped and Ignatius was satisfied he had put it out of action.

Standing back up, he looked at the slab the corpse lay on. Skye had been their accomplice when the Union were looking for the Book of Consciousness. She lay cold and white, naked so they could see her family emblem, the tattoo of the Black Sun, the master of all runes, on her left breast. On her upper thighs were other runes that Ignatius struggled to make out in the dull light.

"Well, this explains her interest in helping us and why she was on a mission on her own. Skye was clearly a mixed-up woman with her own demons to drive out. I just hope no other members of this dark cult come looking for her or, indeed, us."

Skye had been disembowelled and the remnants had been bundled up and placed back inside her gaping wound. Indigo had to turn away for a moment. Without warning, Ignatius grabbed Skye's jaw and opened it. A coin lay on to her tongue in the age-old tradition to call Charon, the ferryman.

A swirling black cloud began to form in the corner of the mortuary. Crimson sparks ignited deep within the unholy sentient cloud, and a blood-red haze began to swirl across the floor, swimming around their ankles and clawing at their legs. An organic mass of fire belched around them, and brimstone filled their nostrils, drowning out the stench of death and decay. The sulphuric smell stung their eyes, and before long the cloud had turned into a sea of naked flesh writing in agony, wailing and filling the room with dread. A large hooded head appeared, its great mouth open. With jagged teeth, it breathed foul air and lapped up bodies with a huge tongue that flicked in and out like a reptile. Three yellow eyes blinked as the Keeper saw Ignatius and Indigo. He nodded his head knowingly and then was gone. But the gnashing of teeth remained loud, and rays of light shot out of every orifice of the remaining throng as they continued to writhe, to shift and change until eventually they started to form several distinct shapes. Terrifying beasts and demons rose to the surface and then disappeared again. Things with leathery skin, one with bat wings and others that looked like deadly insects with venom-injecting tentacles. Hundreds of eyes, bloodshot and sad, stared out and then were gone. Fires burned around them all until at last a hawk-headed man thrust his head out of the burning cloud of misery to come within inches of Ignatius.

"They're here, you know. The gods, they're here. Dirty rats. Like vermin."

Ignatius shot around, and standing there was the man they had encountered on the staircase.

"Dirty rats…" he repeated.

The hawk-headed man rushed out of the cloud, his impossibly enormous muscular frame, all straining sinew and veins popped on every surface of his body, clad in scarlet with a blue cloak and white stockings to the knee.

One sharp eye opened amidst the scarlet haze. It blinked. Sapphire blue sparkled next to a jewelled eye patch. The androgynous face, now fully awakened, raised up out of the mass.

What appeared to be blood rained down gently to cover the seething mass, which writhed in every direction. There were no walls in any direction, just a hazy red mass. Groans could be heard, some soft, some louder. The floor moved; it was alive. Flesh writhed over flesh as the great living mass endured its fate in Limbo. The groans seemed to echo around the unwalled space as the unfortunate horde came to terms with their eternity.

"Adonai," called Ignatius. But the god ignored him and rushed straight for the old man. Indigo bravely moved to block his way.

"No! He is innocent. Let him go," she said, and ushered the man back towards the staircase, pushing him upwards faster than he was able to walk.

"He called me a dirty rat. That may be true, for as you know, I am much more. A demon, a god, a beast. I cannot let such insolence go unpunished." Adonai had a sinister grin. Ignatius knew this was just sport. Killing for killing's sake. Cruelty for entertainment. Calling the Charon often ended in death. They showed no mercy and were known to kill even their own worshippers.

Ignatius intervened. "Leave him be. Please? Such an insult is nothing to mighty gods such as yourselves. Adonai, we have summoned the Charon again as we need help."

"If I'd known you were going to summon us so often and spoil all my fun, I'd not have let the two of you live the last time." His grin now seemed to stretch across his entire beautiful face. It sent a cold shudder down Indigo's spine.

One by one, six more hawk-headed beasts stepped out of the hell-forge with hell-spawn clinging to their limbs, trying to hold them back as they left behind the unnatural broiling darkness as the Keeper released them. Gradually, they all took the shape they used when conversing with humans, their hawk heads disappearing. Paladin stood in his carved ancient bronze armour. Tara, dressed in her black combat leathers and black hooded, red-lined cloak emerged, followed by Aryas the dandy in his purple velvet and brocade coat. Then, Atman with his sombre yet beautiful face, dressed in his black combat jacket and pale blue breeches with white stockings appeared with Darshan in her white tunic shirt and red leather waistcoat. Finally, Devi appeared dressed in a red leather corset and red-leather thigh-length boots.

The seven immortal beings were all familiar to Ignatius and Indigo, who both knew this was a dangerous undertaking; they were just as likely as anyone else to be slaughtered.

"So tell me, Ignatius, why are we here?" asked Adonai, his orange hair flowing around his face.

Ignatius dived right in. "We have been told of another book

that we think you should be aware of. It is the Book of Shadows and is reputed to be written by Calabi-Ya. We thought if that was the case, he may be able to use it to return from his exile. Do you know of it?"

The Charon looked at each other, and their faces all told the same story. "We do not. But if this is true, the book could be, as you say, his key to return. So where is the book?" replied Adonai.

"That is just it, nobody knows."

"But that is your problem, is it not?" interjected Indigo. "This really has nothing to do with us."

Ignatius was surprised to hear this. He was not expecting it. This was the first time Indigo had diverged from his thinking regarding what the Union Jacks were deployed for.

"Why are we the only two humans who can do this? Presumably we are the only two?" said Indigo.

A brief moment of anger flashed across Adonai's face. "Because you are born of the Charon. You asked me once before if you were demigods. I lied. You are indeed like demigods. You are godlings and you wield much power, although you don't yet know what that is. I needed you to remain as you were without that burden to carry, to continue your innocence, until we had found the Book of Consciousness.

As we returned to limbo, I knew there would be weaknesses in the fabric of space and time and if he found one, Calabi-Ya would use it as a portal to return. I just didn't know when. I didn't think it would be this soon,"

"But we have no evidence for his return. This is just a precaution," said Ignatius.

"That may be, but if the Book of Shadows is real, we will need to find out what text it is and secure it. To keep it safe from Calabi-Ya."

"Then how do we find out?"

Aryas stepped in. "Obviously, the name suggests its contents. Have the dark thoughts of the cosmos been gathered into one tome? I suspect they have."

"So what are the implications?" asked Devi.

"I'm not sure, but opening it may be a mistake. It may act as a focus for unimaginable power."

Adonai thought for a few moments, then gestured to Aryas. "We send Ignatius to the Ti-Botta. We can't go ourselves as we have not been called, but we can send Ignatius. They may know more information or perhaps consult the sacred texts and ancient tomes in their library. Aryas, summon Maha-Java."

"Very well."

But before Aryas could begin, Ignatius interjected. "And what of Indigo?"

"She will come with us; we have a different journey to take," replied Adonai.

Indigo cast a glance at Ignatius. She didn't seem very happy with this arrangement, but eventually she conceded, nodding her head to accept the situation.

Chapter 14: The Wind Horse

Darshan stepped forward, a large scimitar hanging at her curvaceous hip, her raven hair tied back with a red bandana. "There have always been legends about a second book, but there has never been any proof. But these were obscure legends, we just dismissed them."

"I have never felt the presence of any other book or seen visions of it with my cosmic eye" said Aryas. "If it exists, it is well hidden, far behind even my mystical powers. And if we find it, it doesn't mean we will be able to open it to see what is written. We plotted for aeons to be able to obtain and open the Book of Consciousness. This may take an eternity to discover."

"We have no choice. We must find out," replied Adonai. "The only people who will be able to confirm this are the Ti-Botta." He looked at Ignatius. "You will have to travel to the mystical city of Sagharta once more and speak with the High Priest."

Ignatius frowned, not sure what was going to happen, but before he could speak to ask about the journey and who would be going, Aryas stepped forward with his usual dandy-like manner, announcing, "Leave it to me."

Ignatius and Indigo were not sure what to expect, or indeed who Mah-Java was. Aryas took his elegant pipe out of his carpet bag, the fluorescent green liquid still bubbling away in the glass bulb, and began to smoke whatever mystical substance it contained. With a dramatic gesture he then took a stance, planting his feet on the ground as if he was about to attack. Pushing the sleeves up on his purple brocaded suit, he began to form arcane symbols in the air with his slender pale fingers, muttering some incomprehensible spell in a low grumbling voice at odds with his expressionless yet beautiful face, his pipe hanging out of one side of his mouth. He began chanting in a low-pitched mumble, his eyes shut beneath his broad-brimmed hat. Plumes of vapour began to fill the mortuary as he moved his hands, describing mystical runes in the air. After a time, those runes became manifest and glowed turquoise, illuminating his face in blue.

After a brief moment, green fire began to dance between his hands and gather speed as he swept his arms around wider and wider, creating more and more flames. The darkness began to recede as all their faces glowed with the eerie green light. As Ignatius looked on, he could see the god wizard's eyes roll back into his head as his voice grew louder and louder, deeper and deeper and a form began to grow within the flames. As the room filled with smoke, and the runes grew larger and brighter, Ignatius thought he heard a horse baying in the distance.

A form started to take shape: flared nostrils, a wild looking eye, an animal's ear, legs, lots of legs. They grew and shifted in the emerald fire, a long leg thrust forward, another, another. They had hooves. Ignatius thought he heard a snort of some sort, an angry sound that echoed round the dead stillness of the mortuary. A long nose appeared attached to two flared nostrils. A horse's head, a wild-looking war horse with solid chest muscles, more legs. Then Ignatius could hear hooves being stamped and making a loud commotion. It was so loud it sounded like several horses. Then it became obvious Maha-Java was an eight-legged stallion with wild eyes and a long flowing mane, its nostrils flaring as it snorted and pranced, almost as if it hadn't taken kindly to being summoned. This was the most majestic horse Ignatius had ever seen, much so due to its eight legs.

It was so brilliantly white, it seemed to glow and emanate its own light. The beast stamped and reared, snorted with anger in its eyes, thrashing his tail and long mane. Rising on its back four legs, it stamped its forward four back down onto the floor, cracking tiles and making so much noise Ignatius was afraid the authorities might hear.

Adonai came forward and took the reins of the horse and calmed the beast until it settled. The long nose and big crazed eyes lunged over and spied Ignatius and Indigo suspiciously. Indigo could feel the beast's breath on her face and stepped back a little.

"An eight-legged horse!" she exclaimed.

"Indeed," replied Adonai, "this is the stallion Maha-Java, a wind horse. He has tremendous power and is lightning fast, capable of taking you across planes and time to your destination. When he runs, he is so swift his eight legs are never all on the same plane at any one time. He is the fastest beast in the cosmos and will take you to the mystical city of Sagharta so you can consult with the Ti-Botta."

Adonai handed the reins to Ignatius.

"Ignatius, this is your steed, this is your journey, only you can do this. We can only present ourselves to the Ti-Botta if they call us. They have not. So, you must go. Whilst Maha-Java is capable of carrying you both, two of you will slow him down. So only one must travel."

"How will I know the way?"

"You will not need to, Maha-Java will take you, but for safety, you may need to look out across the planes using my eye.". Adonai pointed to the eye-shaped birthmark on Ignatius's hand. "The Ti-Botta will be able to give you more information about this grimoire and, perhaps, how to locate it."

Ignatius climbed upon the horse's back. There wasn't any saddle or stirrups. He held tightly onto the horse's mane and gripped with his knees. Before he had a chance to speak, the mortuary was a gloomy blur in his vision as the Maha-Java mounted the staircase in a single bound, and with lightning speed exited the infirmary and was gone into the night, so fast that none of the medical staff saw them leave. As they ran through the cobbled streets of Oxford, Ignatius struggled to hold on as they swept past other horses and a steam gurney or two.

In the blink of an eye, they had left the city and all Ignatius could hear was a faint whooshing sound as the wind horse stepped across planes. Before long, he was racing across golden crop fields, too fast for any of the farm hands at work on the harvest to see them. They crossed lush meadows and into a dark wood, Ignatius ducking just in time as a branch nearly hit him in the face. Explosions deafened him as the horse crossed battlefields and then suddenly, complete silence as magenta nebulae drifted by slowly. He began to get a sense again of how big the cosmos is. No matter how fast the horse was travelling, the cosmic clouds around them barely seemed to move. A bright orange star burned at the side of his face as they passed by, on through a meteor storm, and then back to fields. But these were different to those on earth. They were purple and green, with strange yellow twisted tree-like forms that had bubble-+like growths at the top instead of leaves. Every now and then, one of the bubbles would burst with a loud groan, letting out what Ignatius thought could only be seeds, red orbs that floated away on the breeze and landed some distance from the parent plant.

A sword whistled past Ignatius's ear and an old man appeared mumbling an incantation from an ancient tome that hovered off the ground in front of him. On they continued, passing planets and star systems, through strange worlds, some inhabited, some not. Ignatius began to realise that the journey had no timescale. He didn't know how long he had been travelling. He pulled his pocket watch from his waistcoat, but it was of no use. At times, the hands were racing around the clock face, day after day racing by. At other times, the hands were travelling in reverse. Trying to make sense of his journey, he raised his right hand to his right eye, to make use of the birthmark on the back of his hand. He had learned a while ago that this birthmark was a result of his birth to Adonai and the loss of the god's right eye. It had been Adonai's insurance policy for future use at Ignatius's birth.

As other planes came into view, a monster with long fangs, dripping with venom, snapped at his face. He screamed and automatically removed his hand, the surprise nearly causing him to lose his grip on the wind horse. Maha-Java snorted and looked around at Ignatius with a disapproving look, if a horse could do such a thing.

Suddenly, an ape-like being swinging a club emerged from nowhere. Clearly, they had entered the same plane as the creature. Then there was another, and another. Ignatius felt a heavy blow smash into his shoulder, and his collar bone ached with searing pain. Another blow just missed his head. He felt his horse speed up, but it was of no use, they had already obtained a passenger. Teeth snapped at his neck and he could feel the beast's hot rancid breath on his neck. Muscular arms encircled him and began to crush his ribs. Barely able to breathe or move his arms, Ignatius had just enough movement in his forearm to retrieve his steam cannon. He held it tightly for fear of dropping it. He didn't want to lose his chance. His left arm elbowed the beast in the torso as he lowered his painful right shoulder to swing the creature around just enough for him to aim his weapon backwards. A thunderous hiss of steam rose to obscure his vision momentarily as the bolt hit its mark and the beast howled as he let go and fell backwards with the wind horse instantly leaving it far behind.

A little later, at least it seemed so to Ignatius, three dragons flew by, completely ignoring him and the horse such was their speed. As he continued, Ignatius became aware of a figure way off in the distance. At first, he couldn't tell if it was travelling in the same direction or towards him. At times they appeared to be travelling perpendicular to his course. As they continued, it became apparent that the figure traversed all the same planes that Ignatius did, although not always in the same direction. Whoever it was, they were on a similar path as him. They continued across the breathtaking green and golden nebula that came into view, where fire ignited at its heart instigating the birth of new stars, new life in the cosmos. Then across the pink fields of crops that were being harvested by the local inhabitants of that world. Across the giant sand dunes of another world, so big they would dwarf anything on earth. Then across arid planes with splendid cities on the horizon with slender towers made from gold-tipped crystal. They gleamed and sparkled, reflecting the light of several suns that drifted across a pale green sky. Past squalid alley ways that were full of ragged denizens of the night, high on alcohol and narcotics, past dark doorways where ladies of the night earned a living. Past brilliantly lit buildings and skyscrapers. He couldn't keep up, everything moved so fast Ignatius could hardly take it all in.

The wind horse continued heading straight for a grey mist that lay on the horizon. As they approached, it became obvious they were about to enter an angry-looking sandstorm. Ignatius pulled his goggles from his pocket and quickly put them on. Wrapping his arm over his face to protect his nose, he put his head down and hoped for the best. The stranger he had seen riding the same planes was no longer in sight anywhere, obscured by the lack of light from the storm. Suddenly, Ignatius was nearly knocked from his steed as another horse grazed past his location, heading off at a forty-five-degree angle. But his steed didn't appear to be phased by this and continued. Alone once more, Ignatius found himself travelling a long road through what looked like lush blue grass, passing workers in the fields who didn't even see him, engrossed with working their machinery. Looking to his right, he saw the other horse again charging towards him at incredible speed. He wondered how it could keep up with a creature like the wind horse. He placed his birthmarked hand over his eye and quickly removed it, squinting his eyes to take in the bigger picture. He placed his hand over his eye again and let out a gasp. He could see the traveller on a wind horse set on a collision course with his own horse.

In no time at all, the traveller came alongside him on an identical wind horse. It was almost like riding alongside a mirror. The traveller was clad in clothes like Ignatius's except he was wearing a bowler hat. He had a short cape wrapped tightly across his face, obscuring most of it, even his eyes were behind goggles so could not be seen. The cape and hat were both covered in sand from the storm they had ridden through earlier. Ignatius readied himself for a fight, not really knowing what to do. He placed his hand on his steam cannon and released the safety catch.

"Whoa! Hey! What the…? Who are you?" said the stranger. He pulled his horse away from Ignatius, obviously just realising they were riding identical steeds.

"I didn't expect to see anyone else on this journey, travelling the cosmos, let alone on such a unique horse as mine." said the traveller. "Good day to you, sir," he said as they rode neck and neck.

Ignatius couldn't quite place it, but he thought the voice sounded familiar. It was like he knew the stranger.

Chapter 15: Parallel Lives

"Good day to you, sir!" answered Ignatius. The stranger turned to look at him properly for the first time.

Simultaneously, both Ignatius and the traveller pulled on the reins of their wind horses, but it took time for the horses to respond. They were set on a quest and didn't want to stop. Both horses snorted and shook their heads, their manes flying around in their agitation. Eventually, they reared up, kicking and stamping their front hooves, all four of them. Both wind horses were keen to continue their journey and were clearly not amused at being stopped.

Both travellers circled each other staring intently at the other. After a few moments, the stranger spoke. "Remarkable!"

"What is?" asked Ignatius.

"So, are you some sort of cosmic mirage?" he asked. "Or have I been breathing in celestial vapours and so hallucinating? Who are you, man? Tell me your name."

Ignatius became suspicious and tightened his grip on his steam cannon, eventually answering the question.

"I am Isambard Ignatius," he said politely.

"No! No! You can't be." The stranger took off his sandy goggles to get a better look.

"And why ever not? What makes you think I am not who I say I am?"

The stranger untied his cape and removed it from his face, brushing the excess sand from his eyebrows and cheeks. Ignatius stared in disbelief. It was like looking in a mirror.

The stranger started to laugh heartily. "Well, to me it's quite clear. I am you and you are me. We are doppelgangers. We even sound the same. Don't tell me, you are heading for the fabled city of Sagharta."

"I am indeed. So, you are Ignatius, too?"

The stranger just smiled and nodded politely. "Then maybe we can ride together, and we can learn from each other about what is happening, why there are two of us and what quest each of us is on."

The two horses began to trot, then picked up their pace began to run until they were both running at full pace, travelling side by side and at the same speed, which made it easy for the two Ignatiuses to talk as they continued.

Ignatius felt very uneasy about meeting himself.

"Are you going to keep hold of that steam cannon for the duration, old boy?" said the traveller.

Ignatius released his grip. "So where are you from?" he asked.

"Oxford."

"But that's impossible. I've never seen you around," said Ignatius.

"A different time or plane, I guess."

"So, what takes you to Sagharta?"

"Well, I'm guessing you already know the answer to that." The traveller looked him in the eye.

"We can't both be on the same quest, surely? Has Adonai sent you?"

"He has indeed." The traveller frowned at Ignatius. "You know we now have a fragmented cosmos. Multiple versions. Although we exist separately, our lives, our fates, are entwined. I too seek the Book of Shadows."

Ignatius felt a cold chill run down his spine. There might be two of him, but he was sure there was only one book. Only one source of information they both needed from the Ti-Botta, who were unaffected by the split in the cosmos, as they exist outside of the planes, adrift within them all at the same time. When he realised that and thought this other self was a threat, it was too late. He felt a blinding blow to the back of his skull and slumped forwards, his foot slipping from the stirrup. Then he felt cold steel as a steam cannon was thrust against his neck. However, he could make use of the fact he knew how he would react and attack, giving him insight into his opponent. Trying desperately not to slip from his wind horse and float away into oblivion, he threw himself away from the gun and slipped lower to one side of his horse before his other self could take a shot. Regaining control, he swung back up into the saddle and his fist connected with his assailant's face. He felt the crunch on his knuckles, then quickly, there was a flash of steel as he pulled a derringer from his waistcoat and thrust it under his chin. He hesitated momentarily. This felt outlandish, attacking himself. He closed his eyes and squeezed the trigger. He heard the bang as his shot released from the barrel and through the traveller's jaw. Looking on, Ignatius was confused about the outcome. Blood and flesh were pushed away from the traveller's head, then appeared to get sucked back in until his head and jawline were intact once more. His body healed itself immediately, the wound simply resealing itself. The other Ignatius grinned; blood held in the crevices between his teeth. Then his face grew dark, like a shadow and his appearance took on that of some dark demon.

"How did you do that?" asked Ignatius.

"I have friends in dark places. I am supported by a power far more important than you or the Empire, or even the Charon. Power beyond your imagination with dominion over all. When I have the Book of Shadows, they shall rise up and darkness will reign over all." The stranger gave a hideous, sinister grin. He was clearly more knowledgeable about the book than Ignatius.

The scene changed and the two of them found themselves riding along a narrow bridge of rock suspended in space that arced across a starfield and had no visible means of support. Ignatius had taken the lead but felt uneasy about his doppelganger riding behind him. Just then, some space debris flew by, narrowly missing the two agents. Then one large rock smashed through the bridge behind Ignatius, causing a void that his doppelganger's wind horse could not avoid. They were travelling too fast. The horse found its hooves trying to stand on the great void of space and fell from the bridge. As it did so, Ignatius looked around in time to see the look of horror and realisation of what was happening on his own twinned and contorted face. The wind horse was wild-eyed and snorting, its legs scrambling as it tried to gain footing onto some plane or nebulous aether, but without success. The rock had caused a rip in space and all that existed was the abyss. The horse continued to fall, taking the doppelganger with him, growing ever smaller into the distance as the two of them vanished into oblivion. Ignatius's horse didn't stop but was clearly agitated by events, anticipating that this event could occur again. Before long, they had cleared the bridge and Ignatius noticed he had started to grow cold. They entered a thick white mist, and his vision became limited. Occasionally there was a break in the mist and Ignatius thought he saw mountains in the distance. These grew larger and easier to see. Tall snow-capped jagged mountains that looked familiar. Steam rose and a river of lava belched fire as it wound through the mountains. Ignatius could smell sulphur. Then, as the wind horse flew higher to breach the closest ridge of mountains, Ignatius could clearly see the towers of a magnificent city, black marble veined with red, blue and purple, huge pillars of onyx and obsidian. He could hear the drone of two huge wind harps that flanked both sides of the entrance to the city. He knew they had reached their destination, the city of Sagharta sitting on top of the central peak of the crater in which it resided. It faded in and out of existence as it always does, bridging planes, never settling for long on one of them, surrounded by the Lake of the Celestial Lotus.

Chapter 16: Return to the Mystical City

As Ignatius and his steed climbed the causeway up to the great arched double doors of the mystical city of Sagharta, the city continued to fade in and out of existence, making it difficult for Ignatius to navigate his way. But he felt some familiarity with his surroundings, the mists that surrounded the landscape, the shadows cast by the great sky galleons tethered to the tallest towers, the jagged mountains that encircled the city and the monolithic wind harps that moaned incessantly, interrupted occasionally by the fluttering of thousands of prayer flags strewn from every colourful marbled tower as he approached.

This city, fashioned to be the portal to the Otherworld, was inhabited by earth's oldest race Unknown to history, they had been lost to memory and now resided on multiple planes, meaning Ignatius no longer knew which Earth he was on, but knew his wind horse had crossed multiple planes to get here.

As he reached the gates, a horn blew and the gates opened, whereupon he was greeted by some half dozen Ti-Botta priests who took his steed, his saddle, his weapons and offered him food. After the flurry of activity had dispersed, a wizened old face with a wispy beard appeared dressed in gold and purple robes. "Welcome back, Ignatius. This is a surprise, we did not expect to see you ever again," said the High Priest in a velvet soft voice, his crow's feet wrinkles becoming more prominent around his eyes as he smiled.

"Come, have some butter tea," and he led Ignatius to a side chapel adorned with frescoes of the Charon and their exploits, some too obscene to gaze upon for long.

Ignatius sat and drank, his body becoming warm as he consumed the invigorating drink.

"So, how may I be of assistance? This is an unusual visit. I am assuming the Charon have sent you, unable to visit themselves as we have not called for them."

"That is correct. I am seeking another book, the Book of Shadows, or at least information about it. Do you know of such a book?"

The mood on the High Priest's face changed instantly. He frowned and at first did not reply. Then, with some urgency in his voice, he responded.

"You must not seek this book! It is too dangerous. The Charon should not be looking for this book! Please, I must ask you to leave, your stay is over. I am sorry you have travelled such a long way, but I cannot help you." He motioned to leave, hurrying out of his chair.

"But you must! This is not the reaction I expected," screamed Ignatius. "What is so dangerous about the Book of Shad….."

He got no further with his words before the High Priest had turned and grabbed him by the throat, throwing him to the hard marbled floor with some form of martial art move. Ignatius could feel his cheek pressed upon the cold stone, unable to talk and could see other monks running to surround him.

"You must not look for this book! You have no idea what is in it. You must not even say the book's name."

Ignatius spoke as best he could with his distorted mouth and strangled throat. "Ok! Ok! But please tell me why."

The High Priest released his grip and helped Ignatius back to his feet.

"I am sorry. But this is not like the Book of Consciousness, which you sought the last time. This is far more dangerous."

"You keep saying, but how?" Ignatius was readjusting his collar and rubbing his head, which still throbbed from his hard fall.

"Follow me. I will show you something." The old man walked briskly from the chapel, the other monks clearing a path. Ignatius followed, his head throbbing. The High Priest led him past several side chapels, through the great hall and to a staircase that went down into the bowels of the city. Seizing a burning taper of rush stalks, the old man descended, remarkably swift and agile, with Ignatius hurrying silently behind.

As they eventually reached the bottom of the stairs, the old man turned, the flames illuminating his wrinkled face giving him a sinister visage. "We are deep beneath the city; these walls hold back the lava that gives the land of Fire and Ice its name. Beneath our feet runs the subterranean River of Woe linking the earth to the Underworld."

He pointed at the walls around him. "It is down here that millennia ago, the monks discovered a fracture in one of the walls. Fearful that the fires of this land would flow in and destroy the city, they began repairs. To do them correctly, they had to first demolish part of the inner wall. It was then they discovered a secret chamber. This was not the wall holding back the lava, but the wall hiding a library that the Ti-Botta people knew nothing about." He shone the torch over towards the furthest wall, which lay in the dark. It showed evidence of demolition. Leading the way, the High Priest, took Ignatius over so he could look.

Beyond the wall were row upon row of pigeonholes that each contained several hundred scrolls of ancient parchment.

"We estimate there are seven hundred thousand scrolls, recording the entire history of the earth, the history of the Ti-Botta and the known cosmology. Started thousands of years ago, we are still cataloguing and translating them. Some are in an ancient forgotten script, which takes time."

He then pointed out a large chamber at the heart of all the pigeonholes.

"It is here we discovered Rahu, the Book of Shadows, written by the Elder God, Calabi-Ya. It had lain there for a long time, even before we discovered it. It is not visible to any living being. It hides in the shadows. As we tried to work out what the chamber was used for, thinking perhaps it was a reading room of some kind, our mystics ran some enchantments that accidentally discovered the book."

"So how is it dangerous? Please, you haven't explained." Ignatius was growing increasingly frustrated, his agitated impatience quite clear.

"The book absorbs light and gives off none. It is, as the name suggests, the Book of Shadows. If you look at it, it is invisible. Sometimes, if you are fortunate, in your peripheral vision you may make it out. But the second you look for it, it is no longer visible."

"So how is that dangerous?"

"As an object, it isn't. But there is a reason it hides in the black mire. It is to prevent any creature from opening it. For opening it will bring about certain destruction."

He looked Ignatius in the eyes and with much sobriety explained. "Death will befall you. Not maybe. No chance of survival. The opening unleashes pestilence and death, war and evil, the likes of which have never been seen before. The blackest of souls, way beyond your feeble imagination, lurk within its pages. The cosmos will be filled with monsters, demons and jinn of such eternal merciless malice that the cruelty of the Charon will pale into insignificance. It would bring about total destruction of the cosmos.

However, to prevent this, the Ti-Botta have sealed it with seven enchanted clasps, which cannot be opened unless the correct solution is known. But after our mystics created the enchantments, and when they had finished, they paid the ultimate price and were put to death to protect the secret."

The old man moved the torch over to another part of the chamber to display an ornate mausoleum in true Ti-Bottan style, organic and colourful with all sorts of marble and obsidian, decorated in places with gold.

"But the book became lost and we no longer know its whereabouts. Occasionally, it will move through the cosmos and find a new residence, patiently waiting until such time it is called for and opened."

"So, it's no longer a danger? Then what is the problem? Those who seek it will never be able to find it or open it," said Ignatius.

"We can only pray." The High Priest bowed his head and began leading the way back up the staircase.

"So, who would be seeking it?" Ignatius asked, hurriedly catching up and walking alongside the High Priest.

"Any delusional necromancer, mad occultist or warlock who believes they can harness the book's power. Or, if my thinking is correct, Calabi-Ya himself, to avenge himself once and for all."

"But he was banished! He is back in the Ghost Worlds. Isn't he?"

"That, we no longer know. Since the Charon splintered time

trying to slay it with the Cosmic Sitar. Now, space and time has weaknesses, fractures if you will, that may lead to portals that could allow Calabi-Ya back into the cosmos."

"Won't he be able to open it if he wrote the book?"

"The magic should hold fast even against him, but in truth we do not know."

The High Priest turned and made his way up the staircase with Ignatius following him. As they reached the top, he turned to Ignatius and spoke in a soft wise voice,

"I believe this is all the help we can give you."

Ignatius bowed slightly, thanking the High Priest, "Then I will bid you farewell. Thank you for your hospitality.

"Your wind horse has been given some refreshments and is waiting for you at the entrance. Goodbye, Ignatius. Do not be foolish. Leave the book alone. I repeat, it is not like the Book of Consciousness."

And with that, Ignatius left, with a somewhat anxious feeling in the pit of his stomach. As he mounted his steed and took hold of its mane once more, it began to race back across the planes through which it had come.

Chapter 17: The Oracle

Looking at Adonai, Devi spoke. "Are we going elsewhere for information regarding the book?"

Adonai looked at her inquisitively.

"I think we may need to visit Lyca."

"Who is Lyca?" asked Indigo.

"She is the wise one, the all-seeing Oracle. Gifted with cosmic sight, she may have other information about the book or its dangers," replied Devi.

The seven immortals grouped together, Darshan pulling Indigo in towards the group. They linked hands and Aryas set to work once more with an incantation. After a few moments, the mortuary was empty, the uncovered naked corpse of Skye lying there undignified, uncared for, and alone once more.

Indigo stood once more upon the deck of the great ship Taraka, speedily travelling through the cosmos with the Charon. Whilst Ignatius was away in Sagharta, they were on their way to see the great cosmic Oracle.

She looked up. Although a familiar sight, Taraka still sent shivers down her spine as she saw the usual ash belching out of the chimneys from burning the souls of the dead to power the cosmic ocean-going ship. The ship silently tore a hole through time and space and ploughed on through the starry field, past nebulae and galaxies young and old. New stars formed in a turquoise gas field to the side of the ship. As it continued through the aether, it was buffeted by cosmic wind and a field of asteroids that came crashing into the hull but left no mark as its dark energy protected those on board. As it sliced through the planes, Indigo saw distant lands, both exotic and barren, colourful and so sombre they caused alarm, past planet after planet and through the ocean of consciousness that formed the cosmos.

As Indigo stood observing all the wonders she could, a hand was placed gently on her shoulder. Startled, she looked around. It was Atman, standing firm in his black and powder-blue clothing, his platinum blond hair blowing behind him, his beautiful pale features with his chiselled cheekbones. Indigo let out a gasp and recoiled from his touch.

"My apologies, I didn't mean to startle you, my daughter."

Regaining her composure, she replied defiantly, "Do not call me that! I am not your daughter. You have no part to play in my life."

Retaining his usual softly spoken demeanour, he said, "And yet here we are. Again. I seem to be a part of your life. You are a part of our quest once more. Whether you like it or not, our lives are intertwined. Life has a destiny, and you have a purpose far greater than you can imagine. Daughter! The Charon have spent an eternity plotting from Limbo, as difficult as that is, to shape events that have resulted to us being here now." His usually passive face was now frowning. "We have shaped destiny, without destiny knowing it. You should be grateful. And although we don't know exactly what awaits us at this point in our destiny, we know we had to secure our future, our ultimate fate one day with a plan that would lead to the birth of you and Adonai's son, Ignatius."

He turned and walked away, leaving Indigo trembling with rage. Yes, he was somehow her father, but she didn't want to think of the events that led to that occurrence. Of what her mother had done to reap such a fate.

Time passed at an unknown speed. Various members of the Charon paced about on deck. Tara was the most impatient, strutting around with her long legs, adorned with black thigh-high boots, her red-lined black cloak flowing elegantly behind her. Adonai stood unmoving as usual, at the helm. Paladin sat to the side, cleaning detritus from his ornate bronze armour and sharpening his long, battle-bladed instrument. Occasionally, Devi, dressed entirely in red leather, would approach Adonai and talk to him, her raven curls flowing down her cloaked back.

Despite being surrounded by others, Indigo felt very alone. She had to dig deep within her psyche not to have a lack of confidence and to regress back to the state she was in after her last quest. She reminded herself, she was a member of the Union Jacks. One of the best agents they had seen in the past hundred years. She was the front line of the Empire, its protector, its hope for the future. A soldier of the Queen and defender of the man in the street. Lost in thought, she didn't notice the ship begin to slow. Worlds still flew past, colours changed, some colours never seen on earth, stars were born and died and then the ship was stationary.

The Charon had assembled and as she looked on, the scene changed momentarily, and she saw seven dark and twisted hawk-like hell-beings, with long sharp beaks, dripping with blood, their great long talons wrapped around blood-encrusted scythes. Their black wings wrapped around them. This was the true nature of the

Charon revealed to her once more. She shuddered.

After leaving the ship, the party came to a great plain devoid of any life. Its barren earth grey in colour and furrowed, as if it had once been ploughed, perhaps once fertile. After some hours, a dark line appeared across the horizon. It stretched from left to right, with no beginning or end in sight. As they got nearer, the blackness became a wall. Closer still, the truth revealed itself. They had come to a dense forest of thorns.

Devi turned to Indigo and said to her, "Be cautious, the thorns are long and sharp and will grab at you. Vines will take hold if you get snagged on the thorns, and any drop of blood drawn will attract the forest demons."

"Single file, follow me," demanded Adonai as he led the way. He had drawn his wide battle blade from his back and started to hack a path through the inky dense growth. The Charon had arranged themselves in line, with Indigo in the middle and Paladin following up at the rear in his protective armour.

Indigo was sure that despite a path being cleared, the leafless trees and shrubs moved to close back up again. She suddenly came face to face with a giant thorn, as long as her forearm, pointing directly at her throat. She agilely swerved it. Then, she wasn't sure but thought a vine grabbed at her ankle. Thorns began to move in, thick and fast. Her clothing got caught, steadfastly snagged, and she had to stop. She tore her clothing, leaving behind a patch of fabric. Tara was now caught on several thorns, but she cut herself clear with her broadsword. Indigo removed her short sword and held it out to slash at any further dangers. But the forest was now fully aware of their presence. Branches and vines moved in, snaking over each other to attack the intruders. Indigo, Tara, Darshan and Atman were now all caught up, slashing either side to free themselves. Eventually, Indigo was so tangled her only escape was to tear at her clothing, until she was left in her undergarments, but this was good. This gave her more freedom to move and this is the way she preferred to go into battle, her weapons all concealed in her undergarments.

She felt a tear at her neck and her forehead. Then warm liquid ran down her face and chest, staining her bodice. "Oh no! I am cut!"

Devi swung around to help, but it was of no use. Vines surrounded her and pulled her down. Thorns jabbed at her, ripping her leathers and skin. The onslaught increased in speed, and before long Indigo could hardly see any of the Charon as the suffocating darkness took over. Then the howling started, amongst which she just made out Adonai's strangled cry, "forest demons!"

Black clouds gathered, whipping around each of them, weaving in and out of the branches and vines, like murky fog until they overwhelmed their prey with a vast unbroken blackness, and all that could be heard was the wailing drone of the howling.

Unable to move much, believing this is where she would die, Indigo managed to prise her steam cannon free and took several blasts at the lifeforms nearest to her in the hope she could set herself free. Steam arose as blast after blast removed limbs and she heard the trees scream in agony. She heard voices. The Charon were successfully cutting themselves free and soon Tara could be seen standing on top of a pile of dead wood, her corset torn, one boot dropped somewhere around her ankle, scratches all across her arms and legs and her great broadsword swinging purposely at the demons, some of which were dispersed as the blade swept through their smoke-like forms.

Indigo managed to rise to her feet, short sword in one hand, steam cannon in the other, clearing an opening around her. Atman appeared, free and lunging violently at demons as they flew past. Devi rose, helping Darshan to her feet. As their success grew, so did the clearing. Adonai appeared wild-eyed, his wide blade slashing, branches yielding to his relentless attack. Aryas now had enough space to start some incantation, at which point Indigo saw Paladin put his great bladed instrument to his lips and begin to blow. Indigo instinctively covered her ears and between the actions of Aryas and Paladin, the remaining plants recoiled, clearing a path, and the demons dispersed like cannon steam.

Battle weary, the Charon regrouped and without any delay made their way through the path that had now been cleared for them, Darshan dragging Indigo by the arm to keep her out of any further harm.

They seemed to travel for a long time, but eventually emerged out of the forest to be confronted with a mountainous landscape that looked just as inhospitable. Indigo pulled her arm free of Darshan, asking Adonai, "so where do we go from here?"

He looked at her calmly and gave a rare smile. "We are here. This is the place where the Oracle dwells. This is Vala"

There was a strong smell of sulphur in the air. As Indigo looked up at the mountain tops, she realised they were at the foot of a volcanic range.

"We need to find her cave, it'll be here somewhere."

The Charon split up and Indigo followed Darshan. After a short while, Atman shouted, "It's here."

As they assembled before the yawning black chasm, no light could be seen from the outside. They ventured inside cautiously, eventually finding specks of light that grew larger as they progressed.

As Indigo reached the light, she saw the cave was dimly lit with burning tapers on the soot covered walls. There was a strong smell of incense and the metallic tang of sacrificial blood and sulphur. As she ventured further and the cave enveloped her, she could see a shadowy figure where the cave seemed to end.

The oracle was sat reclining on wolf fur rugs upon a stone dais, her legs apart with her naked body on display without any modesty, except for the golden chains that hung around her neck and waist, and the jewelled gloves and anklets she wore. She was lean and her stomach muscles were prominent, her sinuous legs long and powerful. She looked dirty, unwashed. Her hair was long and unruly and she was grinning with yellow teeth, an unholy grin that sent Indigo's blood cold, the hairs on the back of her neck bristling. The oracle's body was covered in tattoos, and as Indigo looked closer she could see her flesh was a storyboard for the Charon and their endeavours. Reclining around the dais were six naked women who looked drunk on drugs and pleasure, and the floor of the cave was littered with bleached bones of all sizes.

"What tasty morsel have you brought me, Adonai?"

"Greetings, Lyca. We are here for your help."

The oracle stepped down from her dais, ignoring him and moved panther-like in an exaggerated manner, swinging her hips until she brushed up against Indigo. She put her arm around her and pulled her close. Indigo could feel her skin crawl and had her hand on her short sword ready. The dirty hot body of the oracle was tight up against her. Indigo tried to move away, but the oracle possessed a vice-like grip.

"The Book of Shadows!" exclaimed Adonai.

Lyca hissed and released Indigo, swinging round to view Adonai with wild red eyes.

"I cannot help you! You need to leave!"

Devi had half drawn her sword. "That weapon will do no good

against the Book of Shadows. You do not know the dangers you are about to unleash if you are looking for, or have obtained, the Book of Shadows."

"Then tell us," requested Devi.

Lyca returned to her dais. The six women at her feet writhed about her legs and held each other, purring like kittens.

"Away! Away, leave us," and she gestured for them to leave. The six of them scowled and ran out of the cave, holding each other, cursing incomprehensible complaints.

"If I must, I will tell you. In the beginning, there was nothing, not even the First Cause. Eventually, the genderless Omnisoul came into being and created the cosmos, the oldest part, the first creation being Yukteswar, the Well at the Centre of Time, adorned by Omphalos, the Temple of the Dawn. Then, bringing forth all life, they instructed it to seed the cosmos.

The second act by the Omnisoul was to create the four artefacts of the creation. The first artefact was the Book of Consciousness, or Turiya, containing the Omnisoul's thoughts, the very consciousness of the cosmos itself with which it was brought to life. It contains the beginning and end of every atom in the cosmos.

The second artefact was the creation of Rahu, the Book of Shadows. The Omnisoul became bored and tired very quickly at the creation and a lapse of concentration took hold and dark thoughts came into being. This lapse not only created the second artefact but it also led to the creation of the Elder God, Calabi-Ya, the oldest god in the cosmos after the Omnisoul. At least, that is the belief.

In order to try and regain harmony once more, the Omnisoul brought forth the third artefact, Keisu, the Singing Bowl, used to play music to create or restore order to the cosmos, the bowl's vibration working in conjunction with the thoughts of the Omnisoul.

The fourth artefact created was Prajnana, The Flaming Celestial Pearl, which encapsulated the wisdom of the Omnisoul. It represents the purest form of the Omnisoul's wisdom and understanding, it is the reality of the Omnisoul, the truth behind all existence in the cosmos."

Adonai interrupted, "So what is so unusual about the Book of Shadows?"

"There are dark thoughts, but there is nothing as dark as those of the Omnisoul. They exist with such malice and ferocity that they will bring about nothing but misery, pain, disease, plague, and death. It is believed the stuff of dreams, nightmares find their way across the planes and into the book and multiply, grow in horror and depth with such black evil they can no longer be stomached without sending beings wild with madness. In fact, if the book is ever opened, death is the kindest option.

But the book is more complicated than that, legend has it that it was written by Calabi-Ya, the Elder God, who manifested because of these thoughts, collected them, and wrote them down. Other legends say that he is the Omnisoul's brother, or even as old as the Omnisoul. But there is more. Like Ravana, the earthly King of Ceylon, who made himself invincible by hiding his soul in a jar, myth has it that Calabi-Ya hid his soul within the book.

This is why it is so hazardous to open. I believe the Ti-Botta have added additional precautions over the aeons, and nobody but the mystical craftsmen who created them know how to open them. But esoteric knowledge that has spread throughout the cosmos seems to suggest the book can be opened by another enchanted jewel. Somehow the task requires the power of a precious stone. But nobody knows where this jewel exists, or what plane it is on."

Adonai looked at the other Charon. They all had the same knowing look. Indigo saw the look but didn't know what it meant.

At length Adonai spoke, "Perhaps our death, the end to our immortality would be welcome, but despite our lack of mercy, I don't think we should be subjecting the rest of the cosmos to the horrors created by Calabi-Ya."

Indigo was surprised by their decision, but remained silent, she just wanted to get out of there as soon as she could.

"We thank you for the information, Lyca. Do you know where the book resides?" asked Adonai.

Lyca laughed, a hideous grin on her grimy face. "Not exactly, but recent knowledge gives me an idea of its residence. I can see there is much more you are still not aware of."

Chapter 18: The Nadas

Thrusting into the light, Lyca leaned forward, resting an elbow on her tattooed thigh, her face wild and her unkempt hair falling about her face. "Do you know of the Nadas?"

Adonai raised an eyebrow. "We have not…"

"Ha!" She seemed to relish the Charon's lack of knowledge. "The Nadas are two brothers, Viveka and Vijana and their sister, Prajja. They are commonly known collectively as the librarians, but are really titled the Librarian, the Archivist and the Administrator. They are the curators and guardians of cosmic wisdom, and their houses of learning are used to transport information and energy across the cosmos. The archive of all known knowledge is within their protection. They scribe and catalogue that which has been."

"But doesn't the Book of Consciousness already contain that?" asked Indigo.

"It does, but that book is not available. Most beings cannot open it, and although it contains the history of everything in the cosmos, what has been, what is and what will be, it is not for reading. History is recorded by the Librarians. Now tell me your history, you delightful thing," replied Lyca.

Indigo regretted speaking up and she gradually moved back behind Darshan.

"Aryas, do you know anything of these librarians?" asked Adonai.

"I do not. Despite my ability to cross planes and walk the cosmos as my astral self, I have never encountered or heard of them."

Returning her attention away from Indigo once more, Lyca added, "their libraries are secret depositories of ancient and lost knowledge, and are called the Library of Consciousness, the Library of Dreams and the Library of Cosmic Awareness. You will need to locate these. I believe one of them conceals the book, but it arrived recently in this epoch. Or maybe they all conceal the book. It hides in the shadows and can cross planes to do so and each library is on a different plane."

Aryas looked at her and speaking in a direct manner said, "You are the Oracle, are you not? You should be able to find their location!"

"That is true. But they are concealed by magic, and if I try, I shall require payment."

"And what do you suggest?"

"The girl. Leave her with me when you leave. Failing that, you are the mystic, you pinpoint their location!"

"It's a deal!" replied Adonai.

Indigo shrieked. "No! No! You can't leave me here, not with her." As she looked at Lyca, the oracle was grinning, her wild eyes alight with expectation, and she licked her lips. Indigo turned to run but Tara grabbed her roughly by the arm.

"Keep still, girl. We have a quest to fulfil," she said.

Grabbing a steam cannon from her undergarments, Indigo thrust it at Tara, but she was soon overpowered and tightly restrained with no way of escape.

"Ha, ha, ha! Very well," said Lyca, "we have a deal."

She leapt from her dais and picked up several dry and splintered bones that were strewn around the floor of the cave. Rummaging around amongst the wolf furs, she found a long wooden pipe. Stuffing what looked like herbs into it, she lit it and began to disappear in a haze of acrid smoke. When it had cleared she had a drink in her hand and, gulping salaciously, returned back to the dais demanding, "bring me the girl."

The Charon looked on inquisitively.

"The girl! The girl!"

She thrust a heavily tattooed arm out and, with her long bony fingers culminating in extraordinarily long dirty nails, pointed at Indigo.

Tara thrust her forward. Indigo struggled, pulling backwards, but her strength was no match for Tara's.

"Present her arm"

Tara took Indigo's right arm and thrust it forward. Pinning her left arm tightly to her own body meant Indigo was unable to draw any weapon.

"Palm up"

With her arm correctly presented, Lyca ran her fingers down its length. Revulsion filled Indigo's body. "I will avenge this, you demon whore!" snarled Indigo.

Lyca cackled, then shouted "Silence!" and then with her razor-like talons, sliced through Indigo's wrist, drawing blood. The Oracle placed her cup beneath her wrist and collected several drops. She then started an incomprehensible incantation consisting of continuous groaning interspersed with the occasional click and chattering sound. She then drank from the cup containing Indigo's blood, which seemed to turn her wild. Blood seeped down from the corner of her mouth and Indigo had to look away in disgust. Then without warning and with some ferocity, she threw the bones to the floor with a clatter. Then, throwing her naked body on top of them, she writhed around as if in agony, still muttering her incantation. The Charon pulled back for fear of impeding her activity. Then she was finally still and silent. After a few seconds, she stood. Gazing down, she began reading the pattern of the bones with a frown upon her face. Brushing the greasy hair back that was stuck to her sweaty face, she stared as if in disbelief at Indigo. All those standing about the Oracle were feeling a bit uneasy. Indigo was still struggling in Tara's vice-like grip and through gritted teeth demonstrated her hatred for the Oracle.

"I will kill you for this," she said.

Lyca just continued to stare, but she seemed to have changed her demeanour and her vision was as if she was looking beyond the cave entirely.

"What did the bones say?" demanded Adonai.

Withdrawing back to her dais and into herself, the Oracle appeared to be trying to make herself small. Whispering in a hoarse voice, her gaze drilled into Adonai, and she paused after each line of her interpretation.

"Shadows there are many, and come from the dark past,
but seek and find a girl, who is the Iolite, the outcast.
She will bring about complete desolation.
A blue-green world will burn due to betrayal and desecration.
Her mirror soul shall complete the cycle,
to obtain the twin flame shall be vital.
But be cautious of those who dwell in the Dark Lord's crater,
To find the book, seek the wisdom of the curator."

The Oracle was visibly shaken and did not wish to engage anymore. Pulling the wolf furs around her she covered her naked body.

"You must leave. And take the girl with you. I have no use for her. The one you seek is Viveka, the Librarian."

Tara released Indigo, who immediately went to draw her short sword, lunging towards the Oracle, but Adonai intervened with lightning speed.

"We must go," he said, looking Indigo in the face. "Anger has no place here."

"Where will we find Viveka?" asked Tara

"You have the prophecy. Get out! I cannot help you any further."

Gathering themselves together, the Charon and Indigo headed for the cave entrance.

"We shall leave you in peace. Thank you for your assistance," said Adonai as he turned to leave.

On the way out they had to step over the other six women, who were coupling on the hard stony floor, completely oblivious to anyone else present.

Once out into the open, Devi said to Adonai, "What did that mean?"

Adonai gave a slight shrug, displaying a side Indigo had never seen before. "Aryas, any ideas?"

Aryas didn't want to talk too loudly so stepped over to Adonai. "I have some ideas, but need to think on it more on the journey back before I disclose."

The party all headed back the way they had come, thankful that the forest of thorns had remained as it was, the opening they had used still visible and before long they were all on deck again on the great ship Taraka heading back to Earth.

On board, Indigo was confused, disturbed by the way she had been treated and whilst grateful the Oracle no longer had a use for her, whatever unholy pleasure that would have brought, she was perturbed as to why suddenly she was discarded. She had done nothing; she had been held captive against her will once more. This was not the usual bravery the Union Jacks demand of her. She retreated into a corner by one of the cabins and held herself tightly, avoiding the Charon for the entire journey.

Chapter 19: Resolve

The ship Taraka hung in the sky above Oxford, protected with invisibility by Aryas's enchantments and high enough that airships flew far below along with smaller dirigibles ferrying people about during their daily lives, all oblivious to any supernatural events taking place. The huge crystal globe and its black wings sitting on top of a black tower could be seen towering above the honey-stoned dreaming spires reminding the city's inhabitants that the Administorium were present.

Eventually, Darshan looked for Indigo and found her hiding place.

"You have nothing to fear, Indigo. Adonai had no intention of leaving you with the Oracle. You are a strong warrior, and it seems you have a great destiny ahead of you. We just do not yet know fully what that destiny is."

Indigo stood up "I have fought battles across Europe, spied for the Union and done what was needed for the Empire and Queen, but the more involved I get with cosmic affairs, the smaller I seem to feel and all the more useless."

"You must dig deep within your soul and stand steadfast. It is natural to feel some kind of unease."

Indigo composed herself summoning her usual iron-like courage once more and checked her weapons. "So, what do we do now?" she enquired.

"We are awaiting the return of Ignatius to see what information the Ti-Botta have divulged."

Looking over the side, Indigo saw how majestically the airships moved. Looking past the city's spires she saw a disturbance within the far-off clouds, the white fluffy vapour began to swirl and disperse. Then before she could register what was happening, the wind horse was upon her and had come to a halt on deck. Ignatius jumped off. An anxious Indigo ran over to him, taking his arm. "What do you know?"

Ignatius looked at Adonai. The rest of the Charon gathered around as he began to tell what he knew.

"The Ti-botta know of the book, and it was once in their possession. But it is not like the Book of Consciousness. It is far more dangerous. They are talking pestilence and death, evil the likes of which nobody has ever encountered. The book must not be opened. But apparently it hides in the shadows and cannot be located easily and if it is found, the Ti-Botta have added additional locks and enchantments to prevent anybody trying."

"That confirms what the Oracle told us. But she was so spooked she didn't want to tell us much more and as ever with all seers, she spoke in riddles, but it would appear that the fate of the book lies in the hands of Indigo," replied Adonai.

Ignatius shot her a glance. Indigo didn't engage him eye to eye. She did not want to acknowledge the situation. Indigo's mind raced, trying to recall what the Oracle had said, trying in some way to link it to herself, but didn't understand the connection."

"Did they mention the Librarian?" said Adonai.

"No. Why?"

"Apparently, we must seek the wisdom of a Librarian called Viveka."

Ignatius could see that Indigo was troubled and asked why the Charon believed the fate of the book lay in the hands of Indigo.

"We are not sure," replied Adonai.

"Well, I believe the answers we seek lie down there in the Administorium," said Ignatius pointing overboard at the great monolith that towered above Oxford. "Besides, the Watcher said the Administorium are hiding a secret."

"The Watcher!" cried Adonai, Aryas and Devi in unison.

"How have you spoken to the Watcher?" enquired Adonai.

"I'm not sure. He visited me whilst I meditated."

"That's highly unorthodox," said Aryas. "The Watcher should not be contacting mortals. It is beyond his remit and is forbidden. That means the nature of this book is far beyond what any of us can understand."

Adonai looked angry. "Then what do you propose we do, Aryas? Tell me. We cannot leave it to be reunited with Calabi-Ya. We don't know what power he will wield."

"And if he becomes more powerful than the Omnisoul, is that so bad? We may be set free from the shackles that bind us to the will of the Omnisoul. Isn't that what we have all wanted for an eternity? Tell me, if this book is so terrible, what could possibly be as bad as trying to destroy time? Both paths probably lead to total entropy."

"No," replied Adonai. "This way may bring an eternity of unimaginable suffering for all living beings in the cosmos as entropy plays out."

"Has the great merciless Adonai developed a conscience, empathy perhaps?" Aryas almost spat his mocking retort.

"Enough!" cried Adonai. He turned his back on the rest of the Charon and stood at the bow of the ship, peering at the spires of Oxford below, which were made even more golden as the sun went down.

Indigo moved closer to Ignatius, still unable to look him in the eye.

"Ignatius, I am concerned. We are working blind, with little intelligence. We know the book is dangerous, it's magically bound and requires an enchanted jewel to open it. But if opened it will bring death and destruction. I don't think I should be anywhere near it. The Oracle spurned me as if I was evil. I have a very bad feeling about this."

Ignatius looked at her. She had a tear in her eye. He had never seen her like this before. He put a reassuring arm around her and said, "I share your concern, and don't like the situation any more than you do. However, if the book is on earth, and if it is in the Administorium, we have a duty to find it. Protect the Empire, the world, the cosmos. We need to investigate and see if this Librarian is in the Administorium."

Ignatius turned to Adonai for guidance. "Then what do we do?"

"I think you two should go to the Administorium and see what you can find out. We will wait for your signal. I fear if we all go, any chance of finding the book in the first place will be gone. Brute force is no substitute for stealth when looking for the invisible."

Ignatius and Indigo prepared to leave the ship and with some magic from Aryas found themselves on the cobbles of Cornmarket Street heading for the ominous monolith.

Chapter 20: The High Priestess

Ignatius and Indigo waited until nightfall. Then, as the last few dons made their ways back from the taverns and whorehouses, the two Union Jacks made their way in silence to the Administorium building. As they approached, the black monolith was even more menacing than in the daylight. They made their way around the back of the building and felt along its smooth featureless wall. It was cold as ice and except for the familiar patterning upon its surface, a result of the rock's composition and grain structure, it gave no hint of any windows or doorways.

Indigo dared to whisper, "Are you sure this plan will work? Will it get us in?"

"I'm certain of it, I just don't know if it will be silent enough or if maximum disruption may result." He looked at her and shrugged his shoulders. "I'm still fine tuning this weapon, so I'm not sure what to expect." In the darkness Indigo had to stare to make out any expression on Ignatius's face.

"And if it goes wrong?"

"We run! Simple as that!"

Indigo wasn't filled with confidence. She checked her weaponry just to make sure, even though she knew she was fully armed and ready for any event.

Ignatius took his sonic blaster out of the leather holster strapped to his leg. Pointing it at the building, he squeezed the trigger, gently at first and then more heavily, as the cannon fired up and began its symphony. Too noisy, and with no result. Without releasing the trigger, Ignatius adjusted some dials and the pitch altered and became higher, less audible to human ears. Some stray dogs in the neighbouring streets began to bark and howl. There was a lot of commotion a distance away.

"Shut up, you flea bitten hound," shouted a deep gruff voice in the next street. Then another, "Shut that bloody animal up!" More dogs responded.

Ignatius looked at Indigo in way of an apology. Then, as he predicted, an invisible door opened. Ignatius peered in cautiously and then the two of them slipped in, hoping they would be unseen as they scurried deeper into the building, keeping to the shadows.

As they reached the heart of the building, Ignatius whispered, "We need to split up as planned. Look for anything that resembles a library." Removing his pocket watch to check it, he added, "We meet back here in thirty."

Indigo slipped a watch from her garments to check the time, repeating, "In thirty," and she skulked off to the left. Ignatius headed right.

The building was mainly in darkness with the odd pool of light here and there. Ignatius could just make out the familiar site of the carved marble statues of ecclesiastical knights with their arms outstretched and leaning on broad-bladed swords. His mind began to wander. Maybe the statues stood guard over the Book of Shadows, symbolic guardians. He made his way towards them. He heard muffled voices in the distance and realised they came from above. Looking up, he saw two administrators walking a narrow bridge linking two parts of the upper floors. He ducked behind one of the statues and stood a while in its shadow, hoping he had not been seen. His eyes darted left and right, constantly on the lookout for drones, stealthy little spies that flew about ready to raise the alarm. Verifying it was clear, he looked around behind the two statues, expecting to find some kind of plinth or tomb that might hold the book. Nothing. Behind the statues appeared to be a chapel, complete with a stone altar carved from greenest malachite. Candles burned on either end, and strange runes had been painted in gold leaf around the edge of the altar. Either side of the altar stood a gilt chair like a throne, upholstered in scarlet velvet and embroidered with a crest that looked like a dragon. Ignatius thought it looked like a depiction of Calabi-Ya, but dismissed the notion.

As he looked around, checking alcoves and a tiny side chapel, he began to wander: if the book was hidden in permanent shadow, was it possible to trip over it? Or did it exist in the aether, or on another plane? Previously, the Book of Consciousness had been hidden in a vault, so Ignatius began checking the walls of the chapel, looking for hidden passages or movable stones that might be a means to opening a vault. With no success, he came back to the two statues. Across the chamber, he saw Indigo doing similar actions, then she vanished amongst the shadows, presumably entering a side chapel.

A cold blade connected in the dark with Ignatius's throat. He felt the steel bite and a trickle of blood run down his neck.

"Do not move if you wish to live," came a deep voice that was barely a whisper.

Ignatius was shoved in the back and moved into a pool of light towards the centre of the chamber.

The High Priestess of the Administorium silently entered. She walked with such speed and fluidity it looked like she was gliding on wheels. She wore a black satin gown lined in gold, which trailed behind her, swishing the floor as she walked. It was fastened only at the neck with a simple gold chain and a large amulet, and it hung open to reveal her milk-white naked skin. Her features were elfin, with high cheekbones and a pointed chin, slender straight nose and neatly shaped eyebrows. Her eyes were like black pools of pitch and her raven hair was crowned with a wreath of black flowers with twisted ornamental rams' horns protruding from above her brow. She had never been seen in public amongst the streets of Oxford, hence the pale sun-starved skin. Ignatius thought she would strike fear into any member of the public, and so the Administorium obviously kept her a secret.

She was flanked by two dark-skinned muscular guards, each carrying a pike that looked to be made from gold, but steam hissed gently from a vent at the base of each blade, making them no ordinary pikes. They too were naked except for similar black and gold cloaks fastened at the neck and a gold-horned helmet topped with a plume of feathers. The steam surrounded all three, giving the High Priestess the illusion she had just emerged from some magical mist.

As she reached Ignatius, she ordered his captor to release him. The blade at his throat was removed and the man, whoever he was, silently vanished.

"Come!" she said.

As Ignatius approached, the two guards stepped forwards and placed their weapons in front of the High Priestess, in a cross shape, making it quite clear that he was not to get too close to her.

Her cold eyes looked Ignatius up and down, weighing him up

and when she spoke it was like the purring of a cat. "Leave us! I see no concern with Mr Ignatius."

The guards stepped back, withdrawing their weapons, and one of them looked at her quizzically. "Go!" she said, and the two of them bowed slightly and backed away, not turning their backs, sloping away into the shadows behind. Ignatius got the impression they were still close by.

Ignatius went to speak but was immediately cut off. "Well, Mr Ignatius, why do the clerics of the Administorium believe you should be meeting with me? I am not usually available to… well, let's say, the likes of you. You must be a singular man, distinctive in your field. Something special. Well?"

"I am an ordinary person your… Forgive me, I do not know how to address you."

She laughed. "I am Cha-Ya, you may call me that."

Ignatius continued, "As I said, I am an ordinary person who works at the…"

He didn't get a chance to finish.

"Come now, Mr Ignatius, you expect me to believe anything you say. You are far from ordinary, or why would you be skulking about in the Administorium in the darkest hours? Do not underestimate the Administorium. Our intelligence is second to none, we have spies everywhere. I know you always seem to be at the forefront of important decisions around the city. Always on the side of the Empire, but you are much more."

Ignatius felt she was bluffing and didn't know anything more than she had said. The Union Jacks were far older and far more secretive than the Administorium. Ignatius took the conversation away from who he was.

"I am seeking some knowledge of a book. I believe it has a name, that of Rahu. It is perhaps the twin of the Book of Consciousness."

Disturbance clearly flickered across her face, but so briefly it would have gone unnoticed to most. She was surprised Ignatius had heard of either book.

"So you have heard of such a book?"

She didn't answer. "Tell me, what is so special about this book?"

So we are playing chess, thought Ignatius. "I know it cannot be found."

"So if it cannot be found, why do you ask if I know of it? Surely it must be lost, or hidden, certainly from the likes of you, for a reason?"

Ignatius just ignored her comments and questions. "It is also known as the Book of Shadows. I am led to believe it has great power and that anyone reading it should be cautious."

The High Priestess smiled. "You are correct. The book has been drifting through time and space since its creation. It is continually updated, re-written if you wish, by all the dark thoughts, all those dark dreams, nightmares that emanate from all living creatures in the cosmos. It is for this reason it is known by its name, for it is a tome of such darkness it absorbs all light and, therefore, it hides in the shadows. It is impossible to find."

"Thank goodness," he said sarcastically. "Then I guess we will all be safe!"

She eyed Ignatius with both curiosity and contempt. She thought for a while, but wanted to find out more of what he knew.

"I will level with you, Mr Ignatius." She waved her hand majestically and began to recount what she knew. In part, what Ignatius already knew.

"I'm going to skip with the pretence. I know you are more knowledgeable than you are letting on. Nobody is sure what came before the start of the current Celestial Age. It is thought the Omnisoul always is, was and will be. The cosmos sprang from the First Thought and grew out of the consciousness of the Omnisoul. The symphony of thought danced out across the abyss, filling the void with vibrating frequencies that interact to form the offspring that are the past, present and future realities that coincide, coexist and at times interact with each other.

But in man's terms, before the beginning, there was nothing, no earth, no heavens, no stars, no sky, only an empty space waiting to be filled with life and the creation of everything.

During the creation, the Book of Consciousness was formed, containing the life history of every living being in the cosmos, past, present and future. It is the script for being, the entire story of the Hypersphere, just as the Omnisoul decided. The song of the Omnisoul was played on the singing bowl, bringing order and harmony to the heavens, and in order to obtain longevity the Omnisoul wrapped all wisdom up with the Flaming Celestial Pearl and flung it out into the cosmos to drift, eternally maintaining wisdom throughout the conscious thought that is the cosmos.

But even a god can get bored! It is rumoured among civilised kingdoms that in a lapse of concentration, or effort, or playful interruption, the Omnisoul created dark thoughts. At first a spark, a dark idea, but this dark thought grew and began to spread throughout the cosmos, particularly penetrating the domain of the Ghost Worlds and Rahu the Book of Shadows was created. It is the manifestation of all the dark thought, dreams and deeds throughout the cosmos which, left unchecked, would permeate throughout disrupting the harmony of the heavens and the natural order of things and diminish the power of the Omnisoul

With every lapse of conscious thought, the Omnisoul created

more darkness, until this dark matter had woven itself into the very fabric of time itself and this dark energy lay waiting at every weak point and boundary throughout the cosmos, waiting to penetrate and create chaos amongst the harmonious music of the spheres. This dark mass had a name, Calabi-Ya, the Elder God, the would-be usurper, composed of pure dark energy. As Calabi-Ya grew in size, form and strength, the Book of Shadows became more complex, more dangerous.

Together, the Omnisoul and Calabi-Ya form the two aspects, light and dark of the cosmos. To protect the cosmos, the Omnisoul hid the Book of Consciousness and banished Calabi-Ya to the Ghost Worlds, closing every portal and gateway back into the cosmos to prevent him from gaining more power. Periodically, Calabi-Ya attempts to regain a foothold and a terrible battle ensues. The last time was when he found a way back in via Ragnar of Roc but was defeated by gods called the Charon.

So ashamed of his creation, the Omnisoul imbued the Book of Shadows with deepest black so it would forever be hidden in shadow where no being could find it."

Ignatius wasn't sure what to say, The High Priestess had basically filled in or confirmed what he wanted to know. He became suspicious. This was too easy, although he still didn't know where the book was, or what he was going to do if he found it. He didn't know where Indigo was either.

The High Priestess looked confident, superior. "I think you may be of use to me, Mr Ignatius. I want to introduce somebody to you."

She turned her back on him, her cloak swishing, revealing her flesh once more. The two large guards had returned and walking either side of Ignatius, escorted him to walk behind her. Going deeper into the Admninistorium, she led Ignatius into another larger chamber which had at its centre a large pyramid-like structure.

The pyramid gleamed like glass. It looked like it was made from a solid block of black obsidian. It sat directly below the crystal globe that had been carved to represent the world, enveloped by sinister wings that sat at the top of the Administorium building. Moon light that entered the globe was refracted, amplified, and directed in a shaft of brilliant light down the centre of the tower to connect with the apex of the pyramid.

As the cleric led Ignatius towards the pyramid, he could see his own reflection in the black polished surface. Over his shoulder, Ignatius thought he saw the shadow of a dragon-like beast, but as he looked around, there was nothing there.

At the pyramid, the High Priestess was handed a silver tipped ebony rod by one of her guards, which she tapped on the side of the pyramid. A large slab of obsidian slid aside to reveal an ornate metal staircase leading down into the inky blackness of a cavern beneath the Administorium. She led the way, her gold chains echoing as she descended. Ignatius followed into the gloom. As the two of them reached the bottom of the staircase, Ignatius looked up. He couldn't see the light from the aperture of the doorway. In fact, the inside of the pyramid was inconceivably large. The ceiling was non-existent, in its place was a star field with nebulous clouds of colour that drifted about. It was as if the cosmos had been captured and placed inside the pyramid.

Chapter 21: The Repository

Ignatius was led down another staircase. He looked down to see where he was going, but the blackness prevented him from knowing his destination. The stairs seemed to go on forever. He was well beneath the city at a level even deeper than the tunnels beneath the Bodleian. As he looked more closely, he thought the stairs appeared to be constructed of books, huge ancient tomes piled one on top of the other. *Sacrilege*, he thought, *what ancient knowledge could be contained within?* Eventually coming to the bottom, he could see the floor was a mosaic of book pages, thousands of them strewn randomly to form a carpet of text. Each page seemed to murmur as he stepped on them. *Sentient*, Ignatius thought to himself.

"I will leave you now," said the High Priestess. "You have no need for me anymore. This is our library, just follow the pages and you will encounter the answers you are looking for. Our Librarian Viveka is most useful and very knowledgeable. In exchange, the knowledge you possess may be of use to me, so I expect some reciprocation, Mr Ignatius."

Her voice was cold and without any display of anger or any emotion for that matter. When she spoke, she came across as menacing and determined. Ignatius wasn't sure if he was now held prisoner. He was also concerned that he hadn't seen any sight of Indigo but took comfort in the fact that he also hadn't heard any commotion or alarms, so he thought that at least she hadn't been discovered and captured.

As he looked up to where he had descended, he realised the library looked infinite. Shelves around him soared high up beyond his view and although he knew he had ventured underground, the ceiling looked to be sky. A sea of stars filled the void, but it was high up, barely visible. The stacks that held the books appeared to be taller than the depth he knew he had descended and were carved from all sorts of marble and colourful rocks. Blue marble veined with turquoise, speckled pink granite, white marble veined with green and red obsidian. It was breathtaking. Other shelves were made from ornately carved wood, rich in colour, cherry wood, light oak, mahogany, and birds-eye maple were used in abundance. He wondered how all of this could exist beneath Oxford, and no one know of it, not even the spies of the Union Jacks.

Hesitantly, he followed the pages as they went off into the distance, not knowing what he was expected to encounter. At some point, the pages began to entwine to form threads that crossed over each other. They were loosely woven. Perhaps they made up the very fabric of time and the whole of the cosmos. After some time, the threads became looser and culminated in what looked like a giant pulpit of many colours. Colourfully patterned tiles like those he'd seen before in Morocco now covered the floor.

He could just make out the silhouette of a large figure and as he approached, the figure came into view. It was a giant of a man in pale, blue-grey, ornate and battle-scarred armour, similar to that of Paladin. His skin had a green hue and around his neck and draped over one shoulder he wore a heavy cloak with a fur collar. On his shoulder sat a fierce-looking eagle, its talons clinging tightly to the fur. He was sat on top of a large pile of oversized, ancient-looking books. He had several volumes chained to his armour, other smaller volumes, but just as ancient, were locked in cages or jewelled reliquaries. His face looked as ancient and weather-beaten as some of the books.

As he saw Ignatius approach, he leaned down from his pulpit and put a greenish brown leathery finger to his lips and, making a shushing sound, beckoned him to be quiet. This was the Librarian.

Ignatius motioned to speak. "I have come…" and was immediately shut down.

The Librarian leaned forward once more with a furious look upon his ancient face and whispered in a hoarse voice, "This is a library. Silence is sacred!"

Ignatius, completely ignored, thought for a moment or two, the utter silence deafening. Clearing his throat caught the Librarian's attention once more. Suddenly, he felt a tightening of his throat as if he had been gripped by some unseen force. Gasping through his shortness of breath, his eyes bulging, the Librarian looked at him and spoke once more.

"If it is death that shall bring about your silence, so be it!" He then released his invisible grip and Ignatius fell to his knees.

In a hoarse voice, Ignatius eventually managed to ask a question successful.

"What is this place and who exactly, if you forgive me, are you?"

"The Administorium believe they are here to protect the Empire from itself. They confiscate and hide away any heretical texts, any technology they believe to be harmful to the Empire or the public, so they lock it away down here with me, the Librarian.

But that is not the true function of the Administorium. They are here to protect me. They just don't realise that."

Ignatius looked at him quizzically.

"You see, I am not of this plane. I think the High Priestess may suspect that, but even she dare not speak it. The puritanical thoughts of the clerics would not easily entertain such a notion."

Ignatius thought twice before answering, until in a whisper he said, "Then where are you from and why are you here?"

"I cannot say where I am from, I do not know. I am so very old, I cannot remember. I have drifted the cosmos for an eternity until I found what I was designed to look for."

"And that is?"

"It is the Book of Shadows. But generally the Administorium have no knowledge of it."

"So where is it?"

"Ah! A good question. I do not know! It's here somewhere in this library. But as its name implies, it lurks in the shadows and cannot be seen."

Ignatius looked on confused. "Then how can it be found?"

"The answer to that question has eluded me, my brother and my sister for eternity. But what I know for certain is, it is here on this plane, on this planet, in this very Library! I have it on good authority!"

"Whose authority?"

"The author himself"

Ignatius was surprised. How had the Librarian been in contact with Calabi-Ya, who had been exiled to the Ghost Worlds?

"So how do you propose to find it?"

"You are going to find it, Mr Ignatius."

This took Ignatius by surprise. "How? If you have not been able to find it, then how will I? I'm just a human with no powers like yours. What assistance can I give?"

"The book has been here for centuries, but we have only recently discovered that fact. But I am informed that you have the means, and if that doesn't work, we need the Iolite. I want to try both, but you just happened to be the one we have apprehended first."

Ignatius knew he had to get out of there, and that Indigo might be in danger. He made a move to run, but before he was able, the eagle perched on the Librarian's shoulder had spread its impressive wings and looked to take angry flight if Ignatius moved any further. However, Ignatius was equally inquisitive how he could help and what the Iolite was. The eagle took flight and soared above, circling overhead, gradually spiralling lower and lower until he was just above Ignatius's head.

Ignatius relaxed. "What is an Iolite?"

"Ah! The Iolite fulfils the prophecy. It is a purple jewel, the key to opening the book."

"Then how can I help?"

The Librarian looked at him with squinted eyes of suspicion. "You really don't know?"

Ignatius shrugged. The Librarian lunged at him and seized his right arm. Raising it up, he declared in a gruff whisper, "The birthmark! The Eye of Adonai. The Omnisoul's first born of the Seven Sublime Lords."

Using force, the Librarian held Ignatius's hand to his own right eye. He let out a gasp of surprise and Ignatius could see his left eye widen in surprise or awe. It was as if the Librarian had changed, his face becoming veiled with desire and greed. He suddenly appeared to age, lines appeared across his face, he frowned, and his voice was much lower, brusquer, as he whispered, "I can see it! The Book of Shadows is there..." and he pointed into the distance between the bookshelves. The eagle followed his outstretched arm and landed where the book was lying. As the Librarian continued to look upon it, it began to emerge from the shadows for both of them to see.

The book had indeed lain hiding in plain sight. It was enormous, as big as the Book of Consciousness, measuring the same, eight feet by five feet in size, but it looked thicker. But unlike the Book of Consciousness, it did not light the room with any kind of colourful glow. Ignatius thought he heard the odd gasp and scream emanating from it. Violet and black fire swirled around it, giving off an unholy unnatural glow that seemed to absorb all the light from around it, casting nothing but the blackest of shadows. It looked dull grey like lead, lacking any kind of lustre, and it was locked with seven iron-looking clasps, each as thick as an adult's arm. It groaned faintly. Every so often, faces appeared within the black swirling glow, inhuman faces, twisted and contorted in agony. They stretched forward out of the shadows and then were absorbed once more, only to be replaced by other demonic faces, or the heads of wild beasts with huge fangs and bulging eyes. It appeared to Ignatius that the book must contain the souls of all sorts of demons, ghouls and dangers.

It was now obvious to Ignatius that the book should not be opened for fear of unleashing all kinds of unholy scourge, that would most likely result in unpredictable consequences. The Librarian's face changed again, and he looked as giddy as a school boy.

"At last! My siblings will be envious. I have found the elusive, the impossible, the most sacred, most revered book in the cosmos."

He went running over to the book, cautiously not getting too close. All light reflected from his armour was absorbed by the book, and they were both surrounded by a velvet black aura.

"The High Priestess! The High Priestess! I must tell her."

As if by magic, she appeared. Her cloak parted, displaying her long pale thighs, and as her body reflected the limited light available, the book seemed to attract it and draw it in, so none escaped, completely absorbed by the surface of the book.

"You have done well, Librarian. You were right about Mr Ignatius. Now everything is in place to open the book." The High Priestess looked at Ignatius with a sinister grin.

"Now for the girl." Turning away she laughed, fading into the distance as she went pack up the stairs. Ignatius only hoped she didn't mean Indigo.

As the Librarian released his grip on Ignatius's hand, the book faded again, absorbed back into the shadows. But no matter, they now knew where the book lay. Suddenly, Ignatius felt a blow to his skull as the great armoured hand of the Librarian knocked him unconscious.

Meanwhile, on the great ship Taraka that still hung, cloaked in secrecy, in the skies above Oxford, Adonai saw with his blind eye the emergence of the book. Aryas felt the planes shift and the cosmos in the immediate vicinity of Earth murmur in disbelief. The rest of the Charon all looked at Adonai.

"So it's true," said Devi. "Then we must get down there and find it."

Paladin came forward. "I'm ready. Load it onto my back, and as we travel around, we can use it like any other weapon. Maybe that'll quicken the process."

Adonai was silent in his anticipation of obtaining the book.

Chapter 22: The Sacrifice

Indigo was still searching the antechambers that ran off from the main chamber she and Ignatius had started in. There were curious books written in unidentifiable scripts, strange statuary, and several astrolabes and orreries showing how the planets move around the sun. She began to wonder what all of this had to do with protecting the Empire or restricting new technologies. As she thumbed through the pages of an ancient book, she felt the iron-like grip of a muscular arm encircle her, then another pinning her arms by her side so she was unable to reach any weaponry. They squeezed until she was out of breath. She could feel the man's sweat against her skin and taste his foul breath. Her head began to swirl and the world became blurry until she fell unconscious, her body limp and defenceless.

When she awakened, she was lying on the cold tiled floor of the library where Ignatius still lay lifeless. She too remained motionless in the hope that the High Priestess wouldn't see she was conscious.

The High Priestess gave a subtle sign to the two guards she had with her. As they approached, Indigo prepared herself for her two assailants. She was fast as they lunged forwards and Indigo withdrew her short sword and a derringer. As she fired, she pierced the shoulder of one of the near-naked men. Blood ran down his arm, but it only stopped him momentarily.

Indigo took a swipe with her sword, slicing through flesh, but again not deep enough to cause serious injury. She sliced again, this time more successfully. The guard growled with anger as his arm split and raw flesh showed itself. Indigo pulled out her steam cannon and shot him. As the steam cleared, the man dropped to his knees, clutching the red hole in his belly. But the other was too quick and strong. He grabbed her from behind and restrained her by pinning her arms by her side. She felt his large sweaty biceps grip her like a vice, his veins popping through his skin as he squeezed whilst the High Priestess casually relieved her of her weapons. She then struck Indigo across the cheek with the back of her hand, a large, jewelled, golden ring leaving its mark. Indigo's cheek stung as the graze opened and blood ran down her face.

"Strip her!" demanded the High Priestess.

Indigo was confused at this point. What was the High Priestess going to do? Her mind ran all sorts of scenarios, but nothing prepared her for what was about to come.

Another guard took over, and whilst she was restrained by one, the other removed her remaining weapons, roughly searching amongst her clothing with big coarse hands that enquired in every crease of fabric and every body part for any other concealment. Then, taking a large ornate dagger, he cut through the ties holding her undergarments, removing them. Indigo felt the cold steel against her skin as the blade was brought upwards to cut the cords of her corset, revealing her soft white flesh. Feeling vulnerable, she closed her eyes, cursing under her breath as complete indignation sank in when the guard removed her pantaloons. More weapons clanked noisily as they fell to the hard floor, and as she struggled against her oppressors, her skin grew taut with muscle and sinew. She stood naked except for her boots.

"Boots as well!" snapped the High Priestess, and Indigo felt the dagger cut through her laces, and then the cold tiled floor was beneath her feet.

Indigo didn't know what was going on, nor did she care to know. This was perhaps the weirdest event she had ever experienced since becoming an agent for the Union Jacks.

The High Priestess moved towards a green satin curtain, pulling it to the floor to reveal a colossal machine that looked like a giant ray gun. The main barrel culminated in a large crystal surrounded by concentric gold rings, probably some kind of heat sink. There were adjustable dials and gears all over the body of the machine and a punch tape read out, just like the sort Indigo had seen on the calculating machines of Charles Babbage and Ada Lovelace. Towards the one side of the machine was a multi-tiered keyboard with piano-like keys and pipes like those on a church organ, complete with a pedal board and draw knobs. Steam emanated from the sides of the pipes, indicating how the machine obtained its power. Pipework ran off across the floor to a heavy-duty riveted boiler that generated the steam.

Indigo kicked and screamed as the guard threw her over his shoulder and forcibly carried her towards the infernal device. As he placed her down, four other guards each grabbed a limb. Her wrists and ankles were secured with leather straps to the front of the machine, leaving her spread-eagled with the ray gun pointing directly at the centre of her back. In addition to the leather straps, metal clamps were placed over her hands and feet. They pinched at her skin and Indigo knew she had to remain calm so they didn't rub her raw. But as she cast her eyes down, she became aware of cables running from all four clamps, off into the distance where they were linked to a Tesla coil. The guards then attached electrodes to her head. Her heart began to pound in her chest. To what end was she a prisoner like this? She didn't know. What kind of sick experiment was this? Closing her eyes, Indigo prepared to meet her fate. A single tear rolled down her cheek, and she began to think of the life she had led, the joy she had experienced as a girl, playing in the fields behind her house, picking wildflowers and taking them home to her mother. Perhaps now, it was time for her to meet the Omnisoul in the afterlife, perhaps her soul would end up as ash belching from the stacks of the great ship Taraka as it glided across the cosmos.

She became aware of muffled voices around her, shouting orders. She opened her eyes and saw the High Priestess striding towards the keyboard of the machine, flicking her cloak behind her as she sat on the stool beneath the keyboard. Indigo looked around in desperation and became aware that an identical machine had been wheeled in from somewhere and stood beside her. She looked at the High Priestess, then again at the machine before realising that the shackles of the other machine held another Indigo, a doppelganger, also naked and held captive. Indigo noticed the cut on her right cheek. This was the same Indigo she had met in the Bodleian. Their eyes met and the other one took some time for it to register, but she said nothing, just looked on with fear in her eyes and rage in her writhing body. But it was no use, neither could escape.

"You will be the one to fulfil the prophecy. You are the Iolite! The twin flame, the mirror soul that shall be used to open the Book of Shadows. Any last words, Indigo?" She sneered at both women and openly displayed such nonchalance that she clearly didn't care if

Indigo wanted to speak. Indigo had no idea what she meant by the term Iolite, and then she remembered that the Oracle had used that same word. She didn't know if this was some perverse coincidence or if the events really were being played out as predicted.

Without waiting for any response, the High Priestess began to play the keyboards. Indigo saw her long slender fingers become a blur as they danced across the multiple keyboards. She looked like she was possessed as her excitement grew. Her eyes were wild, her hair swinging about her contorted face, her long flowing cloak swishing to give occasional glimpses of her naked body. The music was unbearable, a frequency like siren song.

Meanwhile, the Librarian worked at a panel and the machine crackled and sparked into life. Concentric bands around the cannon began to rotate increasingly faster, generating charge. This was no steam cannon but some electrical music device. It began to hum. As the pitch grew louder, the whole scene began to shimmer and fade in and out as if it wasn't real.

Indigo could feel the air around her begin to change as if it was gathering charge in some way. The hairs on her neck stood on end, her limbs grew tense and the air began to crackle. Then, without warning, the High Priestess released several organ stops. Simultaneously, the Librarian hit a large button, releasing a charge. A lightning bolt hit Indigo in the centre of her back. Her whole body tensed against the awful blow. It hit with such a force Indigo felt it travel through her body. It felt like it had removed her soul. Then another blast, and another. Due to the pulsation, Indigo felt like her limbs had grown weightless, her abdomen trembled and momentarily she believed she had stepped out of her body. Tears rolled down her face and stung her cut cheek. She glanced over and could see the same thing happening to her doppelganger.

Her whole body was surrounded by a purple aura that pulsed with the music, and after a few seconds the light and sound seemed to penetrate her whole body, which fragmented into clusters of molecules and then individual atoms, floating in the air. From this, a deep purple light spread out of her torso to illuminate the rest of the chamber. Indigo's skeleton was clearly visible like an X-ray, every bone displayed like a shadow against the purple background. Her bones drifted apart, her body being dismantled piece by piece. Then her bones were deconstructed, and black orbs of molecules repelled each other until her whole body was a fragmented shell of itself. The doppelganger had experienced the same fate, and as the last remnants of their bodies drifted away, a bolt of purple lightning ripped through the library. As it emanated from their bodies, the fire met above the central chamber of the library and intersected, causing an explosion of purple-black fire. Then, both women could be seen in their shackles once more. The world grew hazy, and darkness enveloped Indigo and she passed out, her head slumping onto her chest.

Rays of purple-blue light continued to emanate from Indigo's limp body, penetrating the darkest regions of the archaic library, and there in the furthest corner, hiding in plain sight, lay the Book of Shadows. It gave off black light of its own and seemed to radiate with pure darkness, pure evil. At last, all could see the unholy twin of the Book of Consciousness.

The Librarian gave the High Priestess a glance, the book now lay permanently in view.

As Indigo continued to be the source of the eerie light, the book appeared to move, to be sentient. It levitated slightly above the ground.

The Librarian adjusted the dials on the machine and the light emanating from Indigo became focused on the seven clasps with their ornate seals that held the book shut. After some time, there was a loud piercing crack, like a great wooden beam being splintered into two. The book released dust and vapour and the first enchanted clasp was thrown open, the first seal broken. Thunder shook the entire library and a deep voice could be heard:

"Come!"

The Librarian and High Priestess continued, concentrating their efforts now on the second seal which, after some time, cracked, throwing open the second clasp. More vapour was released, and again a deep voice was heard:

"Come!"

They continued some more and again, after a short time, the third seal eventually gave way and the splintering crack was accompanied this time by green fire that sparked and fizzed, eventually dying away. The voice was heard once more:

"Come and see!"

This continued until all the seals were broken and all seven clasps were wide open. Then, the book cover opened. Just a fraction at first, and it was as if a thousand imprisoned whispers all came out at once like a great cosmic sigh of relief. Complete silence then filled the library, and three dark seraphs appeared standing behind the book. They looked grotesque, with black wings and tattered black hooded cloaks open at the chest to reveal rotted flesh and rib bones. Beneath the hoods, they wore rusty helmets with broken iron grids where their mouths should be. In their long, thin, almost skeletal hands they each carried a trumpet. Placing it to their helmets they blew in unison and the voice could be heard once more:

"The seals are broken, go your ways, and pour out the vials of the wrath of the Elder God upon the earth."

The seraphs then faded away and the book cover opened fully, and the full horror of the Book of Shadows began.

Chapter 23: The Spawning

As Ignatius regained consciousness, his vision was blurry, but soon he could see the scene before him and looked on in horror. In the centre of the chamber was an unconscious Indigo, stripped and spread-eagled with wires and probes attached to her. The intensity of light that emanated from her crucified body was so great Ignatius had to shield his eyes. He reached into his jacket and pulled out his goggles. Putting them on, he grew accustomed to the light, and there it was. In the furthest shadows lay the Book of Shadows.

He didn't know if Indigo was dead or just unconscious. He felt the full weight of responsibility as leader of the Union Jacks Chapter in which Indigo was an agent. His heart thumped in his chest, great whacking thuds of burden. His stomach churned. He felt empty. It was only in this moment he realised she was more than just another agent, a colleague, a partner; she was the only person in this world he regarded as his equal, his confidante, his friend, his soulmate. It dawned on him: he held great affection for Indigo, but he let matters of the Empire, matters of their work take precedence on every occasion. He had been a fool.

The four brass arms that held her captive glowed with blue-purple light, and a kind of molecular cloud floated around each one and Indigo's body. The faint appearance of her skeleton now faded like a daguerreotype that had not been developed correctly. The same weird light bathed the faces of the High Priestess and the Librarian, giving them the appearance of ghostly apparitions in the darkness, nightmares that had stepped out of the shadows behind a wardrobe in the liminal space between wake and sleep. Ignatius moved quickly and hid behind the nearest bookcase before he was seen. He pulled out his steam cannon to avenge Indigo. As he took aim, he felt a large hand grasp the weapon and pull it from his grasp. A great muscular arm wrapped around him, and Adonai pulled him further away from the scene. Without saying a word, Adonai made a motion to tell him that now was not the time. Ignatius dropped his shoulders and skulked further into the shadows, hiding with the rest of the Charon. From the safe distance, they all looked on to see what would unfold.

Upon the opening of the book, all confusion and despair poured forth. It was like the stars in the sky had fallen to the earth. It was like the whole scene before them had been painted on a scroll and had been rolled up and only blackness filled the void left behind.

Out of the book grew roots of wonderous poisonous flowers that bloomed, letting off deadly pollen. The sound of waves came crashing about their ears. But not waves of the ocean: the waves of a red seething morass of demons. A creeping doom. It was like the four rivers of the underworld had all converged upon this plane, in this library.

Ignatius felt bile rise in his mouth, the stench of putrid death filled his nostrils. The earlier smell of the mortuary paled into insignificance.

This was just the beginning, like dust being released from a long-forgotten artefact. Next came the wailing and gnashing of teeth as obscene shapes and forms of ancient manifestations rose out of the book's pages. Twisted monstrosities born from the darkest recesses of the human psyche surged forward. Some had lobster-like claws, some had tentacles, others oozed and bubbled like scarlet slime. Every so often, a recognisable body part appeared, an eye, some fangs. The blackest hell-spawn, obviously more ancient than mankind, began filling the library.

Next came demons with scaly red skin, their horned heads with sharp features, their long, ridged tails and taloned hands and feet. Some had wings like those of a bat, with throbbing veins on the thin leathery membrane. From between the book's pages, scarab-like insects came in their thousands, releasing a foul odour. The sulphuric smell of fire and brimstone was overpowering, filling Ignatius's lungs, making it difficult to breathe.

Green-skinned ghouls then followed with over-bloated bellies covered in pus-filled boils. Some had burst, releasing their yellow-green contents. Blood flowed from sores covering other parts of their bodies, and rotten flesh hung in places from their bones.

A plague of giant flies then burst forth, deafening Ignatius with the buzz of their wings. He couldn't take any more and, reaching into his great coat, he pulled out a breathing mask and hastily put it on.

The onslaught kept coming, with pale-skinned humanoid creatures covered in pox and carrying primitive weapons like clubs and sharpened flint-tipped sticks. Black vapours emanated like wispy tendrils. These were damned souls flying around at such a speed it was impossible to tell how many there were. They swirled around those present and Ignatius felt them flow under his armpits and between his legs, lifting him up slightly.

"We're all going to die," he mumbled from beneath his mask.

Amorphous blobs appeared and as they left the book, they rolled over some of the other obscenities, absorbing them.

Outside the Administorium, the moon grew blood red and shifted position in its orbit before falling away from the earth, which had cracked, and the dead began to rise up from wherever they lay.

Ignatius thought his ears would burst as thousands of tiny, winged goblin-like creatures flew out, their chattering teeth the source of all the noise. Wild-eyed, Ignatius pulled out his steam cannon and let loose a volley of blasts to disperse them from his immediate vicinity. He had betrayed their presence to the High Priestess and the Librarian. He looked back, seeking assistance from the Charon. Then, the stark reality of their betrayal became apparent. They were stood behind him, grinning with unholy grins, revelling in the anticipation of total destruction. Their eyes were wide with glee at the thought of the total annihilation of the cosmos. At last, they could obtain their desire and rest in peace.

"Well done, Ignatius," said Adonai. "Why fight against the inevitable? You and Indigo have achieved what we could not. This will surely end with the destruction of the cosmos. I can see our attempt to destroy time was flawed. But this, this is perfect, there is no stopping events now the book is open. They will feed off your fear and the fear of all life forms that encounter them. The shadows will grow stronger and stronger from the frequency of these fears. This will continue until there is nothing left of the cosmos for these manifestations to devour. Then they will devour each other. At last, we can find peace. No more cosmos for the Omnisoul to preside over."

As the dead continued to rise up outside, the inhabitants of Oxford were fleeing from the Administorium and cemeteries. The ground around the black monolithic building cracked with a noise so thunderous that nearby airships burst their airbags and began to tumble out of the sky. Pilots were trying to fathom what had happened as they plummeted to their doom.

The front of the building ruptured, and a Hyperquake rippled out across the cosmos, affecting orbits and destroying whole star systems that lay in its path. Alien lifeforms going about their daily business were wiped away instantly without ever knowing what had happened.

The inhabitants of Oxford continued to flee, avoiding the living dead that were randomly emerging and walking the streets of the city. They looked up into the sky and saw a huge fireball streaking across the sky, heading straight for the city. As the ball of fire got closer, the searing heat could be felt, scorching the land around as the projectile smashed through airborne airships and dirigibles. Some unfortunate people were incinerated at close approach, and Oxford's dreaming spires were scorched as the fireball closed in on its target, the Administorium building, and then smashed through the rupture in its façade. Splitting the floor of the main hall, it landed in the library beneath, setting rows of books aflame. The Librarian whimpered and was visibly distraught at the instant loss of knowledge contained within. As the flaming star came to an abrupt halt before all present, the flames dispersed. Standing before them was a slight man dressed in princely finery, the harlequin pattern betraying him as a member of some highborn heritage. The spawning from the book halted and all the demons and plagues stood still, as if waiting for a signal.

"Calabi-Ya!" shouted Ignatius. He turned again to look at the Charon. Their expressions had changed. With the presence of Calabi-Ya, this was now a different situation.

Chapter 24: Soul Searching

The harlequin stood there with defiance, and when he moved it was with swagger.

"I must thank you for your assistance in finding my masterpiece, Ignatius. It really is a find. I had no idea where it had gotten to, such is its nature. Not helped of course by your friends, the Charon." He gave a devilish grin.

Before anybody else could speak, a tiny turquoise spark ignited in mid-air before them all. It fizzed and grew as they all looked on until a familiar pair of giant lips and crooked teeth appeared. As the spark grew in size, the Voice came into full view, followed by a second spark that also grew until another Celestial appeared. Dressed in turquoise robes and seated cross-legged, he hovered some feet off the ground. He had angular features with brushed back black hair, a well-groomed moustache and small pointed beard. It was the Master, leader of the Celestials and the only one who could commune directly with The Omnisoul.

"Ah! Celestials," exclaimed Calabi-Ya. "Things are getting really interesting. Greetings, Master, to what do we owe this pleasure? Have you come to witness the end of all things? Tell me, is the

Omnisoul still so idle that you are sent to intervene? There is still a belief that all of this," he swayed his arms around as if presenting the spawning, "is not a credible threat? The cosmos shall perish, and I will begin creation once more, fashioned to my will."

The Master placed his hands as if in prayer and gave his furrowed brow a slight dip in the way of the smallest of bows.

"Greetings, Calabi-Ya. You are quite correct, I have been sent by the Omnisoul, merely to point out, perhaps, that if you are successful and you make a reborn cosmos your domain, the Charon here, whilst they welcome the demise of the present cosmos, will still survive, and so will vie for dominion over your creation."

Calabi-Ya laughed. "There will be no survival. All beings in the present cosmos shall perish, including you, the Charon and the Omnisoul. I alone shall inhabit the primordial void, free to start a new eternity."

Ignatius was somewhat confused by the exchange. The Charon welcomed the total destruction that was about to occur. They had no ambition to rule; they were tired of their immortality, tired of carrying out the will of the Omnisoul.

It then became clear why there had been a visitation of two Celestials. Whilst this exchange was taking place, the Voice had been in near silent communion with Adonai, whose beautiful pale face erupted into rage. All Ignatius heard from the Adonai was the words, "The Omnisoul orders it. Destroy it!" His voice was filled with sorrow and malice.

Without another word, the Master and the Voice vanished without trace, as Adonai lunged forward, without any willpower of his own, his wide-bladed sword swinging in an arc over his head at the hell-spawn advancing once more. Ignatius heard the crunching of bones, and a fountain of demon blood sprayed the remnants of the library shelves. Calabi-Ya was now surrounded by his creations, protected from the Charon.

Ignatius stepped back cautiously to clear the way, understanding that again this was a demonstration of how the Charon lacked free will when the Omnisoul commanded them. The Librarian was unsure what to do and began gathering up as many books as he could in a vain attempt to protect what knowledge he could and went scurrying off into the shadows.

The other Charon fell in behind Adonai, Tara had drawn her broadsword and slashed at the ghouls nearest to her. Blood and pus erupted as the ghouls let out unearthly screams and gasps. A horde of pox-ridden creatures overpowered her with blow after blow of the primitive clubs, and she fell beneath a mound of flesh covered in lesions and skin nodules. Devi felt her broadsword crash though bone and heard the squelch of organs. Her sword slowed dramatically as it entered the scarlet slime. She tried to withdraw her sword, but tendrils of slime came with it, clawing, rendering her weapon useless. Atman was deep in combat with the demons, some flying around him as he sliced through their wings, causing them to fall screaming on to the library floor. Darshan was cursing as hundreds of the scarab-like creatures crawled across her skin, gnawing at her clothing and flesh. Great holes in her loose-fitting white shirt exposed her body and the giant flies were seeking wounds on which to feed. The same scarab-like creatures were attacking Paladin, trying to crawl their way into his bronze armour. Several ghouls were weighing down Paladin's weapon, part halberd and part musical instrument, so he was unable to raise it to his lips. Had he been able, he would have sent a sonic blast so powerful that all in its wake would be destroyed. Aryas was busy creating small fireballs between his palms and hurling them, disintegrating any beast or demon they touched, but more just kept on coming. The creations from the pages of the Book of Shadows were inexhaustible. This would go on forever, until all in their path were overwhelmed and destroyed.

Ignatius realised several demons were skulking their way towards him. He pulled out his steam cannon and let loose several blasts, steam misting up his goggles. The demons let out screams as the shots hit them and their skin singed. Burning flesh filled the air, but this didn't deter them. Cold claws gripped his neck and arms, and yellow blood-shot eyes closed in, foul mouths dripping venom. Ignatius summoned all his might and pushed back, just enough to pull out his sonic blaster. Quickly turning dials, he pulled the trigger and a high-pitched sound poured forth, stopping the demons in their tracks until the lead one burst, guts and blood raining down all around. Turning the blaster onto the next, then the next, Ignatius succeeded in destroying them. The only evidence they ever existed was the gore that formed a slippery carpet upon the tiled floor. The giant flies swarmed to drink the blood and in a few seconds most of it had disappeared. Then, turning their attention to Ignatius the flies buzzed around his head until complete darkness swamped his vision. A red cloak landed on top, covering him, and Devi managed to sweep most of the flies up in the torn fabric, pulling them off his head and stamping on them, detached legs and wings flying out and lying there twitching and damaged.

Ignatius did not pause. He adjusted the dials on his sonic blaster again and directed his shot at a group of ghouls, but instead of destroying them, it lifted them off the ground and Ignatius was able to direct them away to another part of the library where Atman ferociously cut them down, pieces of rotten flesh falling everywhere.

An almighty roar echoed out around the library as Tara rose up out of the mound of pox upon her. She was covered in blood and her own skin was showing signs of pestilence, her combat leathers torn and tattered, her torso partly exposed and one boot missing, her platinum blonde hair a scarlet mess covering her furious face. Swinging her broadsword in a horizontal arc, she severed several heads and sliced through the limbs of every creature in its wake.

Calabi-Ya muttered an enchantment, his body twisting and morphing until he had transformed himself into his usual form of a dragon. Enjoying the melee before him with glee, he stealthily moved around the edge of the horde, crippling some of his own beasts and demons under foot, but more poured forth to take their places. Venom dripped from his nostrils and burned holes in the floor. He opened his scaly wings and swept forward a whole host of creatures into a position where the Charon and Ignatius had little room to manoeuvre. He approached, stepping purposely, biding his time until it was right to strike.

Adonai had retreated. Not in fear, but to stand next to Ignatius so he could communicate with him. The goblin-like creatures had gnawed at his clothing and skin, exposing sinew and muscle fibre that rippled beneath his fair skin. Blood ran down his face and the tips of his flaming orange hair were stained red.

Having caused a short lull in the fighting, the rest of the Charon had gathered around them. Adonai leaned in towards Ignatius.

"Your weapon, it levitates?" It was rhetorical, he had just witnessed Ignatius using it.

"Yes. Why?"

"Bring the book over here. We cannot get past this hell-horde to obtain it."

Ignatius was confused. "But you will just bring the spawning nearer. There will be no protection!"

Adonai grabbed Ignatius by the lapels and pressed his face against his. Ignatius could feel his hot breath, sweat and blood dripping onto his own face. His vision was filled with a sparkling jewelled eyepatch and angry grinding teeth.

"If you want to survive, just do it! Or I'll kill you, regardless of your heritage, and use the weapon myself! I know what to do!"

Ignatius looked around, searching. It was difficult to see where the book lay, with hell-spawn, flesh and gore piled high. He had to find the source of the spawning again. Aryas summoned his strength and hurled white fire at the throng, dispersing them momentarily, and then Ignatius saw it. He aimed the blaster at the black book, and it began to reverberate. It faded in and out of sight and then lifted, hovering a short distance from the ground. Adjusting the dials again, Ignatius managed to move the book. He took it higher, above the heads of all present. Winged creatures and gnashing teeth poured down on all those around as the book continued to spew death. It wobbled a little, but Ignatius was successful in moving it to his will, drawing it in until it was closer to their position. Green venom poured out, dissolving the spawn beneath it. Sulphur rose from the hissing floor and the Charon struggled to breathe. The filters in Ignatius's mask were growing full, and he started to choke. Steadily, he held the book in place and brought it as near as he dared.

Calabi-Ya saw the book moving and swept a leathery wing out to try and dislodge it, but he fell short of its position. Ignatius thought he saw a moment of panic in the eyes of the dragon, if that was possible. His yellow serpent eyes squinted for a second and then, pulling back his giant scaly head, he came in for an attack and fire roared just in front of Ignatius. Tara and Devi rushed in to attack and their broadswords could be heard slicing at the armour-like scales, seeking his softer underbelly or trying to stab behind his head to pierce Calabi-Ya's brain.

Looking at Adonai for approval on its position, he saw Adonai grin. Then he whispered in a gruff voice.

"Calabi-Ya has hidden his soul in the book. Find his soul. Finally find his weakness!"

Chapter 25: Despatched

With the book so close, the spawning threatened to be overwhelming. Paladin had freed himself and worked his way to the front line. Aryas was close behind; the purple-clad dandy was spattered with blood. Paladin lifted his weapon to his lips and filled his lungs but was unable to blow as he choked on the brimstone and smoke emanating from the still-burning library. He tried again, feeling his chest expand against the inside of his armour, then blew. A shockwave travelled out radially, felling everything in its path. But this was temporary, as the horde regained their positions and more left the Book of Shadows to join them. Paladin tried again.

Next to him, Aryas had produced his glass pipe from his coat and was smoking some concoction of herbs, the green liquid bubbling away, releasing colourful tendrils of vapour. He closed his eyes and began to chant in what sounded like a continuous low-pitched groaning, never pausing for breath, some mystical incantation that made the hairs on the back of Ignatius's neck stand on end.

Calabi-Ya pulled back his long neck, ready to strike with his fiery venom. Fire hit Paladin with full force on his breast plate, his bald head growing red as he began to burn. Within seconds,

Aryas had manifested a dome of blue aether around the two of them, extinguishing the fire and creating a force field that proved impenetrable when Calabi-Ya tried again. His fire bounced back, and several creatures ignited, screaming shrill indescribable sounds as they burned, turning black in an instant. The amorphous blobs just rolled on over the top of them, absorbing them as if they'd never existed. The red slime was now underfoot and trying to gain entry to the bubble that surrounded Paladin and Aryas. Ignatius could feel icy coldness start to creep up his foot and leg and he hastily withdrew to safety. The black tendrils of the damned souls circled the force field and tried unsuccessfully to gain entry. The rest of the Charon were fighting to hold the horde at bay as best they could. Paladin was ready to blow again, and Aryas lifted their veil momentarily and another shockwave burst out. This time, blood, slime and pus splashed out, quenching the fires that still burned around the library. Gore dripped from every surface.

"Get that book closer to me, now!" called Adonai.

Ignatius obliged. Aiming his sonic blaster once more, he lifted the book and passing it over Paladin and Aryas, placed it down in front of Adonai as Aryas momentarily removed the protective bubble. Several deformed creatures surged out and smothered Ignatius, pinning his arms down so he couldn't retaliate. Before all vision was extinguished, Ignatius saw the curved blade of a scimitar flash and cleave the skulls of two of the creatures. He heard bone crunching and felt cold, dead blood run down his face. The weight of corpses was unbearable, but after a short while his burden began to ease and he saw Darshan pulling them off him, scimitar in hand. Her red bandana and the sash around her waist were torn to shreds, her eyes were wild, and clumps of her raven hair missing. Her beautiful face displayed the signs of a pox with greenish pustules covering her cheeks and forehead. Ignatius got back on his feet and backed away from the relentless horde, wondering what Adonai's plan was.

Adonai was swinging left and right slicing through anything that emerged from the pages of the book until he could spot an opening. Without warning, the horde began to ebb and looked like it was slowing, until eventually it came to a halt.

Then came the shadows. These were projections of the blackest souls in the cosmos, containing every evil deed and every nightmarish dream any creature had ever had. They were dark matter and had become a focus for every dark thought that had ever dwelt in the consciousness of all life in the cosmos.

Ignatius felt his blood run cold as the deepest blackest shadows arose from the pages of the book. They were vaguely human shaped, with irregular holes where the eyes would have been, and they had long arms but no legs. Rising, the shadows grew bigger until they swamped the entire library, absorbing all the light from the fires. It was impossible to see any of the now-motionless horde. They were waiting for a signal from Calabi-Ya. Ignatius could hear the rasp of scales as Calabi-Ya stealthily closed in on them. Occasionally, Ignatius caught sight of the dragon's eyes burning like embers in the dark. The library had grown icy cold, resembling the primordial temperature of the cosmos. This was to be the fate of the cosmos once more, now that the Book of Shadows had been opened. Ignatius began to shiver; his fingers numbed by the icy cold.

Outside, ice started to form around the damaged Administorium building. Huge shard-like penitentes had risen, forming wall-like structures around the building. Those Oxonians still in the vicinity looked on in awe, never having seen such ice structures before. The structures rose several feet into the air, but onlookers were wary of the dangers that might lurk behind them. Most had fled and were hiding in the colleges and taverns nearby. Some brave, or foolish, professors had ventured out to look at the structures and to investigate the meteorite that had hit the Administorium. Some regretted their action as the walking dead descended upon them. The writers of the penny dreadfuls were busy compiling their stories on the spot, delighting in the chaos, the unusual ice formations, the shooting star, and the horrors of the zombies now walking amongst them. Little did they know that as soon as the library was ready to burst, death would be released, and their stories and reports would be moot.

The shadows began to multiply and grow. Any other creatures they touched were absorbed and made the shadow grow in size. Soon, the spawning would have to pour forth from the library or risk being enveloped completely by the shadows, feeding their power. Ignatius watched as the two yellow orbs of Calabi-Ya's eyes squinted in the dark, then opened wide as burning venom hit the floor before him and the Charon. He had aimed short but was now moving forward, the horde rushing around him and the shadows waiting in the background. All of Ignatius's training and experience in the field told him this was about to become a three-pronged attack from which there would be no escape.

All this time, Adonai hadn't moved, looking deep into the Book of Shadows.

"Ignatius, I need you," he motioned for him to move closer. The rest of the Charon circled around to protect them. Aryas, who was now exhausted, was trying to replicate the force field he had created earlier to protect them both.

"Give me your hand. I need my eye," said Adonai.

Ignatius positioned himself so the eye-shaped birthmark on his right hand covered Adonai's eyepatch.

Adonai fell silent, his breathing slowed and motionless. He looked even deeper into the pages of the book. All sorts of demons passed his mind's eye, monsters that had not yet been released. A plague of locust-type insects, but as big as dogs, were clicking past his astral mind. Pallid white humanoids, carrying a pox with their intestines bursting through their stomachs passed by.

Adonai realised that none of them could see him. Other indescribable creatures passed him, followed by hundreds of hairy ape-like men carrying huge bones for weapons, grunting and whooping in some unknown animalistic language.

Eventually, the horde began to slow until Adonai peered onto the deepest black he had ever seen. Just shadow remained within the pages of the book.

Ignatius felt his hand begin to freeze. He had never experienced anything as cold, even on expeditions to the Antarctic. The icy feeling started to burn the back of his hand; Adonai's other eye started to ache. An ache that started at the back of his eye and burned into the rest of his skull. Ignatius began to feel Adonai's pain and didn't know if he could continue. Without realising it, he had started to let out a cry of pain. Adonai was silent, still searching the inky blackness.

"Calabi-Ya's soul is that black, it lies in the blackest shadows and cannot be found." But Adonai didn't give up. "Point your sonic blaster deep within the darkness."

Ignatius used his other hand and pointed the gun at the book's pages. He couldn't see anything within the velvet malevolent dimness. He pulled the trigger and the blast entered the book. At first, there was little change, but after some time he could just make out ripples in the black pages, radiating out to the edges of the book. Shadows rose and swirled overhead. More and more shadows until they formed a rotating funnel above them like that of a tornado. An icy chill filled the whole of Ignatius's body like the touch of death creeping down his spine. He didn't know how much longer he could continue this.

The ripples grew in size and began to rhythmically dance to the edge of the book's pages and then, without warning, an almost indistinguishable red glow began as a tiny speck no bigger than a few molecules in the corner of one of the pages. Increasing in size, it appeared as a fiery ball that shifted and continuously changed shape but was no bigger than a thumb. Its sentience became increasingly agitated and the movement within its shell looked violent and desperate, as if it could sense impending doom.

Ignatius looked at Adonai, "Is this it, Calabi-Ya's soul?"

Adonai nodded. Then, drawing his sword, he swung his powerful arms in an arc and plunged his wide-bladed sword into the depths of the book's pages. Harsh shrieks and moans emanated as demons and ghouls felt the full force of Adonai's blade, but it had no effect on Calabi-Ya's soul. Somehow, magically, it had avoided any collision with the blade.

The icy cold death-chill had been replaced by a burning hot fire as Calabi-Ya roared with anger and released more of his venomous breath, hitting the protective cloaking Aryas had provided, piercing the dome and striking Adonai. The soul went crazy, hissing and sparking. The whirling black shadows above were now spinning at such an incredible speed they were just a black funnel from which occasionally a face would appear and attempt to bite the Charon. Ignatius was now face to face with a spectre that tried to grab him by the face, to pull him into the eye of the murderous storm. He resisted and, joining Adonai, reached into the depths of the shadows deep within the book's pages. His arm grew ice cold and burned with the pain as the frost bit into him, freezing his blood and threatening to turn his fingers black with frostbite. The soul eluded him. It was constantly moving, as if it was dropping through the pages of the book, getting deeper and deeper. Ignatius frantically searched but couldn't reach the soul. Then the spectre returned, arms encircling him and trying to pull him into the depths of the pitch-black book. It was then he realised the spectre was female, a succubus with wings and taloned hands and feet. Her skin seemed to absorb the light and give off no reflection.

Her black face appeared before him. Although this was a shadow being, it had a beautiful face with fine features, high cheek bones and a wide thin mouth. Fangs suddenly burst forth and tried to snare him, tried to bite his face. Ignatius could feel the shadowy face nose to nose against his own face. A black cloud came billowing up and out of the book like smoke. It swirled and swayed and on occasion gave way to the form of a woman, then became amorphous once more. It appeared to be wearing a crown of bleached bones, but its movements and transformations were too fast to tell. Then the face appeared once more.

"Maha-Kala, the Queen of Shadows!" exclaimed Adonai. "She is your darkest thoughts, your darkest fears. She will feed off your fear and hatred and grow stronger. She represents the exact opposite of you, all that is bad within you. All that is bad in the cosmos."

Ignatius felt her cold caress and withdrew his arm. He staggered backwards to get away from the Queen and fell on his back. Adonai withdrew also and stood waiting for an opportune moment to strike again. But he didn't get a chance. Calabi-Ya approached nearer. He was the only heat source as venom hissed and burned anything it touched. To distract him, Paladin engaged him in battle, taking the full force of his flames against the breast plate of his armour again. He could feel the warmth through his bronze protection. Aryas had to remove the protective dome because the Queen and her shadows were now trapped inside with Ignatius and Adonai. The rest of the Charon fell in with Paladin to hold Calabi-Ya back until they could find a way to defeat him and then deal with the rest of the hell-spawn.

Ignatius lay bruised and dazed. Looking around him, he took the opportunity to escape the mayhem and move away from the turmoil, heading back towards the entrance of the library.

Chapter 26: Martyr

Ignatius needed reinforcements. He couldn't do this alone. He made his way back towards the great steps that he'd followed to enter the subterranean library. On his way, he saw the machine that still had Indigo shackled to it.

He reached up and began to unshackle her from the machine. He looked across at the other Indigo, her body pale and lifeless, with nobody to care, nobody to grieve for her. Momentarily, he wondered how lonely another Ignatius would be feeling somewhere else in the infinite cosmos. Seated on the floor amidst the debris, Ignatius gathered his Indigo in his arms, pulling her limbs in as if gathering the separated parts the machine had produced. Her poor broken body was so pale, stripped of all her courage and weaponry, of her identity as an expert swordswoman and an agent for the Union Jacks. He held her limp lifeless body tight in his arms, cradling her head, brushing her hair off her face. She looked at peace. Her expression was no longer the contorted terror he had seen earlier. His heart was pounding in his breast. Removing his mask, he held her head and placed a gentle kiss on her forehead.

He rocked backwards and forwards as if cradling a baby, his

eyes shut tight to block out the merciless ugly world that had done this to her. A tear rolled down his cheek. Purple-hued blood ran from Indigo's nose and ears, her inmost soul had been torn out by the infernal device that had imprisoned her and separated her from the surrounding cosmos.

Ignatius searched frantically for the faintest of pulses, to see if the splintering blows her body had sustained had killed her, or if it was possible to revive her. Not picking up a pulse on her wrists, Ignatius put a hand on her chest to feel for a heartbeat, however weak. She was ice cold. It was only then he noticed a violet-coloured burn mark on her left breast. The mark looked a little bit like the shape of a jewel. He searched in vain for a pulse. Nothing. Indigo had left this earth, her body broken beyond repair.

Aryas had followed, feeling it was necessary to disturb Ignatius in his grief, "She is, of course, part of the prophecy. But she yields much power and is a godling. You too are a godling and have power you have not yet tapped into. We cannot intervene, but you have the means…" His voice trailed off.

Although this might be true, Ignatius had no idea what he should do. There had never been any episodes of supernatural ability in either of them as far as he could tell. He searched his mind to try and find out what he should do. Then, instinctively, he placed his right hand over his right eye. His head began to swirl, and he felt nauseated. Furrowing his brow, he closed his eyes, thinking that the exertion of fighting had taken its toll. As he opened his eyes, he couldn't focus correctly. Trying harder, he realised that his right hand seemed to be causing confusion. Removing his hand, all seemed well again. Then, placing his hand back over his eye, he realised he was capable of looking into other dimensions, onto other worlds on other planes. He could see more hell-spawn waiting on another plane, waiting for a weakness or a sign to burst through an unseen gate and add to the attack. He removed his hand quickly and threw himself back, as if trying to somehow escape himself. But he was still cradling Indigo in his other arm. He gingerly placed his hand back again and took his time to focus. Indeed, he realised his view of the world was different. He could see the swirl of energy, invisible usually to the naked eye. The whole scene was a swirl of different colours and textures. He could even see some colours he couldn't identify. New colours not seen on Earth. As he focused harder, he could see bundles of ball-like objects floating around in the aether. He looked down at Indigo, and she had an aura of rainbow colours around her body but very gradually this seemed to be fading to be replaced by a deep blackness creeping in from the outermost edge of the aura and moving towards her body. He could see he was running out of time, but perhaps there was still hope, a chance she might live, but he didn't know what to do.

Radiating out of her heart were concentric circles Within these circles there were other circles that formed a pattern; they overlapped to intersect with each other to form floral patterns like the flower of life, a sacred geometry that Ignatius had studied some time ago. The pattern seemed to be alive. It throbbed and moved. Shifting Indigo's body to free his other arm, he placed his left hand on her chest, and the geometric pattern swirled generating patterns like the ripples on a lake when the surface is disturbed. His hand felt warm and began to glow orange. It began to burn and fade away, blending into the haze of colour that now seemed to be dancing in sharp sine waves on Indigo's chest.

Ignatius felt his hand throb, becoming numb with the pain. He felt sweat run down the back of his neck, and his contorted face displayed his silent pain. He could feel his heart race and the rush of blood through his veins, and then he jumped with surprise as Indigo's limp body jerked upwards and became rigid as a loud gasp left her mouth and her eyes opened fully. She fought to get his hand off her chest, pushing him away and suddenly sat upright gasping for air, her chest rising and falling rapidly as she gulped oxygen as quickly as she could.

It took her some time to get used to her surroundings. As her eyesight returned fully and she could focus, Indigo looked around, confused. Then, looking at Ignatius, she whispered in a hoarse voice, "Where am I? What am I doing here, wherever here is?"

Ignatius held her close again. "The Administorium. It's a long story. We need to get you out of here and to safety, but there is unfinished business."

This was the first Ignatius realised she was naked. He picked her up, supporting her broken body, looking over his shoulder to see the other Indigo hanging there, limp, pale and lifeless. He had no clue if she still lived, but for now he needed to get his Indigo to safety.

Ignoring the Charon and evading all else around him, he made his way to the steps that had brought him down to this strange and weird library. He began to climb, still holding Indigo, heading for the glimmer of light above him, not knowing what he was going to do when he had made it out into the air.

Chapter 27: Reinforcements

Lambeth had seen the fireball streaking across the otherwise grey sky. He gazed out of the window and saw the shadow of a passenger airship darken the street. It had been struck by the meteorite and was free falling with its air bag on fire. It was now so low he could see the passengers in the gondola beneath the envelope starting to panic. Pieces of burning fabric began falling into the street, leaving smoke trails behind them and causing havoc as they landed on the Woodstock Road, spooking horses pulling their hansom cabs and landing on the odd steam gurney. A black and orange cloud rose up about a hundred feet into the air as the airship hit the ground just off the main road.

His experience as a veteran of the Union Jacks informed him that this was no ordinary meteorite, his instincts still as sharp as ever, despite his old age. In the absence of Ignatius, he decided he must act. Placing his chores aside, he went into his room. Shifting his somewhat stark bed across the room he then knelt, his old bones less than amenable to the situation and, lifting a floorboard, then another, he reached in and retrieved his old steam cannon. It was an old model, unlike those of Ignatius and Indigo. It was heavier and more ornate, with the head of a beast cast in bronze around the barrel, so that when the weapon was used it looked like fire coming out of the mouth of some beast. He had no idea if it still worked. He returned to the kitchen and primed the miniature boiler; he added some water and lit the fuse. The gun groaned and started to steam, but after a short while settled down. Lambeth went outside and, taking aim, fired it at the pergola at the end of the garden. It blew a hole in the nearest post.

"Oops! Well, it still works, and without exploding," he said to himself.

He went back inside, put on his bowler hat, stowed his steam cannon in his tailed coat, and set off in the direction of the city centre. On his way, he stopped at the Gentleman's Outfitters in Turl Street, where he met a man not too dissimilar to himself.

"Ah! Lambeth! How do you do? Have you come for a final fitting?" he enquired.

"Indeed, the frock coat is of quality cloth, but the lapels should be wider."

This was enough for the two of them to understand each other; it was a password system that had been in use for many years.

"Have you seen the havoc outside, Alfred?"

"Is it a natural disaster, or is it an attack on the Empire?"

"I don't believe its natural, Alfred. That meteorite was no ordinary rock. I'm sure of it, and if I know Ignatius, he'll be in the thick of it. We need to investigate as I'm certain he'll need our help."

Alfred the tailor gave a slight knowing nod of his head and headed for the door. Turning the latch, he locked it and placed the closed sign in the window. The two of them then headed behind the curtain at the back of the shop where Alfred opened a wardrobe door to reveal an arrangement of gears and levers. He climbed inside the wardrobe and Lambeth followed him. Alfred pushed one of the levers, producing a hiss of steam, and the two of them descended into an underground chamber.

"We need to arm ourselves and call for backup. Do you know how many more agents we have in the city? I know some are in the Far East and Egypt, but I think we have a few," said Alfred, looking hopeful. "I mean, we are not the youngest. We have the experience, but I'm not sure my old bones are up to it any more, old chap."

Lambeth chuckled. "Maybe, but at least we get a bit more excitement for once!"

Once in the hidden cellar, the two veterans armed themselves with derringers, short swords and steam pistols.

"We can call in at the Temple on the way for reinforcements," said Lambeth.

On the way to the disaster site, the two of them called in at the Temple of the Chapter of Albion. This was an unobtrusive stone building near Carfax Tower, which the Union sometimes used as a lookout post. The plain door was solid, unadorned except for the large coach bolts that studded its surface. Whilst Alfred kept a look out, Lambeth gave a strange series of knocks, the code for entry. The door dutifully opened, and the warden beckoned them in.

"Welcome, gentlemen. I am assuming you are here because of the disaster. Do we know anything of its nature? I gather it hit the Administorium."

"We do not at this moment in time. How many Union Jacks do we have here at present?" said Alfred.

"Just three: Hardred, Carter and Lockhart, who has already gone on reconnaissance. And me, of course," said the warden.

"Good," said Lambeth. "But I'm not sure we can wait. Alfred

and I are armed, but we need help should we need to get away from the Administorium in a hurry."

"I can help with that," said Hardred. "I have my dirigible, Windstorm, in the courtyard. The fastest airship in England." He looked really pleased with himself. He was younger than the other Union Jacks, tall with a thin angular face, his blond hair giving him a dashing appearance. He already had his leather flying jacket on with the fur-lined collar upturned.

"Then I think we should go. I don't think we have the time to wait for Lockhart to return." The warden agreed to wait for Lockhart's return. Lambeth made his way to the back door, followed by Alfred and the other two Union Jacks, all armed and ready to fight.

Secretly, Lambeth didn't really know what they were going to do, or if they were capable. The veteran experience of himself and Alfred could be strategically useful, and the young dynamism of Hardred and Carter would be beneficial, but he didn't know what their potential was. Carter was also tall and dressed in a black morning suit with white collar. He had a thin moustache and jet-black hair slicked close to his head. At his side flashed a silver sword.

Windstorm sat ready, its polished brass hull reflecting the golden glow of the evening street lights. From the stern a Union flag blew proudly in the breeze, the red, white and blue of its design a prominent symbol of the Empire, and a reminder of the raison d'être for the Union Jacks' agents. Hardred adjusted his goggles and the straps of his leather flight jacket as he boarded the craft. Lambeth's bones creaked and ached as he climbed into the dirigible, but he said nothing. The four agents held on to the ropes as the warden helped release the line tethering it to the ground. Swiftly they rose and were away, with Hardred expertly adjusting sails and the air bag. As the craft soared higher they passed by Tom Tower on St. Aldates as the bell, Great Tom rang out warning citizens of the danger. Lambeth could see the panic playing out below on the quads of the colleges that made up Oxford University.

Every now and then, Lambeth saw what looked like giant mole hills scattered across these quads and randomly across the streets.

Soon the golden-coloured buildings of Oxford were just a speck and they headed for the Administorium building. Black smoke could be seen billowing from it and fire illuminated the streets surrounding it. Tall shards of ice surrounded the building, and corpses were laid out radially from where the fireball had hit, but moving amongst the bodies were what looked like vagabonds, their clothes torn and tattered. Alfred placed a monocular looking device to his right eye, gears whirred and the scope at the end moved in and out until the lens had focused. He stepped back startled, removing the looking device.

"What is it?" said Lambeth.

"Dead people."

"I know, there are corpses everywhere."

"No. No, I mean walking! The dead have risen, and they are walking about!"

Then he realised the significance of what looked like mole hills. On closer inspection, he realised these had been the resting places of the ancient dead.

Alfred looked terrified. "I've only ever experienced this once before. In Egypt, when we investigated the tomb of Ammon-Thoth, but we never actually saw anything. It was all superstition. But this! This! There are supernatural forces involved here, Lambeth."

The four agents looked at each other.

"Hold steadfast, my friends. I'm sure we can do this, we are more than capable. Besides, the mission is to locate Ignatius to ascertain what assistance, if any, he needs."

"I'll get a closer look," said Hardred. "Hold on tight."

Hardred made some more adjustments and the dirigible turned sharply, then, unfurling wings at the ship's side, they took a dive, heading straight for the Administorium building.

The craft swooped in, and visibility diminished as the plume of black smoke swelled. Lambeth could see the jagged rent in the façade of the monolith. The crystal sphere of the world on its roof had cracked and the wings engulfing it had fallen.

"We need to get closer," called Lambeth to Hardred, who immediately adjusted the sails and the angle of the wings to make the craft drop in altitude.

Lambeth could now see into the damaged building, although there appeared to be no light. Blackness filled the void, except for the sudden appearance of a red fire burning so deep down it must have been in the depths of the earth.

The clerics of the Administorium were gathering outside the front of the building and were in a state of terror fighting off the walking dead.

The dirigible circled the tower and, using the looking device, Lambeth was able to focus in on the burning area. He saw what appeared to be a reptile or dragon, and then Ignatius. He was carrying a dark-auburn-haired body in his arms.

"Oh no! I fear for Indigo," said Lambeth. "We are going to have to drop a line. I fear if we land we will be overrun. Alfred secured a rope to the craft and dropped it overboard. Hardred steadied the craft and flew lower. As Ignatius emerged into the daylight, some clerics tried to apprehend him. Pushing them off, he spotted the rope swinging in front of him. He was relieved as he looked up and saw Lambeth's familiar wispy white hair blowing in the breeze, the old veteran holding onto a cargo pod at the side of the craft with his outstretched arm beckoning Ignatius to make haste.

Ignatius placed Indigo over his shoulder in a fireman's lift and sprinted towards the rope. Tying it around his waist, he held on and braced himself for the lift. Every muscle and sinew in his right arm ached as he held on one-handed.

As the craft lifted Ignatius, a long stream of fire erupted from the building. Ignatius could feel the heat on his back as Lambeth and Carter helped him and Indigo into the craft. Carter took Indigo and lay her down on the bench seating. Ignatius looked back and saw Calabi-Ya climbing out of the building. As the dragon cleared the monolith, the whole earth shook, and any citizens standing nearby were felled as if experiencing an earthquake. As the craft flew up and passed the crystal globe, Ignatius saw the Librarian sat within it pulling levers and adjusting dials. Then the building seemed to explode as it lifted off the ground, killing any administrators and clerics in its wake, and the whole Administorium building soared into the sky, rushing past the tiny dirigible, blowing it off course. Within seconds, the globe was leaving the earth's atmosphere, heading for the stars. Circling high above was the Librarian's eagle, squawking with dismay as he had clearly been abandoned.

Indigo was still drifting in and out of consciousness and was being attended to by Alfred, who had opened his hip flask, offering a strong drink to her lips. As she gulped the rum, her body began to regain some warmth and she started to regain some movement in her limbs. Meanwhile, Lambeth had taken the Union flag flying from the stern of the craft and used it to wrap Indigo's naked body. Ignatius looked on and thought how bizarre and patriotic she looked, wrapped in the flag of the Empire.

Without warning, the craft suddenly jolted as a large scaly taloned claw swiped it out of the air. All looking overboard, they saw Calabi-Ya trying to destroy them. All about him were black spectres flying in circles, swooping in on anything living, absorbing them forever into some eternal cold hell.

The Charon had climbed out of the underground library and were preparing to attack. All seven immortals made ready with their weapons. Behind them the High Priestess climbed out of the ground, her cloak tattered and torn. Her face was distorted with rage.

"The Librarian has deserted us!"

Looking around, she walked purposely over to the nearest cleric. He didn't have a chance to speak before she grabbed his head with both bony hands and gripped tightly, muttering an incantation. The acolyte screamed in agony as she wreaked her unfair revenge on the nearest being. The thin man fell silent and slumped to the floor, whereupon she removed his cloak and replaced her own, wrapping it around her. She then removed his sword and dagger and began killing anyone or anything that got in her way.

Chapter 28: The Four Horsemen

As Ignatius looked on, he saw the Charon suddenly change. Simultaneously, dark grey and purple foreboding clouds seem to roll in above the Administorium. At first, the Charon reverted to their true shapes of winged reavers with hawk heads, their long beaks dripping with blood. Each carried a rusty scythe, covered in dried blood. They were too grotesque to look upon. As black acrid smoke from the fires below filled the air, the Charon changed again. Ignatius felt his blood run cold. He didn't know which would be worse, the horrors of the Book of Shadows, or the four horsemen that now dominated his view.

Adonai had transformed and was seated on a red horse with flames coming out of its nostrils and sharp fanged teeth. He was now wearing full body armour of ornate bronze, similar to that of Paladin's, but stained a dark crimson. A huge crest on his chest displayed a skull and wings. Smoke seemed to emanate from the grill of his helmet and he was wearing a blue cloak the same as he always wore. On his back was his usual wide-bladed sword with the death's-head pommel, and in his right gauntleted hand he carried a huge battle hammer, the head of which was rectangular and several feet long. No ordinary living creature could survive a blow from it.

Next to him sat Atman upon a great white war horse with powerful chest muscles and thick hairy fetlocks leading to hooves that were bigger than any man's head. Its nose and sharp teeth were stained with blood. He was similarly dressed in armour, but this time black and decorated with silver gilt ornamentation and a pale blue cloak. On his helmet was a carving of a silver crown with jewels the size of a man's fist. He carried with him his usual broadsword and a bow with silver-tipped arrows.

Ignatius was growing increasingly nervous. He could not see any chance of survival, given the Book of Shadows was now open, wreaking death and pestilence, Calabi-Ya now roamed the earth, and what looked like the four horsemen of the apocalypse stood before him, members of the Charon who were already known for being merciless and the harbingers of pitiless death.

He could now see Aryas sat on a black stallion. Ignatius had never seen such a large beast, not even in the fields where the Shire horses worked. Again, the horse had fangs, but also had small horns growing from its head. He too was wearing armour, which was purple with gold ornamentation. What looked like a map of the cosmos was carved onto his breastplate, showing golden spheres and galaxies. He carried his usual broadsword but also carried a set of golden scales.

The fourth standing there was Paladin in his usual ornate bronze armour on a pale grey dappled war horse with long teeth like tusks, wild staring yellow eyes and a wild mane. He carried nothing extra but his usual scythe-like instrument.

Nothing moved. It was as though the whole earth stood still. Even the four horsemen were completely static. Behind them now stood Calabi-Ya, in full view of Oxford's inhabitants. About his head swirled the shadows that were now shrieking like banshees with anticipation of complete death and destruction, complete absorption of any unfortunate souls that came into contact with them.

"Ignatius…" whispered Lambeth. "What do we do? Is this the end of days?"

"Four horsemen of the apocalypse. It must be…" Alfred's voice trailed off and nobody saw a tear roll down his cheek.

"I don't know, Lambeth. the Charon, I mean the four horsemen, and Calabi-Ya, the dragon are enemies, and yet they both bring the apocalypse!"

Indigo was now fully conscious, and she peered over the side of the dirigible, letting out a gasp in sheer fright.

"Valkyries!" she whispered hoarsely.

Ignatius looked around and there, flying around the streets of Oxford that immediately surrounded the icy crater where once the Administorium had stood, were three female warriors picking up the dead, leaving only a grey vapour trail when ascended to where the great ship Taraka now hovered.

"They are taking the souls to power the ship," said Ignatius.

These were Devi, Tara and Darshan, who had now transformed into warriors with white wings and ornate helmets on their heads. They were each dressed in white tunics with ornate leather belts and carried golden spears and a shield with the crest of the Charon upon it.

The smoke from the burning library was now billowing up out of the crater and obscuring Ignatius's view. He could just make out the three seraphs who were now standing behind the four horsemen. He could just see them as they put their trumpets to their hooded helmets once more and blew in unison. At last, the evil terror from the other planes began to swarm onto the same plane as the city. Soon there wasn't enough room in the library, despite its infeasible dimensions, and the monsters began to spill up and into the streets.

Without warning, Adonai's horse reared up on its hind legs and as it came back down the earth shook. Adonai continued the movement, leaning forward and struck the ground with his battle hammer. The earth split wide open. The fracture continued to travel and could be seen heading off into the distance towards Cornmarket Street.

"You'd best get us out of here, Hardred. Oxford has become a home for demons!" called Ignatius and without any further instruction the tiny dirigible was away and speeding back towards the Union Jacks Temple.

Looking back, Ignatius could see the four horsemen diminishing in size with the distance as they prepared to create war and destruction.

Adonai looked at the other three horsemen, his single eye glowing red, burning with the desire for the annihilation that was to come. Even their own worshippers dare not cause the Charon to manifest upon their own worlds, for they knew it was likely to end in death.

"And so, it begins. At last, this may be our final hour," announced Adonai. All four horses snorted and raised up on their hind legs.

As the four horsemen began to destroy everything in their immediate vicinity, preparing to bring about and unleash plague, pestilence and famine onto the streets of Oxford, and then the world, guiding the horde of demons and monsters from the book towards the steps to the Administorium above them, the aether in front of them began to ripple and glow with a purple haze. The fabric of time and space warped and the Voice appeared before them in astral form. The familiar sight of crooked black teeth and blue lips came into view.

"May I remind you of your commitment to destroy Calabi-Ya? You have now been instructed by the Omnisoul. That is your mission now and, as you know, the will of the Omnisoul must be carried out." The gigantic mouth grinned an unholy grin, then the bodiless mouth seemed to grow in size as it towered over the horsemen, dominating their view, its foul breath gusting over them like a strong, hot, acrid wind.

"The end of times must wait." A hideous laugh cracked the atmosphere as the Voice displayed an unhallowed thrill giving the Charon their orders. "You shall feel the wrath of the Omnisoul when you return to Limbo. There has been no order to deploy the four horsemen and start the apocalypse. That event shall be for when the Omnisoul is truly bored of the creation. The Omnisoul is keen that you prevent the apocalypse being caused by the Book of Shadows and Calabi-Ya. It is not their place, so banish the demons that have emerged from the book. Your quest to assist in the destruction of all that is, is futile. You shall not be free or have free will, so carry out your mission. The Omnisoul has ordained it! Even if the cosmos begins again with a new order, you shall remain, you are immortal." Then the vision faded, leaving the Charon with no choice yet again.

Although he did not display it, Adonai's heart had sunk. The ever-present hopelessness of failure over-burdening him again. Unseen by anyone, a solitary tear rolled down his face. Once more, the Charon had been thwarted in their quest to find peace, to try at least to end their immortality, their only existence to serve the Omnisoul and when not doing that, to be chained up in Limbo to await their next calling.

Adonai turned his horse and faced Calabi-Ya, who raised his wings and, sweeping them downward with force, lunged forward, breathing fiery venom all over the Oxford streets. It was heading straight for the Charon. Again, all four horses reared up on their hind legs. Then, with wildfire in their eyes, the horses charged, their huge leg muscles straining with power. The earth shook and then came the head-on clash as Adonai struck Calabi-Ya a full blow to the head with his hammer. The dragon roared and pulled his head backwards, then came in with fiery revenge. The burning venom hit Adonai's horse, which seemed to feel nothing but whinnied a little before charging right of the beast's body, where Adonai struck again. A taloned leg shot forth to crush Adonai but it narrowly missed. Paladin raced past on his pale steed and sliced at the dragon's leg. The dragon rapidly withdrew it, trying to swipe Paladin with his wing. A silver-tipped arrow left Atman's bow and whistled overhead to imbed itself just below Calabi-Ya's left eye. The dragon roared, letting his fiery breath splash across the road to Atman, but all four horsemen were immune to the scorching poison.

The Charon now attacked from both sides, with Paladin and Atman on one side and Adonai on the other. With his great bulk, Calabi-Ya was too slow for this coordinated attack, and he sustained several wounds. He took to the air just off the ground to try and obtain an advantage, his wings flapping, fanning the fires he had created, which were now melting the ice surrounding the crater.

The dark shadows were still circling overhead, waiting for the time to come when they could swoop in and absorb everything for their master Calabi-Ya. They wouldn't advance any further without a signal from their Queen.

The giant flies had headed off into the city, the demons had fled and were terrorising the inhabitants. The amorphous blobs were just rolling up out of the crater and the goblin-like creatures were rapidly attacking the Charon. The humanoids were busy beating anyone to a pulp with their clubs along Cornmarket Street and the pestilent ghouls were heading off in the opposite direction towards Summertown. Around the crater was now starting get crowded as a throng of walking dead had made their way there, their flesh hanging from their skeletons, some with rotted bishop's hats and clothing of the clergy, some in armour or leather battle gear and chain mail. Others wore tweeds and flat caps on their yellowed-skinned heads.

Most Oxonians had deserted the streets now and had gone into hiding, which was just as well as the full force of the battle between the Charon and Calabi-Ya got underway.

"How long must we keep battling?" asked Calabi-Ya. "You are just the servants of the Omnisoul and cannot hope to defeat me. I have returned over and over."

"This is the final battle, the end of times. Once we have totally destroyed you, what need has the Omnisoul for our services? We can go free. We are called for very little nowadays other than to battle with you," replied Adonai. He knew this was probably not true, but he had to have hope.

"You are an abomination, you cannot hope to win. The Omnisoul is far more powerful, the First Cause, the spark that ignited creation and life in the cosmos."

"And what if I told you that was a lie?" replied Calabi-Ya. He leaned in close to Adonai, who could feel the hot air emanating from his smoking nostrils. When he spoke he sounded like a multitude. "The Omnisoul is a lie. Why do you think I have the title of the Elder God? I am the Ancient of Days! I have already resurrected the dead, I shall restore the planes for my own creations from the Book of Shadows, to inhabit the planes, and I shall rule the cosmos with the Queen of Shadows at my side and together we shall seed the thirty-one planes. All the fantastic, weird dreams that have floated out into the cosmos throughout time shall become a reality. Every other living being whose story is written in the Book of Consciousness shall die. And for those I spare, they shall bow down and worship me!"

He withdrew, his long neck whiplashing back like a serpent about to strike as he laughed. The air around him crackled as he coughed and spluttered burning venom into the air.

The Charon were unmoving, they were fearless, and they were their usual courageous and heartless selves. They knew that whatever the truth, they must fight on. Their lives were a never-ending eternal battle. As they continued to fight, the Earth shook and cracked as the two armies inflicted vengeance. They were matched blow for blow, without either side gaining any advantage.

Chapter 29: The Drop Off

Ignatius knew they had very little time, if any, to make a plan. After tethering their craft to Carfax Tower, Ignatius looked back and could see the battle taking place in the distance.

"What do you think will happen?" asked Lambeth.

"Who knows? The four horsemen of the apocalypse are here, the Book of Shadows has unleashed all sorts of death, Calabi-ya could destroy us all, yet he has a score to settle with the Charon. I think for now we remain out of the way and regroup."

Indigo was still dressed in just a flag. She had regained her ability to walk after her ordeal and was busy searching for clothes at the Temple. Lambeth helped her, keeping his eyes lowered to protect her modesty, and before long she re-emerged wearing some hunting tweeds, some breeches and brown riding boots, her oversized check shirt tucked in with a waistcoat of finest brown leather. She armed herself with twin derringers clearly visible, a short sword strapped to her boot and a steam cannon strapped to her leg in a beaten leather holster. On her belt she clipped several steam grenades.

"We can't just sit it out. What of the Oxonians and the Empire?"

"There'll be no Empire if all the forces of the underworld are successful. In fact, there will be no cosmos," Ignatius replied.

Every so often, the ground shook as the forces of the underworld fought, destroying everybody in their path and trying to destroy each other.

Just then, Lockhart returned. He was also a younger member of the Union Jacks with jet black hair and a large waxed moustache and small triangular beard. Like Carter, he was dressed in a dinner jacket.

"I say, old boy, dinner will have to wait, it's pandemonium out there! There appears to have been some sort of natural disaster. A meteorite has hit the Administorium, but, and here's the thing, there is talk of dead people and strange creatures coming out of the resulting crater. Although some of the dons at the colleges reckon they are just illusions brought about by some kind of gas given off when the rock scorched the earth."

He looked at Ignatius and Indigo.

"You're not going out, are you? I don't like to worry you, old chap, and you'll think I'm mad, but there's a… and this is the bit I can't explain, there's a dragon out there. A fully grown live dragon! The only thing missing is Saint George!"

His usual dismissive nature was obviously not cutting it. He lowered his voice and, frowning, spoke to Ignatius. "I'm trying to remain upbeat. But the truth is… well, I'm not sure what the truth is. But the Empire, England may not survive this. It really is Armageddon out there. I've never seen such supernatural behaviour, not even in the Congo or the Middle East. By comparison, all their magicians are charlatans. I'm not sure you should be venturing out, Ignatius."

Ignatius held him by the arm. "Don't worry, Lockhart. I can't explain everything, but myself and Indigo are far more experienced in this sort of thing than you could possibly imagine. I can't explain now. But we have battled these beings before."

Lockhart looked alarmed.

"True, we may not return. But we must try and stop this, or you are right, all of England and the Empire shall perish."

Hardred spoke. "What kind of trickery is this, Ignatius? Is it really, dare I say it, supernatural? This is a huge attack on the Empire, and we had no intelligence about it. Is it the French? Or maybe the Belgians? And I'm sure I saw the Administorium building fly into the air; it wasn't destroyed. I'm sure. I'm not mistaken. Am I? It was all so confusing. Can the clerics and administrators access the heavens now? I know they dislike some technology, but how did they do that? What technology have they used that the rest of the Empire knows nothing about? And who are those horsemen?"

"That's a lot of questions, Hardred. It's complicated. I can't explain it all, and now is not the time or place. We need to make a plan to protect the city, to protect the Empire. To survive," answered Ignatius. "But I need to go back!" he announced.

"Are you mad?" said Hardred. "You'll be killed. This isn't some sort of skirmish usually seen elsewhere in the Empire. This is full-scale apocalypse, man. You can't survive. What are those creatures in there?"

"I can't explain right now. I'll be okay, trust me."

He was so calm and sure, the other Union Jacks were confused.

"I'm coming with you!" said Indigo, still looking pale and fatigued.

"Out of the question!" replied Ignatius.

"I'm coming with you!" she reiterated. "That wasn't a request. I have endured the most pain a body can take. I have left my body and drifted through the astral planes, had every atom of my body torn apart and reassembled. I have seen things in the stars that would make you all weep. I am coming with you!" Lambeth, Alfred,

Hardred and Carter all looked towards Ignatius for a reaction.

Ignatius said no more, and they headed for the door. "Hardred, we will need a pilot. Lambeth, you and Alfred start to round up anybody that is still on the streets and give them shelter."

"We will arm ourselves for protection against whatever we encounter. We can lead any strays to the colleges for safety," said Lambeth.

"Good. Thank you, Lambeth."

With that, Ignatius and Indigo made their way to the dirigible.

"Then you'll need back-up," said Lockhart as he followed with Carter, picking up their weapons along the way.

Together they all climbed into the dirigible and took off. Ignatius turned to Lockhart and Carter. "When we get down there, your task will be to destroy the machines that held Indigo captive. You can't miss them, they're like an X-shaped crucifix. Destroy the controls and the keyboards attached to them. Do not fail. Those machines must never be used again."

"Consider it done," said Lockhart as he opened his dinner jacket to reveal several steam grenades attached to the scarlet lining. He grinned, his moustache rising on one side and twitching as he did so.

"So, what do we do?" asked Indigo.

"At this stage, I'm not sure, but we have to try something," replied Ignatius.

Before long they were airborne in the tiny craft and heading for the crater. They could hear the battle raging from some distance away and as Indigo looked below, she saw the demons, the ghouls and the other horrors unleashed from the Book of Shadows.

"What is that black mass behind Calabi-Ya?" she asked.

"Shadows. They absorb any lifeform they touch. But I don't know why they are not progressing like the other terrors. They seem to be waiting for somebody."

The giant flies started to swarm around the dirigible and a few started to attack the sails and wings. It soon became obvious they were trying to eat the fabric to bring the craft down. Hardred took evasive action, trying to manoeuvre the craft erratically to shake them off. It worked momentarily, but then came the boom of a steam cannon shot as Indigo blasted one of the creatures, separating its head from the rest of its body, which was still flying around for a while. As it fell from the sky, it landed in the craft.

"Eww," said Indigo, "they are disgusting!" as she took it daintily between one finger and thumb and threw it overboard. Ignatius followed suit and those flies that were attacking were soon all dead, the rest of the insects having given up, spotting easier prey on the ground below.

Looking into the distance, Ignatius could see Adonai landing heavy blows with his war hammer onto Calabi-Ya as his horse repeatedly charged, its eyes glowing red and flames flaring from its nostrils. Calabi-Ya roared, almost crushing Adonai's horse with his taloned claw. Looking in the opposite direction, Ignatius could just see the High Priestess in the distance.

"Drop myself and Indigo at the crater, then you'd best go after the High Priestess," he said, pointing in her direction. "But don't forget to destroy those machines."

Lowering the dirigible as much as he dared without touching down, Hardred dropped the two Union Jacks off at the crater. They leapt and landed lightly.

As they entered, two clerics came to accost them, Ignatius just pushed them aside, barging past their protestations. Indigo punched one on the nose and he yelped, backing away immediately, allowing both of them to continue down the staircase once more and into the library.

He looked at Indigo, saying, "we need to rid the earth of Calabi-Ya and the Charon once and for all. This really is the apocalypse, Indigo." She looked at him quizzically.

"You were drifting in and out of consciousness earlier. Some of the Charon have transformed into the four horsemen and the others are swooping around like Valkyries sending the souls of the newly deceased to their ship, Taraka, to fuel it. But I fear the worst is yet to come, from the Book of Shadows."

Indigo remembered some of this, and felt a chill down her spine and the hairs on the back of her neck bristled.

"How do we stop them?"

"We'll start with Calabi-Ya. We have to get hold of his soul from within the pages of that book. I don't know if that's possible, but we must try."

Chapter 30: The Weight of a Soul

As the two Union Jacks entered deeper into the library, the surge of hell-spawn continued and the Charon were continuing their destruction of everything in their path, their war horses trampling any demon that came too close. As the fighting continued, Indigo secretly made her way towards the area where the book lay. Although it wasn't visible, having shrunk back into the shadows, its presence was obvious as the hell-spawn continued to exit from its pages. Ignatius took out his sonic blaster and fired it towards the position of the book. The air around it seemed to vibrate, and molecules flew apart then crashed back together and the book appeared. The hell-spawn momentarily stopped, then began again, taking a different path away from the book. The two Union Jacks clambered over bodies and alien lifeforms, feeling them crunch beneath their feet, to get to it. Indigo felt her leg plunge knee deep into a slime monster, and she gasped due to the icy coldness that crept up her leg. She couldn't feel it anymore. But turning quickly she withdrew her short sword and slashed. Red sticky gunge sliced off in pieces as her hard steel bit through the ooze. The monster whimpered and withdrew, looking for new flesh to cling to. Indigo continued, dragging her numb leg as she went.

On reaching the book, Ignatius placed his birthmarked hand to his eye. He didn't know if his plan would work. He looked upon the many planes that intertwined with that of the earth. His mind fought against the madness that threatened to overpower his consciousness and flood his mind. As his mind raced, he began to think that maybe this is what people in an asylum were struggling with, views onto other planes, other worlds, other beings. Then he placed his head into the pages of the book and searched for Calabi-Ya's soul once more. Hell-spawn continued to rush past him, but none could see him as his face peered at them through the pages.

"Can you see it?" whispered Indigo, not wanting to draw attention to them.

"It's here."

The black soul jumped and vibrated, fizzed, and sparked red once more. It contorted, trying to escape detection. Ignatius pointed it out, but Indigo couldn't see it. She tentatively placed her hand into the book. It felt like pushing her arm into the deepest hoarfrost. She blindly searched about with her hand, the chill biting into her skin.

As she leaned forward to search a little deeper, she came face to face with the Queen of Shadows.

"Aarrrgh!" she screamed and tried to withdraw, but her arm was stuck. Maha-Kala had grabbed her arm and started to pull. She pulled back with all her remaining strength, but to no avail. Indigo began to enter the pages of the book. She saw the queen displaying her foul teeth with a sinister grin. She heard her cackle and laugh. Indigo's blood ran cold. The Shadow Queen flew around her like black tendrils with a torso and head. She laughed some more, then closed in on Indigo.

Ignatius had momentarily removed his hand and was holding onto Indigo by her legs, "No! No! Not again, I'm not losing you!"

As Maha-Kala's face came close to Indigo to bite her, Indigo pushed a steam cannon into her mouth and fired. The boom and hiss of the steam were suppressed by the Queen's throat. An ear-splitting shriek echoed around the pages of the book and the Queen retreated, exiting the book high into the air, where she nurtured her injured mouth, joining the rest of the still-waiting shadows. She was injured but not destroyed.

She was relieved, but Indigo still couldn't breathe due to the cold. Frantically searching before it was too late, she found Calabi-Ya's soul.

The commotion with the Queen of Shadows had alerted Calabi-Ya to the Union Jacks' presence. The earth around them shook and he was upon them, his clawed foot slamming down, narrowly missing Ignatius. Then, knocking Ignatius out of the way and pushing his own head into the book, Calabi-Ya tried to gulp down his own soul to protect it. Indigo felt his scaly head brush past her, knocking her aside. He failed. Confused whether it still lay within the depths of the pages, he turned his head and tried again. But the soul had gone. He roared and withdrew from the book, spraying venom across the entirety of the library. More bookcases caught fire, and demons and monsters were set aflame. But he didn't have time to try again before he was being attacked by the Charon.

Indigo climbed out of the book, all sorts of creatures clambering over her to escape into the world. Ignatius got back to his feet, and Indigo gave him a knowing glance. He looked around and picked up some books that were burning and launched them at the Book of Shadows. Flames grew all around, licking its cover and curling around the pages within. But they had no effect. The book was impervious to fire. It just sat there as before until eventually there was no more other material around it left to burn and the fire dwindled and fizzled out. The book was unscathed.

Indigo stood defiantly before Calabi-Ya and casually took something from her pocket. Her hand seemed to glow red with an orange aura. Calabi-Ya shifted a little, uneasy, stepping from side to side. He was clearly agitated. She raised her arm and with her palm held upwards, held the object out in front of her. It fizzed and pulsated. Calabi-Ya looked horrified: there before him glowed his soul.

Without warning, he transformed momentarily, and the now-familiar dragon's head shot up out of his harlequin-clothed body and lunged at Indigo. But she was too quick. She moved aside without Calabi-Ya or Ignatius seeing her move. Ignatius looked on, amazed. How had she acquired such speed?

"Don't be too hasty, Calabi-Ya. A soul is fragile, is it not?"

Returning to his harlequin form fully, he looked clearly perplexed and angry. "So, you think you can outsmart me, do you? You seem to have acquired some speed, but you will need more than speed against me. You are a mere mortal, the lowest form of deity, asura. You are no match for me. I am the Elder God. You have no idea who you stand before. Now give me the soul!"

Indigo slowly closed her hand, gripping the soul tightly. She could feel it pulsing. The vibrations increased in frequency and in strength, as if desperate to free itself. Her hand began to feel warm, the orange aura moving rhythmically with the pulsations. The aura grew and snaked its way along her arm and circled her neck. Like a spectral snake, it coiled its way around her slender neck and began to constrict. She had difficulty breathing but did not release her grip on the soul.

Ignatius could see what was happening and feared for her life again. "Indigo, please! Be careful, I don't want to lose you. Give it to him."

She looked Ignatius in the eye, her constricted voice was little more than a low whisper. "Oh, I'm going to give it him, no fear Ignatius. I know what I'm doing," and she smiled sweetly.

She began to feel the weight of the soul. It felt heavier somehow. Without blinking, she vanished momentarily and then reappeared, free of Calabi-Ya's grip.

She laughed loudly, mocking the god. "Didn't you know? My ordeal at the hands of the High Priestess has left me with some abilities, shall we say! Maybe it's time for you to leave, Calabi-Ya. Leave Earth alone, and I'll hang on to this for a while."

"What do you mean?" asked Ignatius.

"I don't know how, and I don't know when I knew this, but that machine has changed me somehow. I can feel it. I can manipulate matter, manipulate inter-dimensional cosmic energy, just using my mind. The physical laws on this plane no longer apply to me."

To demonstrate, her hand began to fragment into a mass of floating molecules glowing with a purple aura, until the soul and her hand became invisible. The invisibility travelled up her arm. Ignatius stood with his mouth open.

Calabi-ya was pacing up and down, his body contorting every now and again as he resisted the urge to go full dragon. Scaly limbs protruded every so often and the dragon's head flew from the top of his skull now and again and fire shot out of his nostrils. The Queen of Shadows was behind him with the rest of her retinue in formation. The shadows were now getting ready to attack, having waited for their leader.

Calabi-Ya turned to Indigo. "I have been patient with you. At the moment, I am holding back my hell-spawn until I am ready to savour the entropy about to forsake all living beings in the cosmos, all things in these primitive dimensions. And it will start here on this little blue rock you call Earth. All cosmic fabric and life shall disintegrate atom by atom, starting right here. This will be the funnel through which all death and destruction will be sucked. The Charon are running around killing and devouring souls as if they are contributing to this total destruction. But they are fools. It will happen anyway. But whatever powers you believe you have, may only be temporary and are no match for me. Now give me my soul."

It was like a great black cloud had grown up around him as he made himself larger and loomed over the Union Jack, about to pounce.

Indigo wasn't about to be intimidated. She had died earlier that day. Every single part of her still ached, every atom, every vibration caused pain throughout her battered body and, unusually so for a Union Jack, it was not their way, but she wanted revenge, she was only human. Whilst her suffering wasn't at the hands of Calabi-Ya, he was still the cause. It was his Book of Shadows. She stubbornly continued. Today was not the day to die.

It's getting heavier, did you know that? Your soul, it grows heavy." Her arm and hand now visible again.

Calabi-Ya began to look alarmed.

"In fact, it's so heavy, I don't think I can hold it any longer. Is this judgement day? Are you about to be judged, Calabi-Ya? That's the only reason I can think this soul grows so heavy. True, your monsters may be swarming the streets of Oxford, racing to gain control of the rest of the planet, but I think today will not be the apocalypse. For all your darkness, the events played out here have created nothing but light. I am a result of that light. I have been transformed and now you pose no threat to me."

Calabi-Ya was looking a mix of confusion and anger. He looked towards the High Priestess, who was shifting nervously.

"What have you done with your meddling? The book maybe open, but what kind of being have you created? You will pay for this."

The High Priestess scowled. "Without me, without the girl, the book would not have been unlocked and opened!"

She motioned to apprehend Indigo, but she was held back by Devi, who had now blocked her path. "You will let this play out. Even the Charon are intrigued to know how this will end. You truly have created something special."

As Indigo looked around, she could see that the Charon were still. They had gathered and were curious.

"My middle name is Providence; the demi-god of recompense, and I shall restore order. I am the balance to your destruction!"

The Charon assembled behind Indigo. She turned to Aryas, who was still seated on his great black steed, and he offered her the golden scales. She looked Calabi-Ya in the eye as she placed his soul on the scales. At first they were perfectly balanced, but gradually, they began to tip as the soul showed its weight. On the other side, Adonai placed a bag of weights he materialised from the aether. These were large and heavy. He placed another, and another, but it seemed no matter how much weight he added, Calabi-Ya's soul was heavier.

Indigo didn't take her eyes off Calabi-Ya. "Oh dear, it seems you have been found wanting!" she mocked. "Your black soul is full of the darkness of the cosmos, full of sin and is without contrition. The cosmic balance has found against you!"

Now enraged, Calabi-Ya transformed once more into the dragon and lunged forward, snorting venom that dripped to the floor, his forked tongue lashing out as he tried to recapture his soul.

His lack of success gave Indigo a chance to hide the soul fully.

She closed her eyes but could still see everything around her fully. She felt her body drift away, she felt the entanglement of her atomic structure with that of the cosmos. She sensed people she had never seen or met in Oxford crying, she felt their fear, she felt the lives of alien beings elsewhere in the same dimension. For a moment, she was at one with the cosmos. It was within her, and she was within it. Without any thought, she automatically began to chant an enchantment. She didn't know how she knew it, but it came naturally to her. She had knowledge of all sorts of magical energy, sorcerous spells and incantations and sources of great extra-dimensional power that she'd had no knowledge of before her ordeal. She had no fear. She opened her eyes. The soul that had lain on the golden scales had now vanished, the opposite side crashing down under the weight Adonai had placed upon it.

Without warning, all vengeance let loose. Calabi-Ya took to the air, spilling venom across the city, his anger, the herald of death. The buildings around where the Administorium had once stood now burned and melted with the heat. Insects and flying demons filled the skies until it was black, drowning out all light. The red slime and amorphous blobs rolled across the dead and the buildings absorbing them and the fire. Ignatius and Indigo were deafened by the sound of gnashing teeth and the shadows, led by their Queen, now raced at great speed like banshees between buildings, people and hell-spawn alike. Indigo had pulled out her steam cannon and let loose a volley of shots at anything that came close. She pulled a steam grenade from her belt and threw it into the mouth of Calabi-Ya, followed it with another, where they both exploded, sending him shrieking higher into the air. The Charon were now overrun, Devi and the other two Valkyries had taken to the skies permanently, no longer seeking the souls of the dead, and were busy swinging their swords at the flying creatures. Ignatius was also busy shooting at anything that came close. He stood, back-to-back with Indigo, each protecting the other, fighting in formation, turning at every opportunity.

As they rotated, Ignatius saw Paladin put his weapon to his lips. Next to him, Aryas was sat in a meditative pose on his horse, somehow keeping the shadows at bay with an incantation. Maha-Kala circled directly overhead as if choosing the right moment to attack Aryas, or held back somehow by his spells. She shrieked with anger, with anticipation of striking, her beautiful face contorted and twisted, fading in and out of her shadowy body. Calabi-Ya was still writhing in agony mid-flight, but he was not going to retreat. It was as though he had doubled in size as he turned and, like an eagle plummeting for its prey, he flew through the cratered ground and back into the library, striking the ground with such a force the earth cracked beneath him, ceramic tiles and rock being thrown into the air like confetti. He roared and incinerated what remained of the library.

"Lay waste, this world and the next, and the next, and every plane upon which any sentient being stands, for we are the devourer of worlds, we are DEATH!" screeched Calabi-Ya. "The thirty-one planes shall burn, and I will build a new cosmos from the ashes!"

The whole multitude attacked simultaneously. The air was black with shadows, cutting out any shred of light from above and the floor scarlet with demons and slime.

But it was too late. Paladin blew his weapon and the full force of the blast hit the front of the throng. It held them there, but not a single creature fell, and each time Paladin drew breath, before blowing again, the horde advanced, little by little.

The other Charon began to get into formation around Paladin, ready to join as one to try and stem the flow of hell-spawn. Atman took his bow and clipped it onto Adonai's war hammer and loaded it with seven silver-tipped arrows. Paladin offered his scythe-like weapon, connecting it to the hammer so the mouthpiece was like an extension to the handle. The assembled weapon was colossal and resembled some sort of heavy instrument.

Adonai placed the mouthpiece to his lips and pointed the weapon at a confused-looking Calabi-Ya. He filled his lungs to capacity, his chest pushing against the leather body straps he wore to hold his sword in place on his back, and he blew with all his godly might. Simultaneously, Calabi-Ya unleashed his blazing venom as the seven arrows were loosed, flying through the flames and into Calabi-Ya's face, piercing his snout, his forehead and tongue. Adonai blew once more and the hammer was unleashed, thudding into Calabi-Ya full on. The weight of the enchanted weapon was too much to bear, and as it hit the dragon's head, it felled him. He found he couldn't move the weapon; it was too heavy and seemed to be getting heavier. Calabi-Ya was immobilised. Adonai blew once more with the remaining weapon, now just the instrument belonging to Paladin, and after the final sound wave hit Calabi-Ya, Adonai swung the scythe-like blade through the air in a wide arc. As he did so, the unmoving mass of the dragon vanished, along with all the demons, monsters, and retinue of shadows. Once more, Calabi-Ya had been exiled to the Ghost Worlds.

Chapter 31: Invoked

Out of nowhere, three ravens began to fly about the crater. They looked like they were scouting the area and were certainly avoiding the eagle. Ignatius shot a look at the book, expecting to see more black ferocious-looking birds arise from its pages. But nothing. One of the birds swooped down and came almost eye to eye with him, making Ignatius feel uneasy. There was an intelligence he didn't expect. He braced himself, the air thick with anticipation of what horrors were about to come now. But nothing.

Ignatius just caught sight of a figure in his peripheral vision. He was like no other shadow creature so far. He was very tall, taller than any human, naked save for a tattered black cloak and grey skinned. He looked like a corpse, and he appeared to have what looked like plant roots embedded across his skin in places. His features were hidden in his own shadow, which never seemed to be at one with any light source. He was in permanent shadow. His face displayed none of the usual features, just a mouth, thin and menacing. His head was covered in growths that twisted and tangled and rose above his head like the branches of a tree, and his hands had extraordinarily long fingers with long sharp nails at the end.

Ignatius realised this figure was somehow familiar when Adonai exclaimed, "the Stalker!"

He had been sent by the Omnisoul to locate the Charon on whatever plane they were, so the Sleeper could transport them back to Limbo. Back to the care of the Keeper where they would be chained and bound and held captive until the Omnisoul had another task for them to execute. The Stalker moved silently, somehow always in shadow, approaching Adonai. Ignatius began to think that maybe he was related to the Queen of Shadows.

"Your time here is over, Adonai. The Omnisoul has demanded your return. Your transformation into the four horsemen shall not go unpunished. The Omnisoul shall decide when the apocalypse will be, and what form it shall take. It is already written, as you know, in the Book of Consciousness."

The Charon were surprised. The Stalker didn't usually speak. Adonai was thinking that events had been particularly different this time around. They had been used for tens of thousands of tasks, but this had been different. Probably because they had taken their form of the Horsemen and the Valkyries. But also because Ignatius and Indigo had changed permanently. It was like they had begun to grasp their fate.

The Stalker's teeth were black, his thin slit of a mouth twisted and obscene. His breath foul. "When I find the Queen of Shadows, she too will be coming with me, to Limbo, to a special purgatory until the Omnisoul decides what part she will play in the end of the Great Cycle, the end times, the apocalypse. Then the Omnisoul shall decide how the next cycle will begin."

"Whatever happens, the Charon cannot not escape!" said Adonai. "We shall always be the Omnisoul's puppets to be used then chained and bound once more, regardless of which cycle we are in. The sad thing is, and you don't realise this, you and the rest of the Celestials are nothing more than slaves, too. You fetch and send and keep and stalk. Is that what the great Celestials had in mind when they reached such god-like status?"

It was difficult to tell if the Stalker was angry without any features on display other than his mouth. But his mouth twisted and grimaced and the root like growths that covered his face seemed to writhe and contort.

"The Master has a plan, and it needn't concern you. You just need to simply wait for the Voice to commune once more for your next task. Try not to let the weight of the chains that shall bind you, the agony of Limbo and the furnace, dishearten you. After all, immortality is a very long time, especially when you have no real free will. How are you not used to it?"

His thin mouth grinned a crooked, malicious smile. Ignatius kept one hand on his steam cannon, just in case. He didn't like the tension between them and wasn't keen to be involved in any more fighting.

The three ravens still soared above with ever decreasing circles, until they were flying just above the Stalker's head.

"I shall take my leave," said the Stalker. "I have completed my task. I have located you. The Sleeper is on the way."

The Charon all had the same despondent look on their faces. The Stalker's dirty and torn cloak swished around him as he turned and walked towards the shadows, his ravens following him. As he faded from view, another figure appeared.

"He is here already!" said Darshan, her whole demeanour changing. She seemed to withdraw, and sadness weighed heavily on her whole body.

There was a rustle of black feathers emerging from the shadows. The Sleeper wore a heavy horned helmet and his face was a mirrored shield that shone like mother-of-pearl. There were no features, no mouth, no nose, just four holes that looked like they might serve as eyes and nostrils. His wings were wrapped around a tall slender body wrapped with a few narrow scrolls with archaic text written all over them.

The Charon had grouped together, and all looked a little fearful, even the great merciless Adonai. Ignatius and Indigo had started to understand the Charon and their nature in a bit more detail.

Adonai looked at the two Union Jacks "Farewell. Your strength is growing faster than I expected. Remember, you are godlings and if you nurture your true ability in the correct way, you can both fulfil your potential. You were created for a reason. Only with pearls of wisdom can you bring peace."

Ignatius interrupted. "Thank you. We think it is not a power either of us wants, but we are starting to understand more now."

Indigo tried to agree but didn't get the chance as Adonai interjected. "No! No! You do not understand. You have no idea. Your power shall be beyond your imaginings. Your true destiny is yet to be fulfilled. Just one pearl of wisdom can make all the difference."

Aryas stood beside him, grinning. It sent shivers down Indigo's spine.

The Sleeper had begun to move his hands through the air, and orange light started to glow from his fingertips. It increased in luminosity and grew until a circle filled the air before the Sleeper's face. Increasing the speed of his hands and arms, moving them in ever-increasing circles, the light became an orange portal of such brilliance it hurt the two Union Jacks' eyes.

The light began to grow in depth and began to bubble and move, then turned crimson. It looked sentient. A head appeared, then another, then they vanished. It became an abyss of molten fire, an obscene mass of twisted bodies, all writhing amongst the brimstone and shadows. The sound of chains and groaning could be heard. The gnashing of teeth seemed to drown out all other sounds and horror-stricken faces could be seen in the morass of blood and gore that seethed from the portal. Three large yellow eyes could be seen as the hooded head of the Keeper appeared, beckoning the Charon to follow, As the two Union Jacks squinted, they could just make out the silhouettes of the Charon entering the portal, followed by the Sleeper. Then, the dazzling disc rapidly contracted and vanished in a spark of crimson light, leaving behind no trace of the Charon.

Chapter 32: An Unholy Alliance

In the aftermath of the final battle, the two Union Jacks knew they had to reseal the book before it vanished again, carried off into the shadow realms. Silently, the changing state of their powers had started to worry Ignatius. How could they ever return to a normal life, to normal activities working for the Union Jacks? In fact, internally, he was now starting to question what normal was anymore. In the back of his mind, he was also pondering the last words Adonai had spoken to them, but had no idea what Adonai had meant.

Turning to Indigo he asked, "What have you done with Calabi-Ya's soul?"

"I have sent it to the Ghost Worlds, where one day he may be re-united with it again. But for now, he is weak."

They both knew once the book had been dealt with, there was the matter of trying to explain events to the good citizens of Oxford and filing a report that made sense. The Union Jacks didn't take to acknowledging supernatural events or encourage delving into the occult arts.

"We need a plan, Ignatius. Any suggestions?"

Ignatius knew he had to think fast, he was also tired, and his body ached from fighting, his mind fogged and weak.

"What if we try to make a deal with the High Priestess?"

Indigo shot him a look. "Are you serious? After what she did to me?"

Ignatius felt embarrassed. "I know, but hear me out. Perhaps she can destroy the Book of Shadows with some magic, or at least send it someplace where it can cause no harm. We don't have any weaponry to do that. I don't think the sonic blaster is powerful enough to do it, and we don't yet understand our supernatural powers or what we are capable of."

With a concerned look, she replied, "I know but surely the book needs to be resealed?"

"It has lain undisturbed for an eternity, and it was the Ti-Botta who sealed it last time. But that's not an option, not here, not now," Ignatius replied.

Indigo gave a great sigh, resigning herself to asking for help from her antagonist. "Then we will have to be persuasive."

With renewed hope, Ignatius had developed his usual spring in his step again. Indigo followed him and they headed deeper into the smouldering remains of the library. The book was still visible and clearly open. Sat beside it was the High Priestess, her near-naked form covered with black soot and grey ash, her cloak in tatters.

"High Priestess!" called Ignatius. "In fact, it occurs to me, we do not know your name."

She looked at him with displeasure. "What care do you have? You have ruined all of my work. The Administorium is destroyed. The Librarian has fled like the coward he is. What do I care if you know me?"

"Yes, you are right! Let's just kill you now!" Ignatius pulled his sonic blaster out with one hand and a steam cannon with his other hand and pointed them both at her, hoping in reality he didn't have to kill her in such a cold way.

The High Priestess hissed like a scorned cat and got to her feet, "Cha-Ya. My name is Cha-Ya."

"I am sensing that only your magic can reseal the book. Your level of magic is far more powerful and can overcome the physical laws on this plane. Am I right?" said Ignatius.

"Not exactly. But I am powerful enough to summon those that can seal the book. Then what? What do you expect of me after the book is resealed?"

"You can go. Leave this earth, leave this plane, and do not return. You have tried and failed here. As you say, the Librarian has fled, the Charon have gone, Calabi-Ya has been exiled and the book shall be hidden once more. I shall see to that. And your machine is being destroyed as we speak. There is nothing left for you."

"Why should I help you?" she snarled. "I have waited aeons to find that book. My whole life has been devoted to finding the Book of Shadows so I could rule the thirty-one planes as the supreme cosmic queen."

"You know as well as I do, despite your power, you are no match for the Omnisoul or Calabi-Ya. Your dream is just that, a dream! The Queen of Shadows was never going to let you replace her. Her task was to destroy the cosmos, there'd be nothing left to rule." A sneer flashed cross Ignatius's face. "Did you know that opening the book would begin the apocalypse?"

The High Priestess was silent for a while, thoughtful, then spoke, "admittedly, I did not. If it hadn't been for the Queen of Shadows, I believe I could have contained all the other demons and put them to use as my minions."

Her shoulders slumped and she dropped her head. "Are all the demons back inside the book?"

Ignatius looked around and shrugged. "I guess so. I can't see any, but the shadow demons are the ones that are hardest to spot."

"We light up the library," said Indigo. "Those areas not already burning, we light them up, seek any shadows before sealing it." She turned away and whispered to Ignatius. "Then I'll kill her."

Ignatius took her arm. "Let's just get the job done, shall we?"

Pulling herself up from the rubble, the High Priestess looked around, then looked at the book. "We will have to reseal all seven seals for it to be safe. But then it will vanish, sink back into the shadows and be lost once more."

"Can you send it to another plane, away from here?" asked Ignatius.

"I can. But it will still be a danger. The ideal place would be the Ghost Worlds, but Calabi-Ya walks those realms again now. If I cast it adrift, it will wander for an eternity, unnoticed, never resting in one place for very long."

Taking the outer edges of her cloak, the High Priestess extended her arms, so her silhouette looked something like a horned bat. She began to chant in a low-pitched voice. Unrecognisable words came spilling out until they joined up and made a single melodic sound. After some moments, she started to turn her body around on the spot, displaying herself to every face of the library. As the chanting continued, Cha-Ya began to glow with an aura emanating from her naked body. The intensity of the aura grew exponentially and as she continued to twirl, blue rays enveloped her body until her form could just be seen, pale blue and shimmering. Runes manufactured from light circled around her head like a halo, her horned crown in silhouette, whilst others painted her almost invisible body. These were archaic runes in a long-forgotten language, the likes of which could never be read, yet somehow, she knew how to manipulate them and use their magic. The radiating light painted every object in the library and Ignatius and Indigo had to shield their eyes. Occasionally a shadowy form or tiny demon became obvious in the light and made their way back to the book where they climbed into its pages once more. Gradually, Cha-Ya slowed her motion, and her aura began to retreat back to her body and fade. Ignatius was just about to speak when he thought he saw a spectre dash past him. He could just make it out in his peripheral vision, maybe. He turned and looked around. Nothing could be seen in the rapidly dimming light, just the stacks, books, torn pages and the odd fire billowing with black and grey smoke. Ignatius consoled himself that it must have been smoke.

As Cha-Ya came to a halt, she spoke as if in a trance, "'tis done. All shadows, demons and ghouls have returned."

"Are you sure?" asked Ignatius.

She turned and glowered at him with distaste written all over her sharp featured face.

"I can now begin to seal the book."

Releasing her cloak, she began to concentrate on the book itself. Secretly, she had no intention of giving the book up, but knew for now it had to be made safe, and as she began an incantation her mind was elsewhere, plotting how she would dispose of Ignatius and Indigo. The incantation started as before, a low stream of syllables and notes that sounded like an old man mumbling. The book began to tremble, very slightly. Then she stopped.

Turning to Ignatius she said, "This is going to take the rest of my energy. It is not an easy task. The clasps were placed by several wizards or High Priests and their combined energy is far more significant than my own."

Indigo responded. "Then potentially life is over. Yours! Mine! Ignatius! The world will be swept away and the evil that started here will engulf the cosmos, destroying it all. I fail to see what you will have gained."

After a short pause, she continued. "But I am happy to relieve you of your life right here and now. You almost killed me, so I have no sympathy, no mercy left in my battered body."

She pulled two steam cannons from her clothing and pointed them at Cha-Ya. Steam hissed as both guns increased in pressure and power. Before she had time to fire, Cha-Ya hurled a bolt of fire at Indigo, hitting the weapons square on and pushing her backwards. Indigo dropped one of her weapons.

"Enough! Your puny weapons are no match for me! I am losing interest and you are starting to bore me!"

Confident calm reappeared across her face, and the High Priestess composed herself. "If I am to transport the book, which is mine and which shall continue to be mine, then I should seal it. Or at least try. It will then travel the thirty-one planes with me until I decide on a home and make a plan to rule the cosmos, destroying whatever or whoever gets in my way!"

Making hand gestures, she conjured a green vial of liquid from thin air and drank from it. It looked like the kind of liquid Aryas drank whenever he had to perform strong magic. She then did it again, and this time a vial of orange liquid appeared. Again, she drank from it. Then once more. This time it was a vial of foul-looking black liquid, and as she drank from it, she coughed and it bubbled around her mouth, dribbling down her chin and ran down to her navel. She coughed again and black droplets sprayed from her mouth and hung in the air, suspended. Then, looking at the two Union Jacks, her face transformed, her eyes rolled back into her head and her whites glowed bright. Scales appeared across her skin and her fingers grew long with talons at the end. Both Ignatius and Indigo kept a firm grip on their weapons, ready for a fight.

She started an incantation, which rose to a melodic chant that sounded almost like singing. She raised her arms and brilliant white light sparked and encircled her arms like snakes made of pure cosmic energy. She pointed her long talons at the Book of Shadows and thrust her arms repeatedly as the power within her grew in anticipation of release. Then, one by one, seven men, apparitions, appeared surrounding her in a semi-circle. They were semi-transparent and dressed in robes of gold and purple.

Ignatius looked at Indigo. "Ti-Botta!" he exclaimed.

"It looks like it from their clothing."

"When I went to Sagharta, I was informed that they were the ones who had created the seven seals. These must be the priests or wizards who originally did so."

In unison, all seven wizards closed their eyes, bowed their heads and put their hands together as if in prayer. From time to time, they faded in and out like ghosts traversing the planes. One of them was wearing some elaborate headgear. He raised his head and looked directly at the Union Jacks, then, to their alarm, he spoke.

"We knew our calling was for some significant event. Only now have we been brought back from our slumber to assist once more with this unholy tome. I am not sure we have enough power left to reseal it."

Indigo wasn't sure if he was expecting an answer, but she offered one anyway. "But you must. The cosmos nearly fell. The book is of such power and evil, we cannot let it be opened again. "

The grand wizard looked at her with sadness in his eyes, "the last time ended our lives. We gave our lives to save yours and the billions that followed us. Even if we are successful, I am not sure we can ever rest again. I believe we will be banished to Limbo, or the Ghost Worlds. Why should I wish for some sort of purgatory?"

But the wizard didn't have time for any answer. The High Priestess's incantation reached a crescendo, and her song reached a shrill high pitched continuous note. White light flew around her body like lightning. It spread and slithered its way around the seven wizards, circling them until it had reached full potential, then it lifted them all slightly off the floor. They hovered and all pointed their arms towards the book. The light bounced around the library and several times Ignatius and Indigo had to duck to miss being blasted.

The seven wizards joined the song and together they all focused on one spot on the book, which had now closed shut. The first clasp began to vibrate. The book appeared to fight the action and started to give out a sentient murmur, deep and malevolent. It, too, hovered slightly off the ground and closed shut. Then without warning the clasp snapped shut like a crocodile's jaws. Turning their attention to the next clasp, it did the same. Ignatius and Indigo could feel the vibrations beneath their feet, then snap! The second clasp closed. The wizard's song changed slightly in pitch and the light that left their hands changed to have a slightly yellow glow. The third clasp snapped shut.

Suddenly, the book shook violently, and its sentient sound began to rumble like thunder. The noise grew and reverberated deeply, affecting everything around it. The rumble turned to more of a roar and the book hit the ground with such force the tiles beneath it split. Black light began to emanate from it and snake its way towards the wizards, who began to fade until they disappeared.

A startled Ignatius looked towards Cha-Ya, who was frantically trying to recall the wizards, her long talons moving hastily through the air, describing invisible runes. The apparitions began to reappear and the wizards seemed to increase their urgency. There was a shaft of light across the void separating them from the book. Their light force now had a slight orange glow to it and where it touched the book's black light, sparks flew and the air frizzed with energy. Eventually the book's midnight light had no choice but to retreat and where the orange light caressed the book the fourth clasp snapped shut.

At this point, the book decided to try and retreat back into the shadows where it would not be easily discovered again. The grand wizard stepped forward, making a sound as if all his ghostly breath left his body and pushed his arms forcefully towards the book. It came back into view fully. The other wizards changed their pitch again and the fifth clasp snapped shut. The book began to spin, probably in a hope that the wizards would find it difficult to focus on a single clasp. Faces began to appear on the surface of the book cover, twisted, angry and unholy faces with foul grins. They came and went as the book, still spinning, began to gradually move towards Cha-Ya. She backed away, but as the distance decreased, the spinning stopped. The sixth clasp snapped shut.

Wondering where the book was going, Ignatius and Indigo got their answer. Long scaly black arms suddenly burst forth from the book and grabbed Cha-Ya in a last desperate attempt to free itself of its fate. Her talons immediately vanished as she took hold of the arms, trying to release them from her throat. Staggering backwards, she changed her incantation and somehow freed herself from the grip. The arms started to retreat back into the book, and as the last hand was almost vanquished, the seventh clasp snapped shut. The book lay still, insentient, and deepest black, with one hand protruding, looking like a desperate grab frozen in time forever. As time flowed on, the book began to absorb all light around it.

The wizards' spell had stopped and they were silent until the grand wizard announced, "we must seal the clasps."

With that all of them lunged forwards and poured what looked like blood from a glass vial that each of them had concealed in their clothing.

"Blood?" enquired Indigo.

"Our very own," the grand master answered.

All the wizards then surrounded the book. "We must dispose of it before it vanishes from sight again," said the grand master.

They all linked hands and formed a circle around the book. They began to chant in a low-pitched note and a circle of turquoise light began to spin around them. Then, lifting their arms rapidly, the book took to the air high above them, heading for the opening of the crater above. As it entered the light, it seemed to groan, not used to the light, existing only in the dark. As it soared higher, the heavens cracked like thunder and a fiery gateway opened. At its centre was a black chasm, a rent in the cosmos, a fracture on the plane in which the earth circulated. Then it was gone from sight and the portal closed, leaving a dark cloud and rumbling thunder behind it.

Collapsing with exhaustion, depleted of whatever life force they still had, the grand master turned to the High Priestess, Ignatius and Indigo. His face was ancient and red with rage. "The book has been taken from this plane and placed in a realm where it will be lost for aeons. You all deserve to die for meddling in matters that are far beyond your puny comprehension. You are just a minor witch with powers that you cannot master and cannot fulfil to their true potential. You are more dangerous for not having the power than actually possessing it! Now, I and my brothers must rest once more."

The wizards began to fade and then disappeared entirely. The High Priestess was shaken and drained by her ordeal. She looked at Ignatius and scowled.

"I should kill you now. I have nothing but contempt for you both. I have been abandoned here on this plague-ridden rock you call Earth. Crawling with plagues like you and all humans. The Administorium, which took me decades to establish, has gone. I have no reason to be here and when I am rested, I shall find a way to get off this planet and explore the other planes where I can establish all this once more."

Indigo answered, "But the book is too dangerous! You cannot go after it ag…" She didn't get a chance to finish her sentence before a pale, angry hand grabbed her by the throat and pushed her away.

Without warning, Cha-Ya channelled as much power as she had left and with a wrathful vengeance she conjured fire at her fingertips, and threw it at the Union Jacks. It hit them both squarely in their chests, and they were thrown backwards into the nearest bookcase.

"I will not abandon my purpose, my duty. Your words hold no sway over me. I know the book had to leave this plane. I know where it went but finding it may take aeons again, searching the shadows until it reappears. I can live with that. I can live that long. You, however, will be dead soon."

Turning with a dramatic swish of her cloak she walked away.

The two agents lay on their backs, groaning. Indigo was left wheezing trying to breathe. Eventually she quietly croaked, "Are we just going to let her go?"

Ignatius didn't know how to respond. He knew she was still vengeful over her treatment earlier, and rightly so. A shadow passed overhead and, fearing the worst, thinking the shadow demons had returned, he looked up and saw Hardred's dirigible circling the air above the crater.

Chapter 33: The Witch is Dead

The other Union Jacks flew above the crater. Looking down, they could see the High Priestess striding across the remains of the Oxford streets. Hardred pointed to Lockhart, jabbing his finger in the air to indicate the prize.

"What do we do when we get to her?" said Carter. "Hold her captive? Kill her?

"Let's not think about it too much, let's take it as it comes! Clearly she doesn't belong here," replied Lockhart.

The High Priestess was marching with a purpose, her cloak swinging wide. Oxonians who came in to contact with her took one look at the anger on her face and gave her a wide berth. The Librarian's eagle was circling above the dirigible. Looking up, she saw the Union Jacks and began an incantation, swinging her arms wide and describing invisible runes in the air.

"I hate magic!" declared Carter. "I've heard Ignatius is quite used to it, but it's not my cup of tea. Anything mystical or supernatural and I head in the opposite direction. Who is she, anyway?"

"I've no idea" replied Lockhart. "Maybe a witch!"

All of them readied themselves, checking their weapons, steam vapour rising and hissing every so often. Lockhart took out an ancient-looking weapon with a cluster of six barrels.

Without warning, Hardred tilted the nose of the craft, shouting "incoming" as they all dived for their target. As the dirigible hurtled towards the High Priestess at speed, she readied herself, her incantation complete. Bringing her hands together, she conjured a ball of fire and threw it at the craft, hitting it directly on the bow.

The craft shook and all its riders to a man were knocked off their feet. Regaining their footing, a volley of steam cannon shot left the craft and as it closed in on the target, she sent another fireball, destroying every missile mid-flight. But the dirigible didn't change course and ploughed straight into her, knocking her off her feet. As she scrambled to stand again, Lambeth leaned over the side and took a lucky shot. Steam hissed and the bullet hit the High Priestess in the middle of her chest. She looked down in disbelief at the hole that had burned right through her. Turning red with rage, she began an incantation and green fire engulfed the craft, its wings vaporising instantly, and as the craft turned, it hurtled downwards hitting the cobbled street below with such force it ripped a hole in its hull and splintered into three.

"Well, Windstorm has had her final flight," exclaimed Hardred, looking very irritated. "I've been all over the globe in this dirigible, and she comes to an end here in Oxford!"

The agents were all dazed but for the most part unharmed as they looked on, trying to rapidly work out a plot as the High Priestess was obviously uninjured by the shot. Blood oozed from her wound and stained the gold chains around her midriff. Lockhart threw two steam grenades that landed at her feet and as they exploded, she walked free of the debris and smoke.

Casting her cloak aside, she walked briskly towards the Union Jacks with just her crown of flowers and horns, the sword she had acquired earlier held out before her. There was a sudden rush of wind, and suddenly sharp talons appeared from above and dug deep into her shoulders as Manjushri attacked her, disgruntled that the Librarian had abandoned him. In order to brake his aerodynamic dive, he opened his wings. He had an enormous wingspan, and as he flapped he knocked the crown off her head. She swung the sword around but was unsuccessful in hitting the eagle at such close quarters. She retaliated with the dagger a little more successfully, but he succeeded in snatching it from her hand and discarding it. He came in for another attack, his razor-sharp beak pecking at her head, inflicting wounds just above her ear and to the side of her neck. Blood trickled down her torso and she screamed, more in anger than in pain, as the bird released his talons and dug them deep for a second time. Somehow, she broke free from the attack and managed to hit the bird with the flat of her blade and it fell to the ground, mid-flight. Striking it again, she inflicted a blow to one of its wings and the eagle retreated, unable to fly for any sustained period of time.

She turned her attention again to Carter and came at him with the sword, having the advantage due to its length. The blade grazed past his shoulder, and as she went to strike again, Carter knew he was too slow to avoid the blow. Then, he could smell burning flesh as a second hole appeared, just above her left breast, and steam hissed. Through the round hole he could just make out Lockhart standing behind her, steam cannon in one hand, recharging it, ready for another shot, and two grenades in the other. Then, boom, hiss, and another hole appeared. Turning her attention behind her, she expertly sliced through the air and her blade connected with Lockhart's arm. A red gash instantly opened and he dropped his weapon and the grenades as he turned pale and fell to his knees.

The blade was brought over his head and as she brought it down to cleave his head in two, Carter took two of his grenades and, pulling the pins, lodged them into the holes in her back and then dived for cover, his aching limbs slamming hard onto the cobbles. He saw the others take cover as the grenades exploded and red rain came showering down with chunks of flesh and golden chain links. Turning, he could see the remnants of her gruesome smouldering naked flesh with a sword lying beside her.

"Well done, old boy," said Lockhart. "My life flashed before me, then. You saved my bacon."

Carter said nothing, just nodded and gave a faint smile.

"I'm getting too old for this," croaked Hardred, panting for breath as Carter helped him to his feet. "I only hope Ignatius and Indigo have been successful."

"Let's hope so," replied Carter. "But we have to find the machine that Ignatius wants destroyed."

Stealthily, the three agents clung to the shadows, entering the crater, not knowing if danger still lurked. They made their way deeper into the depths of the library until they came to the chamber where the two machines were.

"I'll keep watch," said Hardred.

"Look!" whispered Carter, "It's… it's Indigo. But… how?"

"Let's not worry about that now. Let's just get her down and destroy these devices like Ignatius instructed," said Lockhart.

Clambering up, Lockhart took hold of Indigo's doppelganger's wrists. He recoiled after touching her. She was icy cold and deathly pale. He put his hand on her neck to feel for a pulse. Nothing.

"I fear the worst, Carter. I think she's dead."

"Then let's just get her down and give her some dignity. We can worry what to do with her later."

The two Union Jacks worked with heavy hearts. They had known loss of their comrades before. But this felt a little different. Indigo was always a little different. Fearless, intelligent, quick-witted, she gained respect wherever she went, whatever the mission. Lockhart removed the shackles and supported her by her wrists while Carter unshackled her ankles. Then carefully they climbed down and lay Indigo's body on the hard tiled floor.

"You do what we've come here for, I'll get something to cover her body," said Hardred.

As he did so, he saw Ignatius and Indigo over on the far side of the library. Confused, he did a double take.

"It's not her," he said. "Indigo, it's not her. I can't explain, but she's over there with Ignatius."

They all looked over, then collectively at the corpse before them.

"We'll still need to get her out of here. Whatever the explanation, it's only right," said Lockhart as he opened his coat and took more steam grenades from the lining. Giving some to Carter, the two of them began to strategically place them on the two machines. Attaching them to the part that looked like a ray gun, one under the keyboard, and another beneath the shackles. Then they made a hasty retreat.

Hardred had wrapped Indigo in a cleric's cloak he had found, and the three of them backed away from the two contraptions before throwing a live grenade. The Union Jacks hid behind some badly burnt bookcases, and the ground shook and cracked as the machines exploded, lighting up the library with green fire. The air crackled with energy, which lit the library like lightning every now and again. Shrapnel, gears and hoses whistled through the air and past the Union Jacks, with some debris embedding itself into the bookcases and walls. Dusty dry volumes began to burn and smoke began to fill that part of the library. Smoke came billowing out of the crater to blanket that part of Oxford with a green haze. It seemed alive, shifting and twisting in unnatural ways, as if it writhed in its death throes.

Looking at Carter, Lockhart grinned, his thin moustache twitching. "Mission accomplished, old boy," he said, then slapped Carter hard on the back to celebrate.

"We'd best get out of here, we have company!" said Hardred.

They all turned to see two escaped demons on their way to apprehend them. They stood their ground, Indigo lying on the floor behind them. All three agents charged their steam cannons and fired in unison. Shot after shot ripped holes in the approaching enemy. Their firepower increased in intensity and smouldering dead flesh filled the air. Lockhart threw Indigo onto his shoulder and together they carved a route beyond the hell-spawn to emerge at the crater's edge.

As they did so, a steam gurney came chugging to a halt at the crater's edge. Wisps of white hair blew in the breeze as the driver poked his head out of the side window.

"Lambeth! Good man, and just in the nick of time," said Lockhart.

Scrambling, they placed Indigo in the back with what reverence they could under the circumstances and then piled in. The vehicle sped off away from the scene, heading back to the Temple.

Chapter 34: The Other God

Ignatius looked at Indigo with some compassion, but knew there were more important issues to attend to just now.

"As much as I don't like saying this, I think we need to clean up down here first. Besides, with our comrades above, I don't believe the High Priestess is going to get very far if they haven't already dealt with her."

Indigo looked annoyed, hating the fact the High Priestess was allowed to walk away from them, but she agreed. "What did you have in mind?"

"This place needs to be destroyed. We don't want the public, or even the academics from the University, to come probing about down here. I don't believe that is in the best interests of the Empire. I also want to eradicate any evidence of the Administorium. We do not want them returning."

Indigo looked slightly alarmed. "But what of all this knowledge? We can't just destroy it. It'd be like the library of Alexandria all over again. This knowledge could advance the Empire, no, humanity enormously!"

Frowning, Ignatius retorted, "I don't believe for one second that humanity is ready for any of this. It would cause panic and competition from which it would not recover. I'm talking unwanted rivalry between colleges, governments, countries. It might even lead to all-out war. Besides, look at it, just trying to understand the vastness of this library, how it's bigger than the space it fits into would be enough to cause panic. The fewer people who know of this, the better."

Ignatius began to look around for some means of destroying the antiquity that lay before him, some means of a plan. Before he could formulate one, he noticed that Indigo had wandered off and could just be seen in the distance browsing the stacks. Intrigued, he followed.

"Come on, Indigo! We don't have much time."

"No! You destroy this place around me if you must. But look! Here we have knowledge that may be useful. There are several volumes by Enoch Slipnot. Plus, an old ancient book about the Ti-Botta. So old it's crumbling as we look at it. If we are going to keep encountering the Charon, we may need to know more."

"I guess, you're right. Take what you can, I'll look for anything related directly to the Charon."

Before too long, the two Union Jacks had acquired several volumes of interest and stacked them near the staircase that led back up to where the Administorium building had once stood.

"So how are we going to do this?" asked indigo.

"I'm not entirely sure, but my sonic blaster seems to be the most powerful weapon we have right now."

Ignatius pulled out his blaster and started to tune the dials. He pointed it at the pulpit where the librarian was first seen. Feeling the resistance of the trigger, he squeezed gently and a sonic ray emanated and snaked its way across the library until it encountered the ornate carvings of the pulpit. The whole thing started to vibrate and tremble. At one point, it looked like it faded to nothing, then was visible once more. As the frequency increased and equalled that of the material of its manufacture, it appeared to become two pulpits, then one, then three, until it ruptured and disintegrated, showering the tiles with tiny debris. The flame on the lantern that stood on the pulpit didn't blow out. It danced around as if alive, and sparks flew off in all directions. Several sparks ignited single, dry and dusty tomes and the lantern itself eventually fell into the nearest stack of books and set them alight. The fire was quick to spread, helped by Indigo and Ignatius, and before long the whole library was an uncontrollable conflagration. Out of the black and grey smoke came the screeching of the Librarian's eagle, soaring above the flames and dive-bombing in and out of the fires, perhaps trying to extinguish them or save the odd book. The bird came flying above their heads, fury in his eyes and smoke being given off from the tips of his feathers on one wing. The great bird of prey circled above Ignatius, then swooped to land on his shoulders, sharp talons digging in and drawing blood. Although alarmed, Ignatius remained still so not to distress the bird any further. Folding its wings, the bird remained in place, turning its head towards Ignatius, who feared the worst and waited for it to attack. Face to face, Ignatius could see there was intelligence in the bird's eyes. Bringing his razor-sharp beak close to Ignatius's ear, the eagle spoke.

"You had better hope, for your sake, that I have been able to absorb the entirety of the knowledge contained in this library, so it has not been lost for all time. When Viveka finds out, he will skin you alive and make book pages from your skin, and the tale of your death shall be described on your own flesh."

Ignatius's blood ran cold. How could a bird speak? Before he got a chance to ask the question, hesitating to question his own sanity, the eagle offered some explanation. Shifting from side to side, the bird spoke again.

"I am Manjushri, the scribe who was tasked by the Omnisoul to record the history of the Celestials, documenting their rise to power from mere alchemists to the god-like status they hold today. I was betrayed and swapped for knowledge in a bargain made between the Celestials and the Librarians. I was once a god. Now I am imprisoned in this body of an eagle."

Indigo was stunned. "What are you going to do? The Librarian has fled, and the Celestials have shown no interest in you. What can we do to help?"

The eagle turned to Indigo. "There is nothing anybody can do. But I shall have my revenge on the Celestials. I have been waiting for an eternity. But my day shall come. But you should be more concerned about your own fates. You have destroyed a universe of knowledge here. It will not go unnoticed. You are oblivious to the untold damage you have caused in the cosmos. The ripples of your actions travel out as I speak, and the entangled threads of the cosmos fabric twist and knot and break in places as a result of your actions. Merely trying to destroy the Well at the Centre of Time as the Charon had previously tried was nothing in comparison. This library links all thirty-one planes on which great Temples of knowledge and great learning houses are crashing down, returning to dust, and the denizens of those planes do not know why. But they will investigate and find out. Your lives are at risk. You are fools. To save questions by the people of this city, or wider, you have destroyed the knowledge that could have set them free. You are ignorant and humanity is doomed to never progress much further beyond walking out of the forests on two legs."

The eagle flapped his wings, demonstrating his powerful and enormous wingspan. Then he lurched forward and took flight, rising high into the air, circling the rim of the crater above.

Ignatius said nothing. He looked at Indigo with some sadness in his eyes. Indigo felt uncomfortable regarding their fate. In their delay, the fires had spread. Bookcases had begun to come crashing down or fall over as one side burnt away leaving them unstable. The heat was beginning to reach the two Union Jacks. Ignatius thought he was going to lose his eyebrows, so they made a hasty retreat, climbing the staircase back to the floor where the Administorium had once stood.

The two of them stood at the crater's edge watching the library burn. They waited long enough to be convinced that nothing would be left. In their arms, they each carried a number of books liberated from the shelves. In silence, they both turned their back and walked away, heading in the direction of Summertown. Other people they encountered were, without exception, heading in the opposite direction, towards the site of the chaos. Arriving at the door to his house, Ignatius turned the key and let them both in. They headed for his study where they carefully placed the treasure they were holding on his book shelves.

"We need to start studying these without delay. But tomorrow is a good day to start," he said and the two of them sat down, exhausted, Indigo in a large comfy armchair and Ignatius on a daybed. There was a large thud as Ignatius relieved himself of his sonic blaster and steam cannon as they both disarmed themselves, placing their weapons aside. Indigo removed her usual array of twin derringers, her short sword and two steam cannons, all hidden, as usual, in her undergarments.

Chapter 35: Concealed

Ignatius lay there looking quite exhausted, his face, although still handsome, was somewhat pallid. He seemed to have permanent frown lines upon his forehead and all joy had gone from his gold-flecked sapphire eyes.

"Do you think I did actually die today, Ignatius?"

She knew the answer but was trying to keep Ignatius occupied. She could feel a dull ache in the pit of her stomach. Ignatius said nothing, he just stared at her blankly. As she looked at him, she thought she saw a pale shadow move across his face. But then nothing. She continued to stare at him intently, but saw nothing else, so she disregarded it. Despite all their adventures together, nothing had ever brought them closer together than the adventures involving the Charon. She had grown very fond of Ignatius over the years and was only now beginning to understand her feelings for him.

Suddenly, it was as if the light began to fade. The room turned cold, and Indigo could see her breath fog in front of her face. She looked into his eyes. It was like he wasn't attached to the real world any longer. As she peered into the blackness of one pupil, she thought she saw a figure moving. Looking behind her, she realised it wasn't a reflection. A black shadow snaked its way around Ignatius's body like a wispy evil tendril. It wound its way around him like a boa constrictor, threatening to squeeze the life out of him.

The walls began to darken and became a mosaic of black shadows shifting, fading in and out, maybe even crossing planes to achieve this. Dark runes floated across the kaleidoscope of pieces that had now fragmented all around them. Adjusting her eyes, Indigo thought she could see an altar with Ignatius on it. He was struggling, fighting for his life, but unable to move, his body in the throes of death. The scene became liquid, and blackness enveloped all, circling everything in the room, like an archaic ghostly phantom made of deadly vapours, before giving way to the slightest of dim light in which Indigo could see the ancient crepuscular shadow deepen and fully form into the upper body of the Queen of Shadows. She had concealed herself and had escaped the destruction earlier and was now a phantom bent on revenge. Her beautiful face appeared before Ignatius and she kissed him, her blue lips locking on to his as she pulled him closer, her slender arm locked around his neck. He had no escape. She looked directly at Indigo and sneered. The Queen knew this would hurt Indigo the most.

As the Queen kissed Ignatius again, then withdrew her face, Indigo could see she was sucking the lifeforce from his rigid lifeless body, revealing her black fangs as she pulled back, black tendrils draped between them like foul saliva.

The Queen was now fully formed, her naked body displayed, her legs wrapped around Ignatius like a succubus in the night. Black tattoos covered her body, and as she moved, so did the tattoos. They writhed and changed shape, sliding over her skin, caressing her, absorbing energy from her.

Indigo knew it was only a matter of time before Ignatius would be an empty husk, a living zombie. She looked around frantically, trying to come up with a plan. The queen broke off once more, momentarily, and gave Indigo a foul sardonic grin, then returned to her activity of emptying Ignatius of all life.

Indigo spotted the sonic blaster Ignatius had placed aside earlier. She picked it up, and it seemed to purr in her hand. Adjusting the dials, she pointed the weapon at the Queen of Shadows. If she got this wrong, she could injure Ignatius or, worse, disintegrate him, his innards violently exploding all over his study. She took her time and could feel the pressure as she felt the resistance on the trigger, the Queen at this point seemingly preoccupied with drinking Ignatius's soul, was completely oblivious to Indigo's actions.

Then unexpectedly, the Queen transformed before her like a female version of Calabi-Ya. She was dressed head to toe in what looked like a skin-tight harlequin outfit. But on closer inspection, Indigo realised this was not cloth but her tattoos, the checkerboard pattern inked onto her lithe naked form.

She grinned again at Indigo, her long arms and legs still wrapped securely around Ignatius.

"You look surprised!" she said in a low husky voice that seemed to reverberate around the room. "His mind is so weak, it was easy to enter it, to hide amongst his greatest fears, his darkest thoughts and nightmares until the time was right. He is so feeble. I'm going to enjoy killing him and watching you suffer as I do it. Did you know that he loves you? Shame he'll never get to tell you. You will never know his touch!"

Indigo could feel her blood begin to boil. The rage inside her was rising, but she knew she had to keep her cool so she could think straight and save Ignatius.

"You may have exiled my consort, Calabi-Ya, but I am far more dangerous. Even now, I grow stronger, feeding off your fears, for I can exist in the shadows for an eternity, where nobody dares to go. The human mind is weak, and fear is all around. I have an endless source of energy on this plane. Free from the shackles of Rahu, I can grow stronger with every minute that passes. I can become stronger than Calabi-Ya himself. If you only knew the power of your thoughts, you would never have a negative thought again."

The Queen looked away for a moment and stared into Ignatius's eyes, then closed her own. The room began to sway, like onboard a ship, and one by one, several copies of the queen appeared around the room, doppelgangers, created to take control of the city, the earth and much more.

Simultaneously, all heads turned to Indigo and grinned before speaking in unison, "disciples of the shadows are many and with their power this Earth shall fall. Even now they get stronger, you are feeding them all with your fear and rage, your thoughts of revenge. Your hidden emotions are all just food for my vassals. A never-ending supply. And what's more… you simply can't help it!"

Every identical face in front of her began to laugh, their mouths wide open, showing hideous teeth and a thrashing tongue, foul breath and wide, wild eyes. Indigo closed her eyes but could still clearly see the faces.

Completely immobilised now, Ignatius was doomed. Was this to be his last adventure? Indigo had no choice. She took aim, her hands trembling a little with fear, but at the back of her head she knew this was only making the Queen stronger. Her trigger finger pulled back and she fired the sonic blaster at the queen, who laughed mockingly as she continued to suck lifeforce from

Ignatius. Her form began to fade in and out and ripples began to flow up and down her body like waves on the ocean. She moved like a serpent, her face coming dangerously close to Indigo's. She hissed and began to sing, a high-pitched wail like that of a siren, attempting to cancel out the sound waves inflicted by the sonic blaster. She writhed and moved her body from side to side, the ripples subsiding. Indigo turned the dials on the back of the gun and fired again. This time the Queen of Shadows, unable to match the pitch, unable to sing in symphony with the weapon, began to writhe in agony. Her body seemed to fade, then return. Parts of her lithe form disintegrated momentarily, until at last, triumphantly, she was back in her full form and ready to strike.

Indigo placed the gun aside. She felt a warmth grow deep inside. A fire burned within her, a cosmic fire that linked her to the billions of stars that drifted throughout the heavens. She summoned the power of creation that dwelt within every speck of stardust, within every nebulae and dormant in every living being in the cosmos. The fire grew and moved up her body to her chest. Struggling to breathe, she felt it move through her arms, which she had subconsciously stretched out before her. Her fingertips tingled. Indigo heard every particle of light across the cosmos sing in harmony, reaching perfect pitch against any darkness that got in their way. And then the full force of her power rippled across the divide between her and the Queen of Shadows and hit her with full force between her breasts. The black tattoos on her torso quickly retreated and moved down her arms and across her back, away from danger. A musical hyperquake rang out from the earth and made its presence known across all thirty-one planes. The queen's dark malevolent features seemed wracked with horror, her eyes bulged in disbelief as she released Ignatius and stumbled, her wild eyes staring at Indigo.

As she stepped backwards, her harlequined form blended with the black and white tiles on the floor, parts of her disappearing and reappearing. Lunging with long claw-like nails, she threw herself at Indigo, who had picked up the sonic blaster once more and without warning a red flash burst across the Temple, spraying walls, floor and Indigo's face. She tasted the foul metallic tang of blood on her lips. The Queen of Shadows lay on the floor in bits, her lifeless body a gory mess, ripped apart by the sonic blast. Her tattoos faded until they disappeared. Simultaneously, all the other copies of the Queen faded from sight.

A great sigh and gasp emanated from Ignatius as his lungs struggled for air, and his mind and body re-entered the present. Indigo threw herself at him, wrapping her arms around him to comfort him.

"Ignatius, I thought I'd lost you."

He coughed and wheezed and eventually managed a faint smile. "I'm going nowhere," he whispered struggling to speak. "What happened?"

"The Queen of Shadows had secretly followed us and attacked you."

"Has she gone? Is she dead?"

"She's gone," came the reply, "but I'm not sure if that just means she has returned to the underworld, the pages of the book or some other hell. But I have no intention of hanging around in dark corners for the foreseeable future."

Ignatius rested in the arms of Indigo. When he eventually looked out the window, where the light dimmed, he thought the worst, his heart skipping a beat, thinking it was another shadow demon as he heard the flapping of wings. Looking out, he saw Manjushri sitting on the stone windowsill, preening his injured wing. Ignatius smiled, thinking silently that maybe the Union Jacks had a new recruit.

"It looks like this mission, this catastrophe is finally over. You and I have survived the shadows and twin souls. But I don't know what the citizens of Oxford will make of this. Already, word is on the way to London and the penny dreadfuls are in print with tales of dragons and demons and a night of the living dead," said Indigo.

"Then our work is done. Nobody will believe those dreadful papers and it all sounds far too fantastical to be even remotely real." Ignatius thought for a while. "I know. We'll put word out that there had been a meteorite crash, which has destroyed the Administorium and left the crater that now exists. I'll get Carter and the others to work with the local bobbies to close the area off with a tale of dangerous gases, hallucinatory vapours which will explain visions of the dragon and the walking dead."

"And you think that'll work?"

"Worth a try!"

Ignatius shrugged his shoulders in a carefree manner, but he was just trying to reassure Indigo, whom he now realised he loved dearly. Deep down, silently, he had a feeling this was not the end. Something much larger was at play.

Chapter 36: Funeral

It was a grey morning. Unremarkable, just like any other. The sun had just about risen over the Temple roof and was peeking through the clouds. It was a cold white sun, sitting amongst the grey clouds. No heat could be felt in the atmosphere as the entire Chapter of Albion came solemnly through the high-arched, gothic doorway and onto the cobbled street. A fitting start to such a grave occasion.

The horses with their feathered plumes bobbing about on top of their heads neighed and stamped their hooves nervously. The black carriage they pulled was constructed mainly of glass so when it was pulled through the streets, passersby could see the casket and doff their caps to pay their respects.

Last out of the Temple came Ignatius, dressed in a black mourning suit, carrying a cane with an ornate, bright silver cap. As he stood waiting, a woman came around the corner behind and slipped in next to him unseen. She was wearing a black dress and heavy black veil obscuring her face. They were arm in arm.

The graveyard was only a short distance and as the officiant replaced his top hat and began striding away, the horses followed with the Union Jacks following, with Ignatius and his lady friend at the back of the cortège.

Slowly, they neared the graveyard. Passersby stood to the side, holding their various headwear, and bowed until the long black line had completely passed. The silence was deafening. It seemed that even the birds had stopped singing.

A simple ceremony took place in the old ancient chapel that stood crumbling in the corner of the graveyard. Looking around, Ignatius could see the ashen look on some of the faces, comrades, men-at-arms. Each one willing to give their life for their Queen and country, the Empire, the Empress. Nobody spoke, not even to each other. Not a whisper.

The wind had increased a little since arriving, and when the Union Jacks had all exited the chapel, it felt colder and greyer than before.

The chaplain said some words, most of which Ignatius heard, but didn't really process as his mind was elsewhere. His heart was elsewhere. He vaguely heard the chaplain say the familiar words of, "ashes to ashes, dust to dust…" but that was it. He squeezed the slender arm that was locked into his and to reciprocate, the woman placed her other hand on his. She leaned in, cautiously, scanning around to see if anybody was watching, looking beyond the railings and onto the streets.

"I'm fine," she whispered. "I am ok with this. Besides, we had to give her a decent burial. Regardless of where she is from. She will be missed on her own plane, but at least we have lain her to rest with dignity."

Ignatius turned his head slightly to gaze into Indigo's eyes.

"I know. But this could just as easily be you. I'd never forgive myself if …"

Indigo interrupted him with a quiet hush. "But it's not me. Besides, this gives us a huge advantage. To the rest of the world,

Indigo Gemstone is dead. So nobody is going to be looking for me when I carry out any missions. It may be advantageous, it may not." She shrugged her shoulders. "Only time will tell."

"True. But at some stage, we need to tell the rest of the Chapter. Half of them here think that's really you!" He nodded slightly towards the coffin as it was lowered into the ground, four burly men, grave diggers, each holding the ends of a leather strap that had been slung beneath the casket.

In all, the service lasted about an hour, and on the way back to the Temple, Ignatius was starting to wonder how he was going to break the news to the other Union Jacks in his Chapter. However, he knew he could rely on Lambeth, Carter and the others to assist if needed.

On returning from the funeral, Ignatius was in a quiet, sombre mood. He was thinking of Indigo. He couldn't get her out of his head. He didn't want to see any harm come to her, and the funeral had been a very real reminder that her life was precious to him. Burying her doppelganger was very real and had given him an insight into the pain he would feel if any harm came to Indigo.

As they all stood in the Temple reflecting on the morning, sherries were handed out. Indigo had not left his side once. Inevitably, another Union Jack came over to enquire.

"Good morning, Ignatius. My condolences to you. I know you and Indigo were very close."

"Thank you, James," was just about all Ignatius could say.

"Well! Are you going to introduce us, Ignatius? To whom do I have the pleasure, my dear?"

Before Ignatius could speak. Indigo lifted her veil. "It's me, James. I am alive and well!"

At first James recoiled, alarmed and confused. He looked

around for support and was greeted by Carter, Lockhart, Lambeth and Hardred, all laughing at him.

He looked back at Indigo. "So who did we just bury?"

"It's a long story, James," Ignatius interrupted. "We did bury Indigo, but another Indigo. Her doppelganger who, it seems, could travel space and time and came here on an adventure, but unfortunately will not be able to return. We have no idea whether this is a good idea. But at least now we have one agent who nobody will ever be expecting on any mission from here on."

The other Union Jacks all crowded round to congratulate them. How many more roads were to be travelled, how many more missions to be carried out, none knew, but what they did know was, as usual, the Chapter of Albion were more cunning and successful than any other Chapter, mostly due to the brilliance of Ignatius and Indigo.

Epilogue

Report Number: 01/1857

Type: Classified

Agent: Isambard Ignatius

Chapter: House of Albion

With reference to my last report, I am now urgently requesting a meeting with the First Lord of the Union Jacks as my information is above classified. What follows is even more incredible in some ways than my last report. Therefore, I do declare myself fully of sound mind and body and can provide witnesses to the events herein who can testify if required. These are other Union Jacks member from the House of Albion – Lambeth, Hardred, Carter and Lockhart. Indigo Gemstone can also bear witness; however, she almost lost her life during the mission and is not yet fully recovered, so her statement may be called into question.

The mission that Indigo and myself have been on was not a planned mission, but came about from intelligence received. It would appear that further to the Book of Consciousness, there was a twin volume, the Book of Shadows. It had been hiding in plain sight, although I do not know for how long. This possessed incredible power when opened and caused the affray that took place.

You will be pleased to know that The House of Albion have been able to curb any further questions related to events by persuading the local Oxonians that there had been a natural catastrophe in way of a meteorite strike that hit the Administorium building, destroying it in its entirety. The Administorium now ceases to exist, although it is unclear at the moment if any clerics or administrators successfully escaped. During the battle, certain supernatural events were witnessed, such as demons, ghouls, the living dead, shadow monsters and a dragon. These were so prominent that it was not possible to keep them secretive and so many Oxonians witnessed them. As you can imagine, this has sent the city into a panic.

We have managed to declare these were nothing more than apparitions brought about by the noxious gases given off by the meteorite strike, the nickel-iron vaporising with the local limestone to give off vapours unhealthy to the human psyche. Several scientists at the colleges questioned such fanciful ideas but again we have managed to silence them. Others have decided to research such a notion, but I don't believe these professors will cause us any issue. The police, who are unable to come up with any other explanation, have been only too happy to perpetuate such a story, lacking any explanation or evidence of their own.

Again, with reference to my previous report, I explained that the mystery of the universe lies in sound and that all matter can be destroyed if the frequency can be matched. I requested permission to start investigations into the development of such a weapon. I have concluded my research and produced one, which I am calling a sonic blaster. This has been successfully tried and tested in the field. For future missions I believe it would be advantageous for all

Union Jacks to be armed with such a device.

Furthermore, we have discovered that humans do not just dwell in the universe but are a part of the universe. All matter is linked. By following the correct path, a being's mind can dwell constantly amongst other planes until he or she can make it a permanent abode. Man's mind can become the thoughts and the nature of the universe, his neurological patterns, maintain the harmony of the spheres, his breathing creates the cosmic wind – we are capable of cosmic union. Dark thoughts can twist and manipulate reality, contorting it to create horrors that manifest as shadows that were never meant to be.

It is my belief that Indigo has mastered such a power. Therefore, she has become one of the greatest assets the Union now possesses. During this mission, Indigo died but we had been able to revive her. How, exactly, I do not know. But I believe this process has changed her abilities above and beyond all other humans. Therefore, she is worthy of study.

The knowledge we have gained in this mission has provided us with intelligence that at the same time the two books were created there was another artefact, called the Flaming Celestial Pearl. I request permission to seek it out and decide if it carries any danger to the Empire or the world.

We have also obtained some ancient texts that may be of interest to the Union that help explain the cosmos to give us a better understanding of our position in the universe and perhaps how the Empire may expand towards the stars. These claims and ideas may seem fanciful for the moment, but I can vouch for the validity of them.

Meanwhile I am concerned for the safety of both myself and Indigo having been informed that our lives may be in danger for the

part we played in destroying the library beneath the Administorium.
As ever, I can elaborate on any part of this report if required.

I. Ignatius

Oxford.

254

Glossary

Asura   Calabi-Ya refers to Indigo as Asura. In Buddhism, Asura is the lowest rank of deity or demigod.

Calabi-Ya The Elder God, the great dragon. As old as The Omnisoul he represents the first division within the consciousness of The Omnisoul to form dark matter and energy, created from the dark thoughts of The Omnisoul.

The Celestials   The Celestials are powerful sorcerer lords who have obtained god-like status from an otherwise extinct civilisation in the Netherworlds who have gained access to the cosmos. They are known as the Master, the Watcher, the Keeper, the Stalker, the Sleeper, the Guardian and the Voice.

The Charon   The Charon (pronounced Kair-uhn or Karon) meaning fierce brightness, have many guises; they are the Seven Sublime Lords. They are also known to humans as **The Beautiful and the Damned** – damned because they are immortal and have little life of their own. They are held captive and used to carry out the will of The Omnisoul as directed by The Celestials. They are Adonai, Devi, Aryas, Tara, Atman, Darshan and Paladin.

Cha-Ya   The name of the High Priestess. Chaya (or Chhaya) is the Hindu personification and goddess of shadow or shade.

Enoch Slipnot   An anagram of the author's name – Colin Sephton. Enoch is the author of the manuscript Ignatius reads in the Bodleian Library,

Iolite   An Iolite is a gemstone of the mineral cordierite which has a violet or blue colour. In gemology it is a vision stone which aids clear thought and aids understanding. It is said to aid eyesight. In folklore it was used by Vikings and is called the compass stone because thin layers of the gemstone were used as filters to reduce glare or as a polarising filter. Purple gemstones generally thought to have the ability to guide the Third Eye. The Oracle refers to Indigo as the Iolite as she is the purple light, the gemstone used to reveal the Book of Shadows. This is how we find out why Indigo has the name Gemstone.

Keisu   A Keisu is a bronze bowl-shaped drum used during chanting by Buddhist sects in Japan. It is the name of the Singing Bowl that the Omnisoul brought forth as the third artefact and used to create music to restore order to the cosmos, the bowl's vibration working in conjunction with the thoughts of the Omnisoul.

Lyca   The name of the Oracle. It is from William Blake's poem Lost Girl, who wanders out into the wilderness. It is symbolic of the Oracle living in the wilderness.

Maha-Java Sanskrit for very swift (Mahajava). It is the name of the eight-legged wind horse which is based on the eight legged horse of Odin called Sleipnir which means 'slippy' due to its speed.

Maha-Kala   The Queen of the Shadows. It is from the Sanskrit, Mahakala meaning the great black one. Maha (great), Kala (time of death). Or meaning beyond time of death. She feeds off a being's dark thoughts and fears.

Manjushri The name of the Librarians eagle. It is a Buddhist word for knowledge. He was once a god, the scribe who was tasked by the Omnisoul to record the history of the Celestials, documenting their rise to power from mere alchemists to their god-like status. He was betrayed and swapped for knowledge in a bargain made between the Celestials and the Librarians.

The eagle symbolises strength, courage, wisdom and immortality.

Nadas   Three siblings who attend to the libraries. The name is from Nadis that are energy channels with crossroads and junctions and bring information and energy from one point to another in your body. Similarly, the libraries are used to transport energy and information across the cosmos. Viveka, Vijana and Prajja (female) are the Librarians. These are all Sanskrit words for 'wisdom'.

The Omnisoul   The genderless creator of the cosmos. The movement of the stars and planets is governed by the laws of vibration and rhythm that are played out by the energy field of The Omnisoul and the Cosmic Sitar. The cosmos is the entanglement of The Omnisoul's consciousness.

Oxonians The inhabitants of Oxford, England.

Penitentes Shard-like snow formations that form elongated blade-like walls of hardened snow and ice. They are formed by sublimation and high pressure, and are found at high altitudes. They can be found in the Andes and other planetary bodies within the solar system, such as Pluto and maybe Europa.

Prajnana The name of the Flaming Celestial Pearl, the fourth artefact used at the creation of the cosmos. It is Sanskrit for intelligence, knowledge, wisdom. Derived from Jnana which is Sanskrit for the wisdom of the reality or Brahman. Prajna in Hindu is the highest and purest form of wisdom, intelligence and understanding.

Ravana An earthly Indian King. He placed his soul in a container to make himself invincible in battle. He is referred to by Lyca when she tells the Charon that Calabi-Ya may have hidden his soul in the Book of Shadows.

Rahu The name of the Book of Shadows. It is a shadow planet and is king of meteors. Rahu represents fear, dissatisfaction, disappointment, obsession, confusion and mischief. In Vedic astrology, Rahu is responsible for causing the solar eclipse.

Sagharta Sagharta is a cathedral like city and home of the Ti-Botta. Surrounding the city is the Lake of the Celestial Lotus, into which runs the River of Woe. It is said the River of Woe links the earth with the underworld, where the Charon dwell.

Seraphs   Seraph is from the Hebrew Saraph, meaning 'burning one'. They are celestial beings that are the highest rank of angel in Christian tradition.

Skoto   The name of the two doppelgangers who kidnap Indigo. It has a Proto-Indo-European root meaning 'dark' or 'shade'.

Tamas   A Sanskrit word meaning 'darkness'. Enoch Slipknot's book is known as the Tamas Codex.

Taraka   Taraka is the name of the Charon's ship. Taraka is derived from the Sanskrit tāraka meaning crossing or ferryman. It was used as the name for the Charon's ship as they are the ferryman from Greek mythology. In Hindu the name can also mean star, so it is also appropriate as the ship travels the cosmos.

The Ti-botta   The Ti-botta live upon the earth in the land of fire and ice. It is a strange mystical land that exists across more than one plane and therefore, cannot be found easily, sometimes fading in and out of the planes it crosses. The Ti-Botta are based on the Tibetans.

The Union Jacks The Union Jacks are a secret organisation, invisible and omnipresent, without beginning or end; with no recognised recorded history. They are individuals of Engineering Science, technological masters without borders. Their story is long and complex, and entwined with the established history. The secret

Brotherhood that preceded them traced their origins to Brutus of Troy.

Vala   The name of the place where the Oracle dwells. It is the anglicized form of Völva, the Norse name for an oracle, shaman or witch.

www.ingramcontent.com/pod-product-compliance
Lightning Source LLC
Chambersburg PA
CBHW031027310726
48969CB00007B/1900